EXPOSURE

Alex could see Steph's reflection in the mirrors on the toilet wall opposite them. The anticipation of being discovered and the reflection of Steph tonguing her in this public place were more erotic than any of her fantasies. It made her more turned on than ever. She wanted and needed to come. It needed to be quick so she put her hands behind Steph's head and guided her mouth gently towards her clit.

'It's locked,' came a posh, pissed voice from the other side of the door.

'Oh, for pity's sake, Flicky, it can't be locked; it's probably just stuck,' came another voice. 'Let me have a go.'

Alex was on the verge of coming. 'Don't stop,' she mouthed to Steph who was looking towards the door. Just as a broad, horsey shoulder heaved against the flimsy door, Alex grabbed Steph and hauled her into a cubicle, swinging the door shut just as the outer door crashed open.

Steph quickly took up where she had left off, massaging her hard clit with her left hand. Just as Alex was about to come, Steph covered her mouth with a juice-soaked hand.

Flicky and horsey friend were washing their hands when they heard Alex's stifled groan. Horsey leaned towards her companion and whispered, 'There are people having sex in there!'

EXPOSURE

JANE JAWORSKI

First published in 2001 by
Sapphire
Thames Wharf Studios
Rainville Road
London W6 9HA

ISBN 0 352 33592 0

Cover Photograph by Michele Serchuk

Typeset by SetSystems Ltd, Saffron Walden, Essex
Printed and bound in Great Britain by Mackays of Chatham PLC

CONTENTS

ONE

Come Here Often?

'For pity's sake, Stephanie, you're desperate for this woman. You want to spend the foreseeable future shagging her senseless. Your one and only aim is to get into Alexandra's knickers right now; not after a period of prolonged courtship, but now. So what are you doing holding her hand?' asked Marsha incredulously.

'I didn't –' Steph tried to explain herself as she squirmed in embarrassment.

'Use your body, Stephanie. Get close to her, touch her, dominate her because at the moment she's dominating you.'

'Do you really think –?'

'Make her look you in the eye. Look at her. She's crying out to be fucked until she screams. She's not going to say no, but you've got to persuade her that what you've got between your legs is worth sticking around for,' Marsha continued, now on a roll.

'But it's really hard doing this in front of all these people,' Steph blurted out with enough force to stop Marsha as she started to move in on a nervous-looking Alex.

Stephanie was ruing the day she'd clapped eyes on the notice advertising this particular acting workshop on the notice board at drama college.

'But this is a sexuality and gender class, petal. So like it or not, you're going to explore sexuality and gender.'

Steph wanted to kill her mate Bev for encouraging her to get involved in this ridiculous scenario. She glared at her best friend who was among the fifteen other students sitting crossed-legged on the floor of the draughty drama studio watching her feeble attempts at portraying a predatory male. Bev was the one with her hand over her mouth snorting with laughter. 'Manly' wasn't the first word that would leap to mind when describing Steph. In her clingy jeans and spaghetti-strap top, she liked to think she looked a little like Davina McCall and, with a few minor adjustments, she wasn't far off. But, in spite of her voluptuous tits and curvaceous hips, a 'masculine' side had been known to rear its head on occasion.

Tuning back into her tutor's voice, Steph heard Marsha ask if she was uncomfortable playing the man. Not wanting to appear prudish or unable to push her acting ability to its limits, the fiercely competitive part of Steph made her protest that she was perfectly fine with the situation and that she would like to continue with the improvisation.

'That's the spirit, luvvy. It's all about understanding power dynamics,' encouraged Marsha. 'When I was in Rep back in the 70s, I had to go on as Macbeth for a couple of nights, would you believe! Yes, it's a long story, but the point is I would have given anything for a forum like this to help me understand just what it's like to have a bloody great donger hanging between your legs.' There was a slight titter at Marsha's sudden enthusiasm for bloody great dongers.

'That's enough of that,' she said sharply. 'There is nothing amusing about this whatsoever. After all, you boys will be up here in a minute.' As she concluded her lecture, she spun round in a flurry of chiffon and silk and said nonchalantly to her assistant, 'Remind me to bring the strap-ons in tomorrow, will you, Glenda, darling?'

Steph turned her attention to Alex who had been standing patiently in the centre of the room during this interlude. Alex was playing what Marsha called the 'gender anchor' in this exercise in order to keep some semblance of reality. They had only met about three hours previously and until that moment Steph had been too intimidated to look at her fellow performer properly. She knew from the introduction circle earlier that morning that Alex was a little older – 28 to be precise – and a far more experienced actress than herself. She'd got her Equity card and had done several tellies already, whereas Steph, a mere kid of 20, was still stuck at drama school working her way towards her graduation show, an event that could make or break her career.

Eventually Marsha stopped talking. Dramatically, she hunched over, backed off the stage and into the audience leaving the women to pick up the scene where they had left off. She pressed 'play' on the beaten-up portable CD player and the Isley Brothers' swirling guitar riffs filled the room. Marsha had obviously never left the 70s.

Steph took in the way Alex's black, curly hair licked round her neck. Then she stared at the face it framed and thought she looked like one of those gorgeous models you see splashed on the side of buses advertising clothing for Gap – all lips and eyes. One of the store's most recent advertising slogans, 'Everybody In Leather', flashed across her mind and an image of this sensuous woman clad only in tight black leather pants replaced the real image of cord bootlegs and tight T-shirt that stood before her. No stranger to Sapphic sexual fantasies, Steph tried to put the bright blue eyes, slender nose and full, parted lips into a sexual context she could recognise and was not surprised to find that flirting with this woman was incredibly easy.

The scenario Marsha had set for them was simple and left lots of scope. Steph's character had taken Alex's character to a bar with the express purpose of getting off with her.

'So . . . do you come here often?' Steph's opening gambit provoked unanimous groans from her audience.

'Why don't we go and sit down?' asked Alex, as she directed Steph to the shabby sofa that the class had set out to represent the interior of a bar.

'Control, Stephanie!' Marsha's voice wafted through the music. Twisting round to face Alex, Steph flung her arm loosely over

Alex's shoulders but although she had started talking she didn't have a clue what she was saying. Her mouth had gone into seduction autopilot because her attention was being diverted by the way her body was reacting to this situation. Far from taking control she was quickly losing it and getting more and more unwilling to rein herself in.

Alex's brief was to respond to Steph positively if she felt like it or not if she didn't. It was up to her to react to what she was offered. As Alex ran her hand up and down Steph's thigh, it was obvious that she wasn't going to 'block' the scene that Steph was now directing and the younger woman automatically flexed her muscles so that they strained against the faded demin of her jeans.

Steph had come up with a line about the music being loud so they were wedged together on the sofa with each woman's mouth hovering over the other's ear as they talked. Steph was aware that Alex's breath on her skin was really starting to turn her on and silently praised herself for being so into the role. She slipped her hand round Alex's neck to pull her in closer and daringly kissed the soft skin just below her ear.

Enjoying her fellow performer's audacity, Alex moved her hand further in between Steph's thighs that were spread wide apart. Steph remembered what Marsha had told the class about what it might feel like to have a cock instead of a clit. Judging by the throbbing in her fanny, hers would have just grown into a good seven inches. No, make that eight. Alex's hand nudged the fabric covering Steph's crotch, brushing against her cunt lips. It was a fleeting and almost imperceptible movement, but Steph had to stifle a moan. Nobody would have believed a reaction like that wasn't real.

The two women explored each other's bodies with their hands as they talked until Steph gently guided Alex's face up to her own. Not a very brutal or aggressive move, but it felt right and Steph wasn't really thinking about acting any more. For a brief second they looked at each other, wondering if they should go this far. Lust got the better of caution, however, and they kissed each other in short, tentative bursts. The attentive atmosphere in the room changed completely as the women felt fifteen pairs of eyes not just watching them but boring into them.

When they parted their lips and Alex thrust her tongue into her partner's mouth, Steph felt as if a fireball was surging through her veins. She was practised in the art of stage kissing and no one had ever stuck their tongue in before. All mouth, no tongue action; that was the unwritten rule but Steph wasn't complaining. All the right parts of her body were throbbing and wet, when the music faded and Marsha's hushed voice broke into the scene.

'Now, Mike, you're this man's girlfriend,' interjected Marsha in a semi-whisper to the class. 'Let's say your name is Kathy. You've arrived at the bar with some friends and have just seen your boyfriend locked in an embrace with this other woman. Go into the scene and let me see what you do. Now remember, you're a woman so be aware of how that might inform your whole physicality. OK. And, enter Kathy.'

Stupid bloody 'Kathy', thought Steph to herself as she felt Alex instinctively pull away from their embrace.

As You Like It

'You ever snogged a woman before, Steph?' asked Bev as they made their way up the metal stairs to the canteen for lunch.

'What kind of question's that?' Steph asked nervously, wondering whether it had been obvious to the whole group just how turned on she was.

'Looked pretty damn horny, that's all, hen,' joked Bev.

'Let me put it this way. Who would you rather snog? The gorgeous Alex or the less than gorgeous Mike Lomas?' replied Steph as she gave her friend a playful poke up the arse as they neared the top of the narrow stairs.

'Oh yeah. Point taken,' said Bev without needing time to weigh up the pros and cons.

'Get a move on then. At this rate all the strawberry Slimfasts'll be gone by the time we get there.' Steph had tried all the diets in all the books in all the world, but whether she was currently trying to lose weight or not, she did favour a Slimfast for lunch.

5

As they troughed down their food in a small, afterthought of a room that passed as the canteen, Steph scoured the room for Alex. She wanted to find out more about this alluring, somewhat enigmatic woman but Alex was nowhere to be seen. Steph was always open to having adventures, but she'd never before experienced anything like her adventure that morning and, after years of dreaming about doing it with a woman, was hoping she might be able to engineer an opportunity to do a bit more exploring.

A fart and a belch from Bev signalled that lunch was over and the two friends went down to look at the notice board to see what the afternoon held in store for them. Steph's moist crotch still reminded her of the morning's activities, and her heart beat faster as she ran her finger down the list hoping that she'd see her own name in a pair with Alex's. She searched for a way to hide her excitement at seeing she was going to be rehearsing a scene from *As You Like It* with Alex. All she could blurt out was: 'Oh no! Not frigging Shakespeare!'

'I'd take Shakespeare over Adrian Mole any day,' said Bev when she saw she'd been cast as the schoolboy secret diarist. Bev's words fell on deaf ears, as Steph was already on her way to the rehearsal studio.

Flinging the door open, Steph's eyes scanned the room hoping to find the newest object of her obsession. Alex was the only person in the room and Steph watched her as she lay on her back, knees bent, lost in a typical relaxation pose. She hadn't had a chance to speak to Alex about the improvisation they'd done earlier on, but she hoped her gut reaction that it had been a mutually agreeable experience was right. Bev came tumbling in the door behind Steph and broke into both women's dream worlds.

'Oh, hi, Steph, I didn't know you were there,' said Alex as she rolled over onto her stomach and looked up at the two women.

'Yeah, hi, Alex,' stammered Steph, a little ashamed at being identified as a voyeur. 'Have you met my mate Bev?'

'Pleased to meet you, Bev.' Alex got up off the floor and came over to shake hands. It struck Steph as being rather formal considering she and Alex hadn't so much as said 'g'day' before sticking their tongues down each other's throats. 'I gather we're going to be working on a bit of Shakespeare together this afternoon, Steph,' said Alex. Steph wondered whether it was her imagination or whether Alex's voice had been that deep and sexy earlier that morning.

'Yeah. Who do you want to be, Rosalind or Orlando?' joked Steph.

'Oh, I think it's my turn to be the man, don't you?' replied Alex. Steph was amazed that her clit started to throb at the mere thought of it. She wondered whether this woman was the one who would finally make her fantasy world redundant. The other students began to enter the room and Marsha took centre stage to address her class.

'Now, I know there's not a lot of space at the moment, so we're going to have to use the rehearsal rooms in shifts. It's up to you to work out who goes first, but don't forget that you've got to present these scenes in less than forty-eight hours, so going off to have a cigarette and a bit of a sunbathe in the garden isn't going to be a productive use of time,' barked the tutor. 'Now, I'm going to be roaming around the building all afternoon and will drop in on all of you at one stage or another to see if you need any help. So don't panic, you won't be on your own.'

Alex led Steph out into the garden for a fag, a coffee and a bit of a sunbathe while they waited for a room to become free. Steph suddenly felt a little nervous about being with this woman without any class or character to hide behind.

'What made you sign up for this class then, Alex?' asked Steph in her 'polite conversation' voice.

'Marsha.'

'You know each other?'

'You could say that. She used to teach me voice at drama school and often phones up when she's got these kind of things going on.'

'You've done this class before?'

'No. I have to say that this is one of her more interesting ventures.' Steph took the fag that was being passed to her and smiled at Alex as the smoke seeped from between her lips. Alex smiled back. From the way Alex was looking at her, Steph knew that nothing had to be said about the morning's performance. They sat in silence for a moment or two, enjoying the cigarette and the warmth of the spring day.

'Why don't I give you a neck rub while we're waiting?' Alex asked out of the blue.

'Sounds good,' replied Steph as she swivelled round so her legs were astride the back of her chair. With her head lolling forward Steph saw Alex's cigarette being tossed onto the grass and ground out by a pair of heavy leather boots.

'So where do you live, Alex?' Steph managed to squeeze the words out through her compressed windpipe, such was her enthusiasm to know more about this woman.

'Questions and neck rubs aren't really a good combination,' replied Alex, not wanting to give away a thing. 'Just relax into my hands.' Alex pushed her hand up through Steph's shoulder length brown hair and started kneading her scalp. She moved her body closer so that Steph could feel the warmth of her thighs pressing against her own. She was so aroused by this woman's touch that it was fast getting to the point where either a wank or a fuck would have to take place. Steph had had enough of being brought to the brink of orgasm by Alex and was eternally grateful when she recognised Bev's voice shouting out that there was a room free and that they should go up and grab it. Steph was not at all nervous or apprehensive as the two women made their way silently up the stairs and along the corridor to Studio B. She knew Alex wanted to shag her and as a total dyke virgin whose dreams were about to come true, Steph had never been so turned on in her life.

They walked into the room and Steph shut the door and pulled the roller blind down over the glass panel so nobody walking past would get a glimpse of what they both knew was about to happen. The door didn't lock, but neither Steph nor Alex were worrying about intruders. Dropping her bag onto the floor, Alex moved in on Steph and kissed her hard on the mouth. She pushed against her so forcefully that Steph started to stagger backwards. Sensing that she was going to break away from her, Alex grasped her around the waist and guided her over to the wall.

'You know, I haven't been able to stop thinking about fucking you since we kissed this morning,' gasped Alex as she leaned over her and reached down to run her hands over Steph's arse.

'Me too,' confessed Steph.

'Do you want me to show you exactly how turned on I am?' Alex said, toying with her eager partner.

'God, yes!' said Steph, wondering what she was going to do. Alex plunged her hand down into her own trousers, dipped her finger in her fanny and, with it soaked in her juices, used it to trace the moist outline of Steph's lips. Steph's tongue licked her lips, hungry for the taste of Alex's sex.

'I would say that is the taste of a pretty horny woman.' Steph's expectations about how the afternoon might pan out were being surpassed already.

Intoxicated by the strong smell of sex, Steph reached inside Alex's T-shirt and dragged the material up and over her breasts. She thanked her lucky stars that there was no bra to contend with and pulled away from Alex's demanding kiss to get a better look. Alex's tits were beautiful; round, firm and a perfect handful. Mesmerised by this stranger's body, she ran her fingers over the dark red nipples that were erect and aching to be licked. Alex let out a gasp of excitement as Steph bent her head and ran her tongue over her expectant flesh. Steph looked up to see Alex's blue eyes looking down at her, her kiss-smudged lips were slightly parted and her breath was coming in short, sharp gasps.

'Christ, that feels so good,' moaned Alex, 'but if you don't lick me pretty damn soon, honey, I'm going to explode.' With her mouth still exploring every inch of Alex's breasts, Steph reached down to Alex's crotch. She rubbed the seam that ran in between Alex's legs and heard her partner groan with pleasure.

'Easy! Someone might hear us,' said Steph. She turned round to look at the door for reassurance, suddenly scared by the thought of being so exposed.

'That's half the fun, don't you think?' Alex whispered huskily in Steph's ear as she reached down and cupped her new friend's crotch in her hand. Her mouth was so close to her ear that Steph could feel Alex's lips touching her skin as Alex reminded her about the job in hand. 'Now, what's more interesting: Marsha paying us a surprise visit or my cunt, which, I can assure you, is wetter than you could ever imagine and crying out for your mouth.' Alex reached for the waistband of Steph's jeans and flicked open the button. The only sound that filled the air was Steph's zip being pulled down, slowly but surely. Leaning against the wall and almost forehead to forehead, the two women stared into each other's eyes, mouths open, sweat glistening on their skin, anticipating what was to come. Never breaking eye contact, Steph reached down, slipped her hands inside Alex's trousers and watched the pupils of the woman opposite her dilate with desire.

'They're too tight,' declared Alex, 'undo them.' Steph found the button and released it from its hole just as Alex had just done to her. Steph pushed Alex's trousers over her hips and pulled at the elastic of the black cotton pants she found underneath. The feel of Alex's pubic hair was driving her crazy, but the clothes were still preventing her from reaching her fanny.

'Take your trousers off and open your legs,' Steph hissed. Alex wasn't about to argue and struggled to release one leg from her cords to allow Steph to get at her crotch. Pulling her pants to one side, Steph plunged her finger into Alex's sex. Using one hand to keep her underwear out of the way, Steph began to move her middle finger in and out of Alex's moist cunt.

'Jesus, that feels good,' said Steph. The smell of Alex's juices rose between them and Steph inhaled them readily.

'Eat me, Steph. I want to feel your tongue in my cunt,' Alex commanded. 'I can't wait any longer.'

Suddenly the sound of the bell that signified lesson changeover filled the room. With Steph's finger in Alex's cunt and Alex's hands massaging Steph's tits, the two women froze. The sound of feet could be heard tramping along the corridor and voices dissected some class that had just taken place.

'I want you to make me come, Steph,' whispered Alex as the noise got closer to their studio.

'But what if they're coming in here?' argued Steph who for once was being outdone in the risk-taking stakes.

'Then they'll get the thrill of their lives.' Alex smiled. Spurred on by Alex's bravado, Steph let herself be pulled away from her position against the wall and allowed her head to be guided down between Alex's legs. Using the wall for support, Alex tilted her pelvis forward and presented her aroused cunt to her lover. With the school alive with the noises of students on the move, Steph parted Alex's fanny lips to reveal her protruding clit. There was a bang as someone lurched against the door.

'What the fuck . . .?' asked Steph urgently pulling away.

'Steph! Do you wanna have sex with me or think about them?'

'Jesus, Alex, you're good!'

'Steph, please,' groaned Alex, seemingly oblivious to the potential intrusion. She placed her hands on the back of Steph's head and guided her into her crotch. Alex's knees buckled slightly with the intensity of her desire.

'Get on the floor,' ordered Steph. Alex did as she was told and let Steph spread her legs as wide as they would go. Steph marvelled at the beauty of the cunt that was being presented to her.

'So, you want me to lick you out, do you?'

Alex shut her eyes and nodded in reply. With that, Steph plunged her tongue into Alex's hole and tasted a woman's juices for the first time. She replaced her thrusting tongue with her thrusting finger and turned her attention to her partner's clitoris.

Next door, a rehearsal of *Whistle Down the Wind* had started up and singers of various standards were warming up. 'Oh, yes. That's beautiful. Oh, babe, right there,' said Alex, her voice rising with her impending orgasm.

'Shhh!' urged Steph. Protected by the building noise in the adjoining room, Steph abandoned the slow, tantalising route and started to tongue Alex's clit faster and faster as Alex's hips bucked up to meet her mouth. Totally intoxicated by Alex, Steph had ceased caring about intruders when she heard her gasping cries: 'I'm coming. I'm coming! Oh fuck, Steph, I'm coming!'

Steph hung on to Alex's waist and continued working on her clit until her hips stopped thrusting and her orgasm subsided. Sitting up, Alex took Steph's face in her hands and licked her own juices from her partner's face and mouth before quickly pulling her trousers back on.

11

'I never thought I'd say this, but thank fuck for *Whistle Down the Wind*!' Steph said, laughing, elated at the thought of having made Alex come so violently.

'What are you doing with these still on?' Alex teased as she fingered Steph's gaping trousers. 'Don't you fancy me?' Alex went to pull the offending trousers and knickers off, but Steph suddenly wanted to feel this sensuous woman on top of her. She opened her legs and let Alex's lithe body slip in between. Alex covered her face with soft kisses and began rubbing her pelvis up against Steph's fanny.

'You want to come like this?' she asked. Steph nodded. 'Will you be able to come like this?' she probed, concerned that Steph shouldn't miss out on the fun.

'What do you think?' replied Steph who grabbed Alex's arse urging her to thrust faster. 'Just being in the same room with you would be enough to make me . . . oh my God!' Clutching Alex's arse with her fingers and sinking her teeth into her shoulder, Steph's climax was intense. With Alex between her legs and a post-orgasm flush taking over her face and chest, Steph ran her fingers lightly over the smiling face that hovered above her.

The opening door sounded like a gunshot to the two women who were lost in each other's bodies and their own thoughts. Alex turned round quickly to see Marsha standing just inside the doorway looking slightly puzzled.

'We thought we'd work on the wrestling scene instead of going straight into the main text,' piped up Alex, thinking on her metaphorical feet. 'That's OK, isn't it, Marsha?'

'Oh, yes. Lovely. Perfect actually. Clever girls!' said Marsha who seemed to be satisfied with this explanation. 'Wonderful idea for finding a way into Orlando,' she continued. 'So which one of you is playing Orlando?'

'I am,' chorused the two women from the floor. Marsha raised an eyebrow and gave the women a knowing smirk. In their heart of hearts, Alex and Steph knew they'd been rumbled.

TWO
Falling Off the Wagon

That evening Steph was sitting in her north London flat wondering whether her afternoon of sex had been a figment of her imagination or not. Alex had left shortly after Marsha had walked in on their 'rehearsal' but there had been no reference to what had happened between them, no 'we must do it again sometime', no hint of how she felt. As a result, Steph was in the rather unusual position of feeling slightly used. Bev had called to ask if she wanted to go for a few jars down the pub, but she was too busy feeling incredibly turned on at having finally discovered the delights of lesbian sex and also a little put out that Alex hadn't been more . . . well, 'friendly' was the only word she could think of that fitted her expectation.

She cracked open a bottle of Australian chardonnay and poured herself a glass. Learning lines seemed more than a little dull in the circumstances so she flicked the TV on. Soaps turned into quiz shows which turned into the drone of a newsreader's voice which, mixed with the wine, succeeded in sending her to sleep. When the doorbell went at around 10.30 p.m., Steph thought it would be Bev, pissed and too lazy to get her keys out of her bag. Begrudgingly, she heaved herself out of her TV chair and went to answer the door. As soon as she saw Alex standing in front of her, she regretted the manky old track-pants she was wearing and the unattractive sneer on her face.

'Hello,' said Alex as if it were the most normal thing in the world for her to turn up unannounced at strange women's houses after the nine o'clock watershed.

'What are you doing here?' asked Steph in astonishment.

'I was in the area, so . . .'

'But you don't know my address!'

'I am quite friendly with the course tutor, you know.'

'Oh, yeah. Of course,' said Steph, feeling a bit silly.

'So, are you going to let me in?'

'Oh, yeah. Of course!' Steph moved aside and let Alex through.

'Are you OK?' Alex asked, noticing that Steph looked a bit flustered.

'I'm just a bit surprised that you're here, that's all.'

'Surprised? In case you'd forgotten, we've got a scene to put on and, as I recall, we didn't do an awful lot of rehearsing today.'

'But you practically ran out of the studio after Marsha burst in on us this afternoon. To be honest, I didn't think I'd be seeing you again.'

'I had an audition I had to be at, that's all. Sorry, hon,' soothed Alex as she reached out to run the back of her hand across Steph's cheek. 'But look, I'm here now, so why don't we get down to some work?'

'Fucking weirdo!' Steph said, trying to hide her delight, and showed her into the living room. Steph retrieved her abandoned book from the floor and the two women worked their way through the scene, talking about motivation, objectives and all the other wank that actors love to bang on about. Around 12.30 there was a phone call from a very drunk Bev. She wanted to let Steph know that she was going to stay over with Tina and that she shouldn't worry about her. She told Steph that she loved her very very much, that she was the best mate in the world and that she would see her tomorrow in class.

'So we've got the place to ourselves?' said Alex who had discarded her script and was stretched out on the TV chair tossing back the last of the wine.

'But it's gone midnight, Alex, and surely way past your bed-time,' taunted Steph.

'Come here and say that!'

Steph couldn't resist sinking to her knees in front of Alex to accept the long and luxuriant snog that was being offered. Alex automatically reached for Steph's tits but was pushed away.

'Not going all coy on me now, are you?' asked Alex in surprise.

'As much as I want to spend all night fucking your brains out, there are too many questions I need answers to,' declared Steph, amazed by her self-control.

'What do you mean?'

'Christ, Alex, we've groped each other in front of a class of students and had fantastic sex in one of the drama studios but I don't know anything about you!'

'And you want to?'

'Yes!'

'So what do you want to know?'

'Why you're being such hard work would be a good place to start.'

'Steph, do you really think I go round hitting on every cute woman I work with?'

Steph thought about this for a moment and then had to admit that she did. Alex burst out laughing at Steph's image of her.

'Well, I'm sorry to shatter your illusions, but I don't. Although after today, I am beginning to think that I should!'

'So, what then? You've got a boyfriend, is that it?'

'Good God, no!'

'So why are you being so goddamn secretive?'

'I want you to try and understand, Steph, that it's not because I don't like you. This is going to sound really odd, but I have an arrangement with my agent. Really I shouldn't be here at all.'

'What? Some sort of business deal?' Steph was fascinated and apprehensive about where this was leading.

Alex looked as if she was having a hard time deciding exactly what she was about to say but eventually came out with: 'I've kind of made a promise to my agent that I will remain celibate.'

Steph started to laugh and was pleased that Alex's imagination seemed to be as fertile as her own. 'It's no joke, Steph.' The seriousness of Alex's tone meant Steph knew immediately that this outlandish statement was not some sort of bizarre wind-up after all.

'Why on earth would you do that?' asked Steph, despite being a little wary of the answer.

'This is really hard to say without sounding totally hypocritical and arrogant, but I struck a deal with my agent when he took me on. He would only put me up for the high profile, starry stuff – you know, movies, big tellies, blah, blah – if I kept the dyke thing completely under wraps.'

'So you are gay?'

'As a goose, sweetheart!'

'Fucking hell,' exclaimed Steph.

'I know. It's shit. It is like selling your soul to the devil, but I've dreamed about being in the movies all my life and now I've got someone who's powerful enough and interested enough to help me make it happen. Believe me, Steph, when you're standing in front of someone who's offering you a screen test for "the next big movie", giving up sex doesn't sound like such a big deal.'

'You're not doing a very good job then, are you!' Steph laughed at Alex's serious tone. 'So where do I come in? Are you going to cut off my tongue and condemn me to a life of kiss-and-tell-silence?'

'You wouldn't be much good to me if I did that, would you?' Alex started to lighten up.

'So this is sort of finishing something that should never have started?'

Alex paused and silently nodded her head. 'I know I have no right to ask you, but will you keep quiet about what happened? Not a word?'

'Not even to Bev.'

'So why did you have sex with me in the studio, Alex? Anyone could have walked in and seen us. Why would you do that if you're so scared about people finding out you're a raving lesbo?' Steph was tired, disappointed and confused.

'I can't help what turns me on, can I?' Steph waited for her to continue. 'I just find the idea of having sex in unusual places really horny, that's all. I know it's stupid, but that's how it is.'

Steph was beginning to wish she hadn't opened this conversation as she was approaching information overload.

'Trust me to land a freak like you on my first go.' Steph got up from her position at the foot of Alex's chair and produced a bottle of Grouse and a couple of glasses from the cabinet. Serious drinking seemed like the right thing to do at this stage.

'You are allowed to drink, aren't you?' remarked Steph sarcastically as she poured too much Scotch into the tumblers. 'No deals, pacts or restrictions on that one?' Alex dealt with the jibe by just ignoring it totally.

'Today was really your first time?' Alex's surprise seemed genuine. She took the drink that was passed to her, but held on to Steph's hand.

'Yeah,' Steph admitted shyly and looked up at Alex hoping she wasn't going to be made fun of.

'Well, you were wonderful.' Alex slid off the chair to join Steph sitting on the floor. She swung herself round so the two women were sitting face to face, their bent legs entwined. Alex took Steph's hand again. She guided Steph's hand up to her mouth and gently sucked on her fingertips and licked down the shaft of her fingers.

'This is the first time I've fallen off the wagon, you know.' She was trying to make her feel better.

'Am I meant to be flattered?' Steph was almost in a sulk.

'When you kissed my neck in class, I thought I was going to come on the spot.' Alex continued sucking and licking and caressing Steph's fingers.

'That's only because you haven't had sex for God knows how long. How long has it been?' Steph suspected Alex knew the precise answer to her question but instead Alex just shrugged her shoulders.

'What made you think you could trust me though?' The thought of Alex choosing her to have sex with did make Steph feel a bit special.

'I don't know. Instinct. Gut reaction. We clicked, didn't we?'

Flattered by her comments, Steph was still aware that her click had been bigger than Alex's. 'Steph, I'm trying to tell you how much I fancy you!' said Alex, apparently eager to get some sort of reaction from her.

'Yeah, well, I'm trying to tell you that I'm sick of fantasising about various unattainable women and this afternoon I really thought I'd finally found someone I might be able to start a real relationship with and now you turn out to be a complete fucking ambition-crazed wacko!'

They sat in silence both trying to digest what the other had said. Steph watched Alex as she glanced round the room taking in the *My Friends & Neighbours* poster on the brightly painted green walls, the books lined up on the shelves according to colour and the solitary customised Ikea cabinet in the corner.

'So which unattainable women have you been fantasising about?' She smiled at Steph, took her glass from her hand and put it on the carpet beside them.

'I'm allowed to have secrets too, you know,' Steph teased.

'Well, you're not going to be doing that tonight.'

'Really?' Steph was fascinated by the way she could say something like that and not sound arrogant.

'Why should you have to touch yourself when you've got me to do whatever you want?' Steph's heart raced. She knew it would be madness to have anything more to do with this woman, but some reactions can't be controlled by logic.

'Just for tonight?' asked Steph, hoping that she'd misunderstood the whole warped scenario.

'Just for tonight,' confirmed Alex. Steph put her hand on Alex's thigh. 'But not a word.' The touch of her bare leg made Steph tingle with desire. 'Promise?' Steph kissed Alex full on the lips in a move that sealed their pact.

She ran her hands through Alex's soft curls and pulled her tighter into her body as their tongues met. As she pulled away from the kiss a string of saliva joined their mouths for an instant and glistened in the light of the muted TV. Steph's hands were shaking as she reached for the buttons of Alex's shirt. Slowly she undid the first button to reveal her bra. She ran her hands over the flimsy material that covered Alex's body, wanting to savour every moment of this affair. Motionless, Alex offered her body to Steph's exploring hands. Steph popped open the buttons one by one until she was able to push the garment off her lover's shoulders and onto the floor. Alex's tanned, semi-clothed body was more erotic than Steph could have dreamed. Reaching behind her, Alex undid her bra and let it fall to the floor before easing herself down onto the cushions behind her.

'I don't know if I can,' Steph whispered almost overcome by the sensations that were wracking her body.

'Give me your hand,' Alex murmured. Gently, Alex placed Steph's hand on her exposed breast. Steph felt the nipple harden underneath her palm and squeezed, enjoying the soft moan that escaped from Alex's lips. Sitting astride her hips, Steph bent over and dragged her tongue from the hollow of her neck round to her ear. Pinning her arms to the floor she breathed in this beautiful woman's scent and took her earlobe between her teeth, biting it just as she liked hers to be bitten. Steph could feel Alex's hips grinding against her. 'Not so fast. This is my night, remember,' she chastised Alex, pushing her pelvis into the cushions with her crotch. 'I'm going to get up now, but I don't want to see you with your hand in your crotch, OK?'

Alex nodded and seemed to be pleasantly surprised by the way Steph had decided to take control. Steph stood up with her legs either side of Alex's body and peeled off her T-shirt. She hooked her thumbs inside the waistband of her track-pants and pulled them down and off. Instead of the white, lacy knickers she'd had a glimpse of earlier that day, Alex found herself staring up at Steph's naked cunt instead. Unable to contain herself, she sat up, wanting desperately to plunge her tongue into Steph's sex. Steph tutted as she held Alex's head inches away from her fanny. 'I thought we were doing things my way . . .'

'But I just –'

'You can look, but don't touch. Not yet.' Steph was really getting into her role now. She could feel Alex's breath on her clit and although she yearned to have Alex touch her, she was enjoying the woman's desire too much. Steph ran a finger over the length of her cunt so it was covered in her juices and put it in Alex's open mouth. 'Think of that as an appetiser,' she teased as Alex licked the offered finger noisily. Moving away from Alex's impatient tongue, Steph turned her attention to her partner's remaining clothes. Assessing the situation, she guessed that the cotton skirt wouldn't pose much of a problem and began to pull it down over Alex's legs. The prostrate woman lifted her hips obligingly. The wet crotch of her pants confirmed just how turned on Alex was. Steph couldn't resist taunting her even more and ran the finger that had just been in her own wet hole over the drenched material. Alex gasped and thrust her hips forward but, knowing that she had to let Steph orchestrate the scene, made no move to touch her.

Kneeling between her open legs, Steph lowered her head and brushed her lips across Alex's navel, pulling her pants down as she went so she could reach in and touch her pubic hair. She reached behind to the small of Alex's back and gripped onto the only item of clothing that was left and tugged the pants down over Alex's arse. Lifting her crotch, the offending article was eased away from her body.

'Sit on my face,' Alex hissed, impatient to get to the main course. Steph positioned herself so that she was kneeling astride Alex once again.

'Wait for it,' she whispered, lowering herself so that her fanny skimmed over Alex's stomach, smearing it with her wetness. 'Everything comes to those who wait.' Gradually she moved up Alex's expectant body and, running her hard clit over Alex's erect nipple, she shuddered with excitement. Not wanting Steph to come before she'd got a chance to taste the cunt she'd been deprived of earlier, Alex took this as her cue. She moved down between Steph's legs so that her lover's swollen red lips were inches over her face. Alex ran her fingers down either side of Steph's erect clit so it thrust out of her cunt even further. Flicking it with her tongue, Alex plunged her tongue into Steph's sex. Steph's groan of relief at finally giving in to Alex's tongue came from deep inside her and Alex could feel the thighs either side of her head trembling with lust. Steph's breath was coming in short, heavy bursts as she thrust her clit hard into the mouth below her. Taking her weight on her arms she started to slide her cunt over Alex's mouth so urgently that Alex didn't know whether she was tonguing her cunt or her clit. Her face covered in Steph's juices, Alex grabbed hold of her hips so she could force her tongue even further inside her hole. Steph's moans were turning into screams of delight and she pumped her taut, throbbing clitoris into Alex's mouth.

'Jesus, Alex, you're going to make me come!' She could feel her clit grinding against Alex's teeth. 'Jesus Christ!' she screamed as her orgasm built inside her. With one final thrust Steph let out an enormous groan as her climax thundered through her whole body and her come poured into Alex's hungry mouth.

Steph leaned down to lick her own come from Alex's face. Reaching behind her she ran her hand in between Alex's legs and felt the stickiness that had seeped out of her sex and onto her thighs.

'I want you to fuck me with your clit.' Alex's voice was husky and barely audible but straight to the point. Steph didn't need to be asked twice to try out her favourite sexual fantasy. Alex looked almost pained with anticipation as she lifted her right leg up to let Steph position her open cunt lips over her own. Between their scissored legs, Steph could see Alex's clitoris was engorged with lust. Alex put her hand in her cunt and parted her lips further to give Steph a better view of her sex.

'I want to feel you rubbing against me, babe,' Alex demanded. 'I want to feel you against me.' Steph was frozen with intense excitement. 'Fuck me, Steph.' The command was enough to stir Steph into action and she lowered herself onto Alex's clit. She heard the sound of their drenched fannies coming together and thought she'd died and gone to erotic heaven. Both women gasped loudly when they felt the pressure of the other's clitoris on their own.

'I never thought anyone could be so –'

'Oh yeah!' shouted Alex as her lover hit exactly the right spot. Steph was once again building towards a climax. Concentrating hard on giving Alex pleasure, she moved her hips in time with the thrusts coming from below. Steph saw Alex's face start to contort and knew from the way Alex was digging her fingers into her arse that she was about to come.

'Come with me, Steph. Come with me!' Alex screamed as her orgasm swept through her entire body. The noise, the sweat and the smell of two women coming together was intense.

As Steph sank into Alex's arms, there was a bang on the wall from jealous neighbours. The two women grinned at each other, proud that their performance had provoked such a reaction. Steph looked at the clock. The realisation that it was nearly four o'clock suddenly made her yawn. Alex twisted round to look at Steph who had curled herself around Alex's body. 'You're not going to sleep, are you?' she said, disappointed.

'I'm exhausted.'

'But we've only got a couple of hours left together – you can't go to sleep.'

'How about we just go to bed then?'

'OK.' Leaving the room strewn with their clothing and reeking of sex, Steph led Alex into her bedroom. Under the duvet Alex put her arm around Steph and pushed strands of sweaty hair away from her face. 'I can't get close enough to you,' said Steph who was already beginning to panic about Alex leaving and walking out of her life. Alex drew Steph in tighter and trapped her between her legs.

'Close enough?' she asked.

'Ummm, feels good.' Alex began to stroke Steph's back and arse and neither woman was surprised to feel their bodies start to respond. Pelvis to pelvis, their hips started to rock backwards and forwards and they started to make love all over again.

Stupid Mind Games

It was Alex's mobile phone that eventually woke the pair up. Alex leaned over the side of the bed and scrabbled around in her bag trying to locate the source of the intrusion. Tipping the bag upside down, the phone came tumbling out. Alex looked at the display and recognised Marsha's number.

'What does she want at this time in the morning?' groaned Alex as she let it click onto voice mail.

'Who?' croaked Steph who was even less awake than Alex.

'Marsha.' Alex turned and looked at the clock. 'Jesus Christ, it's 11.30!' she yelled and leaped out of bed. 'Come on, Steph, you're going to be late.' Steph gripped on tightly to the covers that Alex was trying to pull off her.

'I'm not going.'

'What do you mean, you're not going?' said Alex as she looked around the room for her clothes and then remembered why they weren't there.

'I can't go back there and work on a scene with you after all this!' Steph mumbled through the duvet. Alex sank down onto the bed.

'Look, you go and I'll phone Marsha and tell her that something's come up, OK?' enthused Alex.

'I'm not going, Alex, and that's final.'

'What are you going to do all day then?' Alex appeared reluctant to leave whilst Steph was looking so unstable. 'For Christ's sake, Steph, we hardly even know each other. We had a shag –'

'Or two.'

'Or two,' continued Alex. 'It was fun. It was good sex. But a couple of orgasms and a shared fag doesn't automatically make us lesbian-fucking-life-partners, you know!'

'Why are you talking like this, Alex? Stop it.' Steph was disappointed by the sudden change in Alex's attitude but knew exactly what she was trying to do. 'I'm not as naive as you think, you know,' she said sharply, too tired to play stupid mind games. 'I know you're panicking because you don't know any more if you can trust me, but that's just something you'll find out in time, won't you?'

'Steph, I thought we'd agreed . . .'

'Look, Alex, I really like you. Fuck knows why, because anyone who agrees to obliterate their private life for some tenuous promise of money and fame must be a total idiot, let alone a complete bastard for taking out their frustration on defenceless young women. But I do like you. You are the horniest, most gorgeous woman I've ever clapped eyes on and I think that what you're doing is just such a fucking waste!' Steph was pleased that she'd said her piece and flopped back down on the bed, pulling the duvet back round her.

'I'm sorry if I've hurt you, Steph,' replied Alex. 'I never thought it would be like this. I fancied you in class but should never had let it all get out of control. I really am sorry.' There was no reaction from Steph and Alex looked a little frustrated that things hadn't turned out as neatly as she'd planned.

'I mean, how was I to know that I was your first?' Alex continued. 'It wasn't very fucking obvious in the studio yesterday!' There was a humpf from under the duvet. 'Well, it wasn't,' protested Alex.

'It shouldn't make any difference whether I've shagged one woman or a thousand. The fact is that you shouldn't go round giving people a bite of the cherry then whipping it away!'

'So you only want me for my body?' asked Alex. Another humpf from under the covers. 'Jesus, Steph, all you've got to do is put yourself around a bit in some of the bars in town and you could shag a different woman every night!'

'Well, I might just do that!'

'Good.' Alex's phone went again. This time she saw it was the number of her agent's office. What impeccable timing she thought to herself, smiling at the irony of the situation. She answered the phone and went over to the other side of the room to speak to the caller in hushed tones. Steph pulled the covers down slightly from over her face to try and hear what she was talking about. She only caught a couple of words but could tell it was an important call.

'Alex, it's Quentin.'

'Quentin, this isn't a good time.'

'I don't think there can be a bad time to tell you that you've been called back to read for the Brett Torento movie, is there?' came the voice of Alex's agent down the line.

'Seriously?'

'Couldn't be more serious. They want you to do a couple of scenes with Brett this time. It's a good sign, Alex. A very good sign.'

'That's fantastic, Quentin. Listen, I'll finish up here and call you when I get home. OK?'

'Speak to you later.'

Clicking the phone shut, Alex returned to sit on the bed. 'Look, honey, I'm really going to have to go now; there's somewhere I have to be.'

'OK,' said Steph calmly, rolling over to look at Alex.

'Mind if I take a quick shower before I go? I'll have all the dogs in the neighbourhood following me down the street if I don't!'

'Sure. Take some clean underwear too if you want.'

Alex went over to the drawer Steph was pointing at. 'Cheers.' Holding a pair of Steph's knickers in her hand, Alex walked slowly towards the door.

'I'll let you get some sleep then, yeah,' Alex whispered to the shape under the duvet.

'Whatever,' was the muffled reply. Alex gathered up her stuff, grabbed a towel off the back of a chair and made her way to the door.

'So you won't go saying anything –' Alex tried one last time to get some reassurance before she left.

'Oh, please!' said a frustrated Steph. Alex paused a moment.

'Don't forget to go and cruise around some of those bars I mentioned,' said Alex in lieu of a goodbye.

THREE

Cruising and Surfing

A slurping noise echoed round the sides of the glass as Steph sucked the last of her vodka Red Bull up through her straw. She looked intently at the mound of ice lurking in the bottom and knew, if she wanted to avoid making eye contact with anyone and have something to occupy her attention, she would have to go to the bar and order another one. Going out alone wasn't something that Steph usually did. Going out alone to a women-only bar was something she never did and now she was there felt so nervous that she'd made a big dent in the contents of her cigarette packet and downed three vodkas – she'd only been in the bar an hour. Even Bev would think that was quite impressive.

Steph smiled as she remembered the look on Bev's face when she told her she was gay. Her friend's Glaswegian accent had got broader and broader as she gasped and howled and finally squealed with delight. Bev had trotted out a couple of stories including one about an experience she'd had with some chalet maid on a field trip to Bognor and then suggested they go down to the pub to celebrate. They had had a good time in the pub and talked about all kinds of stuff that Steph couldn't now recall and was sure wasn't worth remembering anyway. She had alluded to her liaison with Alex but had stopped short of mentioning her by name. By the time Steph had got to the end of her confession, which had got more and more convoluted as she steered as far away from the truth as possible, Bev had been given the impression that her friend had been used and abused by some sex-starved vixen-from-hell who had taken advantage of a poor, inexperienced dyke who was looking for friendship and maybe more. Bev had encouraged Steph to get out and about on the scene and during the intervening days had taken to reading out the descriptions in *Time Out*'s gay bar section in order to map out an agenda for her friend.

As Steph squeezed in between two women sitting on stools at the bar she realised the woman to her left was wearing the same cologne as Alex had been wearing that day at college. Standing on the rail at the bottom of the bar so she could been seen better over the tall counter, her arm outstretched with a cashpoint-fresh tenner signifying her intention to buy a drink, it was all Steph could do to stop burying her face in the gorgeous-smelling stranger's hair. She felt something tug on the note in her hand and gripped on tighter before she became aware that someone was talking to her.

'Do you want a drink or not?' shouted the woman behind the bar over the music, which had segued from early evening moderation into a serious late-night drinking and dancing vibe. With more vodka in her glass and the thump of dance music in her ears, Steph decided she should go and check out the talent on the dance floor while she still had a grip on her faculties, albeit it loose.

If she was going to get anywhere that night Steph realised that she was going to have to start looking like she was having a good time, maybe even allow the odd smile to flicker across her face. Bolder with booze, she looked up and began that kind of half dance people do when it's cruising not dancing that is on their mind. Her eyes began to scour the room for a possible shag and she was pleased to find there were at least a couple of cute possibilities after just one circuit of the floor.

Suddenly she caught sight of a tall, slim figure across the other side of the room. The woman was bending to put her mouth close to the ear of the person she was dancing with. Steph wasn't sure whether the palpitations she felt were due to the intense amount of caffeine that was coursing through her veins or because the woman had dark curly hair. She cursed the strobing lights that made it impossible to see for sure. Was it Alex? And if it was, what the fuck was she doing here?

As Steph was squinting through the flashing lights, Alex was in fact pacing around her flat in St John's Wood. Holding a gin and tonic in one hand, she held the script her agent had passed onto her in the other. After the recall she'd had earlier in the week, the director had been in touch again and had asked her in for one final reading. She would be reading one of the love scenes with Brett, the movie's leading man and Quentin had told her the director was trying to decide between her and one other woman for the part of Brett's love interest. It was a good role and Alex had played the sophisticated, hard-nosed type who melted at the sight of a chiselled-jawed man a thousand times before so it wasn't exactly a stretch for her. Basically it was down to the chemistry she could generate with Brett. He was cute enough, but was never going to light her fire. Alex had read her Stanislavski, however, and knew if she allowed pictures of her love-making with Steph flood her mind she would have no problem.

Trying to push thoughts of her big break out of her head, Alex went to sit in the window that overlooked the garden of the basement flat directly below her. The sultry April evening was beautifully quiet and only the sounds of voices from the local pub wafted into her space from time to time. In a way she found it quite reassuring to know that there were people out there having fun on a Saturday night while she stayed in and fantasised. She wondered what Steph was doing and with whom and her fantasies took on a different nature. She felt her nipples going hard underneath the tight white vest she was wearing and automatically slipped her hand into the opening of her cotton pyjama bottoms. Her pubic hair felt good to her touch and her mind wandered back once again to the day and night she had spent with Steph. She had been a prolific lover in her old days on the scene and certainly recognised a good shag when it happened. And Steph had been just that.

★

Steph didn't know whether to feel relief or disappointment that the woman she had been scrutinising on the dance floor was not Alex at all. Liberated from her fleeting fear that Alex had duped her into believing the celibacy thing simply as a means of not having to see her again, she turned her attention back to the job in hand. Aware now of the scene going on around her she realised that she had almost been subsumed into the group of women standing next to her and Steph decided to follow their lead and throw herself into the music that was bouncing off the walls of the small, packed room. Steph smiled at the woman with short white hair and a stunning tan who was dancing opposite her. It was returned and there was something in her smouldering brown eyes that made Steph realise that this was her chance. She smiled again and the woman beckoned her over. It was as simple as that. She was dancing in a dyke club with a gorgeous woman who was coming on to her . . . she hoped. Steph moved closer and the woman placed her hands on her waist. With one leg in between the other woman's they moved to the music, their crotches getting closer and closer. Steph could smell the woman's perfume as she was drawn closer into her body.

'You here with anyone?' asked Blonde Woman in a thick Spanish accent that was so horny Steph couldn't believe her luck.

'No. I mean yeah,' replied Steph. 'She had to go earlier.' She didn't want to seem like a total sad-fuck-no-mates.

'Girlfriend?'

'No, she's just a friend.' Steph was so close to Blonde Woman that she could feel her tits brushing against her own breasts. Steph felt her fanny starting to throb as she put her hand behind Blonde Woman's head and put her mouth next to her ear to ask the same question.

'No. All alone. Except for them. We're all here on our holidays,' explained Blonde Woman, pointing at her friends on the dance floor.

'What's your name?' asked Steph.

'Conchita. You?'

'Steph.'

'So, Steph, what do you drink?' They made their way through

a sea of glistening bodies that had lost all concept of space, personal or otherwise, and arrived at the bar. Conchita sat on a stool and leaned against the bar while Steph shuffled awkwardly nursing her umpteenth vodka. She didn't really know what to do. It was too loud for small talk and too soon for a snog, so she ran her hands up Conchita's thighs and stared into her eyes. Steph realised that etiquette must be different in Spain, as Conchita reached down and kissed her gently on the lips. Steph happily moved into the space between the muscular Spaniard's legs and returned her full-lipped kiss. With her hands brushing the thin band of exposed flesh between Steph's hipsters and her top, Conchita pulled her even closer and pushed her tongue into Steph's mouth. The mixture of fags and booze on her breath was intoxicating and Steph opened her mouth wide to take Conchita's tongue even further in her mouth. Steph reached behind Conchita and under-neath her T-shirt to run her hands up her back. Her body felt so tight and sculpted that she had to be an athlete of some kind. Pulling back from their embrace, Steph felt more than a little horny as well as more than a little drunk and was happy that conversation didn't seem to be uppermost on this perfect Spanish woman's mind. She reached up and traced the outline of Con-chita's jaw with her finger, not quite believing that the experience was real.

One of Conchita's friends came over and they had a short conversation in Spanish. Steph didn't have a clue about what they were saying but the rhythm of their voices and the way Conchita was hooking her fingers down inside Steph's trousers was enough to hold her interest.

'My friend says they are going now,' translated Conchita as her friend disappeared off into the throng.

'Oh. Right,' said Steph, hoping that Conchita wasn't going to vanish into the night so quickly.

'And you? Are you staying?' Conchita asked.

'If you are,' came the reply.

'Sure.'

It was late and everyone was wasted on either pills or drink so Steph didn't think it was too out of order when Conchita pushed her knee into her crotch. With her hands on Steph's arse, Conchita started to rub her knee against the thin fabric that covered Steph's cunt.

'Where do you live?' asked Conchita as she moved her hands up to Steph's tits. The young Spaniard's breathing was heavy with desire.

'Finsbury Park,' replied Steph.

'Is it far?'

'No.'

'Good. Shall we go?'

Steph didn't need asking twice.

Frustrated and excited by thoughts of her meeting the next day and vivid memories of Steph's beautiful, wet fanny, Alex took her glass and went into the small study where she turned on her computer. On the Internet she could be whoever she wanted. No faces, no names, no repercussions and certainly no promises to be broken. She went to her bookmarks and selected one of her favourite women-only chat rooms. There was bound to be someone there who was as eager as she was to have some fun.

Signing on using a profile that was guaranteed to get dykes from Alaska to Zanzibar tempting her into a private room, Alex sat and waited for a response. It didn't usually take more than a couple of minutes before someone started mailing her with interesting invitations and in the meantime she sat and watched a rapid conversation unfold in the usual Internet jargon that was almost unintelligible to the unaccustomed. She was following a familiar interaction that focused largely on the sexuality of various tennis players before she got a bite. She moved some papers off her desk and put her glass down next to the keyboard.

'Hi, Alex. My name is Laura. Would you like to come visit?' were the words that appeared across the screen.

Alex quickly had a look at Laura's profile. It said: 'New York woman-who-likes-women-about-town; based in LA; into fun, fun and more sex, sorry, fun. Mail me. By the way, dykes – that means women – only.'

'You got a picture?' came the next message.

'Sorry, no. I'm a bit new to all this,' lied Alex as she clicked on the send icon.

'Wanna see mine?'

'That's what I'm here for.'

Alex waited a few seconds and went to her mail box to collect her delivery. She opened the file and pixel by pixel an image of Laura – or a picture of whoever Laura wanted to be – built itself on the screen. Alex was presented with an image of a sophisticated-looking woman sitting in a luxurious leather chair wearing a business suit with her skirt pulled up round her arse, one leg flung over the arm of the chair and a dildo hanging out of her cunt.

'I hope that's not the one you send out on your CV,' typed Alex. Although it wasn't terribly funny, having a joke with someone was always a good way of gauging how a cybersex session would go. Some Americans just weren't on the same wavelength and turned out to be hugely disappointing in Alex's experience, but she was relieved when a message came through saying: 'Of course not. It's my crotchless leather panties and cupless bra ensemble that gets me the job every time!'

'So what do you look like, Alex?'

'Short curly hair –'

'Dark?'

'Yep. About 5 foot 11. Quite fit, I suppose.'

'How old?'

'28.'

'You?'

'35.'

Alex's hand was back in the opening of her pyjama trousers. The image of this elegant New York businesswoman plunging a dildo into her cunt was incredibly horny and Alex wanted to get down to business.

'Alex?'

'Yes.'

'You still there?'

'Yeah. Just finding it hard to type and wank at the same time.'

'Tell me about your fantasies . . .'

★

Steph took Conchita's hand and led her quietly through the hallway of the flat she shared with Bev, praying that she would be out or at least in bed already. The bus journey home had been excruciatingly long for both young women but the opportunity to finally explore each other's bodies was within reach.

Steph closed her bedroom door quietly as Conchita came up behind her. Leaning into the door, Steph pushed her arse into Conchita's crotch and felt her lover's hands slide inside her blouse and pull her bra up and over her tits. She rolled Steph's nipples in her fingers so they became hard with desire before plunging her hand down into Steph's trousers and inside her pants. Steph tried to turn round to face Conchita but the Spanish woman pushed her back so she was spreadeagled, police-search style, facing the door. Conchita reached down and unzipped Steph's trousers and pulled them and her knickers down to the floor. Obligingly Steph stepped out of them and spread her legs again so Conchita could get to her cunt. With one hand stroking Steph's arse and cunt lips, Conchita struggled out of her T-shirt. Steph could feel Conchita's nipples rubbing on her back and the woman's pubic hair that was poking out of her unzipped trousers rubbing on her arse. Steph turned to face Conchita and guided her onto the bed. Conchita's half-open jeans and skimpy, black thong had to come off. After easing them down, Steph climbed on top of her eager lover. Astride Conchita's lean, muscular frame, Steph started to rub her pussy on the pubic hair below . . .

'So, you want to know about my fantasies, Laura.' Alex's words seeped down the line to the woman on the other side of the Atlantic. 'Seeing your cunt in that picture, wide open, dripping and aching to be fucked, I would like to do nothing more than strap on a real fucking dildo, not like that small-shite thing you have flapping around in your hole in the photo, but a real, huge, thick bastard. I would like to fuck you with it, hard so that it presses against my clit . . .'

'Alex. I'm making a bit of a mess of my keyboard! Have you got a number?' Laura's typed words appeared on Alex's screen. 'Can I call you?'

Alex made it a rule never to give out her number on line, no matter how horny she was or how delicious the other person sounded.

'How about I give you a ring?' suggested Alex.

'But my husband is still asleep in the next room,' said Laura.

'Oh, so I've got a closet case on my hands, have I?' teased Alex.

'If you could see him, you'd understand, honey!'

'You don't need to justify yourself to me,' said Alex, intrigued by the scenario she had stumbled into. There was a pause and then a number flashed up on Alex's terminal together with the words 'call me in five'. Alex could hardly wait. Phone sex was so much better and easier than cyber, although she had pretty much perfected the art of typing with one hand during her period of enforced celibacy.

The clock clicked to 2.35 a.m. when Alex put her freshly mixed gin and tonic on the table in the living room and picked up the phone to dial the number she had been sent. The phone didn't even ring for half a tone before it was snatched up.

'Hey, Alex?' Laura's voice was deep and more Sharon Stone than Christine Cagney.

'I wish you were here so you could lick my throbbing clit . . .' breathed Alex into the phone.

'Jesus fuck, you're horny, Alex. What are you wearing?'

'I was wearing my pyjama trousers; you know the kind with the drawstring and the slit that is just made for wanking. But I've taken them off now and am just sitting here in a tight, white vest, with my legs open and my juices dripping down onto my thigh . . .'

'Imagine, Alex, that I'm there,' whispered Laura softly into her mouthpiece. 'Imagine I'm kneeling in between your legs with my mouth just hovering over your clit so you can feel my hot breath in your cunt. What if my hands were to come up and caress the inside of your naked thighs. Just touching the soft skin of your inner thigh. My fingers are massaging the very top of your thighs now just brushing your hair and the lips of your cunt that are red and swollen . . .'

Alex moaned with pleasure as her fingers translated Laura's

words into reality. Wedging her phone under her chin she reached for her drink and pulled long and hard on the liquid.

Hearing the clink of ice on glass, Laura continued bringing herself and Alex off.

'I reach into your glass and take out a cube of ice and put it in my mouth . . .' Laura's voice tailed off so all Alex could hear was her heavy, erratic breathing.

Responding to Alex's moan and urges to continue, Laura went on.

'I'm taking the ice between my teeth and passing it over the lips of your pussy so you can feel the coldness of the ice and the hotness of my breath at the same time.' Alex moaned louder as she took the cube of ice out of her own mouth and smeared its cold wetness around the lips of her fanny. Her clit was aching for her touch, but Alex didn't want to rush the moment.

'Laura – are you touching yourself?' asked Alex, suddenly concerned for a moment that she wasn't giving as good as she was getting.

'You'd better fucking believe it, girl!' replied Laura and Alex could hear her breath coming in shorter, sharper rhythms.

'Laura, I want to hear you come,' said Alex urgently, afraid that the husband's presence in the other room might spoil the show.

'You will, honey, you will,' Laura gasped.

'Are you wet?'

'I'm fucking gushing here, sweetheart. I'm parting your lips, Alex. I can see your clit and am flicking my tongue over it.' Alex's hand moved to her clit. It barely took a second before she could feel her orgasm rising inside her . . .

Conchita lifted Steph off her torso and onto the bed next to her with ease. She rolled her over onto her front and climbed on top of Steph so their bodies were totally connected. Letting her thighs slide down so they were either side of Steph's beautiful, voluptuous arse, she reached down and gently parted her buttocks. When Steph felt Conchita's clit gently rubbing on herarse hole, she clenched her muscles and heard Conchita gasp with pleasure. The feel of the Spaniard's pubes and cunt on her hole was exquisite.

'Move with me,' urged Conchita as she thrust harder between Steph's parted flesh. With Conchita riding her, Steph tensed and released, squeezing Conchita's clit between her buttocks as she did so, and drew Conchita's orgasm out of her. The flood of Spanish that accompanied the flood of come that seeped all over Steph's body was exuberant in every way.

Sliding down so she was kneeling between Steph's legs, Conchita guided Steph round so they were draped over the side of the bed. She licked both women's juices that were saturating Steph's thighs. Her firm hands at the back of her knees, she opened Steph's legs wider and pushed them up and over her shoulders and started tonguing her arsehole. Steph gasped with excitement at the sensations that were taking hold of her body.

'Suck my clit,' begged Steph hardly able to contain her desire.

'What is this word you use?' asked Conchita innocently. Steph knew a reply wasn't needed as Conchita took her clit in her mouth and started flicking her tongue over it and began to suck, lick and chew on it for all she was worth. Steph could feel the orgasm growing inside her . . .

'Suck my clit, Alex,' said Laura as she worked on her clit with one hand and poked her cunt with the middle finger of the other hand. 'Fucking hell, you're gonna make me come,' drawled the sexy American woman down the phone. Laura's voice was getting breathier and louder as Alex continued to talk her to climax. Alex heard the sound of something falling off a table as Laura reached for a cushion to smother the sound of her orgasm.

With her fingers working furiously on her clit and in her cunt, Alex knew there was nothing she could do to hold back. The sensations seemed to gather from the pit of her stomach until they exploded in her cunt. Alex's orgasm was loud and extreme and made even more intense by the fact that she could hear Laura coming on the other end of the line.

'You are one horny bitch, Alex,' said Laura as soon as she could collect herself. 'Will you call me –' Alex heard the sound of a door opening and a man's voice calling out, 'Honey, are you OK?' just before the line went dead. She smiled to herself, looked at the clock and decided it was time to go to bed. After all, she had to look gorgeous for Brett in something like six hours' time. Even though it was late she couldn't stop herself from making sure those images of Steph were fixed in her mind.

Two of the four women fell into a deep sleep after their night's various sexual adventures. Alex lay awake going over all the reasons why she had to let Steph go while Steph lay awake looking at the stunning woman sleeping next to her and, in spite of the great sex she had just experienced and all her promises to Bev, couldn't help wishing it was Alex she was lying next to.

Two's Company

'Wakey, wakey, Steph!' said Bev as she burst into the bedroom. 'I've got enough tea and Marmite toast to sink a battleship and want to hear all about your evening.'

Steph became aware that someone else was in the room being obscenely chirpy and chatty. She poked her head out from under the duvet just as Bev was about to rip the curtains open and flop down on the bed to share their usual Sunday morning debriefing. Lifting her head Steph managed to signal to Bev that she wasn't alone. Bev was just doing a comedy, slow-mo retreat from the room when Conchita stirred and spotted her.

'Buenos dias,' Conchita croaked through a fag, booze and sex-drenched voice.

'Ohh, we have a foreigner in our midst,' teased Bev, her hand lingering on the door knob. She mouthed a half-hearted 'Sorry, mate' to Steph as she made no sign to move. A hand came out of the duvet.

'Conchita,' said the mound lying next to Steph by way of introduction. Bev shook the outstretched hand and introduced herself.

'Sorry, I didn't know Steph had company,' Bev explained.

'It's OK. Did I hear you talking about tea?' Obviously Conchita's need for a drink was greater than her need for privacy.

'I think I miscalculated the numbers but there's enough to go round.'

'Fantastic,' said Conchita while Steph looked on aghast at the scenario that was unfolding. Bev scurried out of the room and before Steph could retrieve the right words from her vodka-addled brain, she reappeared with a tray of tea and toast and plonked herself on the edge of the bed.

'So where do you come from in Spain?' asked Bev who was always Johnny-on-the-spot as far as small talk was concerned.

'Barcelona.'

'Really,' said Steph, quite proud of the fact that it was more information than she had gathered in more than ten hours with the woman. To Steph's dismay, Conchita was more than happy to welcome Bev into the bed as the three women drank tea and Bev chomped her way through the toast she had prepared.

'You have lived with Steph for a long time?' asked Conchita.

'Oh, yeah. We go way back,' replied Bev, fascinated by the new addition to the household.

'Girlfriends?'

'Yes. We've been sharing for years. She's the best girlfriend ever!' said Bev, trying her best to sell a product that had already been sold several times over.

'Sharing?'

'Yes. We've been most places and done most things together, haven't we, hen?' Bev gave Steph an affectionate hug.

The normal Sunday ritual had taken too much of a surreal turn for Steph to handle, however. Not knowing how to let Bev know that Conchita was obviously trying to lure Steph's best straight mate into a threesome, Steph turned over and wriggled out of the situation and under the duvet. Bev, in all her friendliness, bless her, remained oblivious to the whole situation.

'Why didn't you just tell me to go?' hooted Bev after Conchita had left.

'Jesus, Bev! I bring a woman home for the first time, like, ever and you come and get in bed with us. What the hell you do think she thought was going on?' retorted Steph, at once amused by Bev's behaviour and frustrated by her lack of tact.

'You could have told me that was what she was after!' said Bev.

'How could I? Bev, I thought you were a bit more savvy than that!'

'She just seemed so friendly.'

'You can say that again!' Steph laughed, remembering which part of her anatomy Conchita had chosen to kiss goodbye.

'So are you seeing her again?'

'She flies out tonight.'

'Oh. Bad luck,' said Bev, ready for an emotional-damage limitation conversation.

'No. It's OK. She was nice, but, oh, you know . . .' Steph's voice tailed off as she lost herself in her thoughts. There was a Pinter-like pause while Bev sat in the armchair in the living room, hugging her knees, nodding in taciturn agreement. Sheryl Crow's voice filled the room asking them if it made them happy why the hell were they so sad? Bev's voice finally cut through the music.

'But she was fucking gorgeous!'

Steph couldn't hide the fact that she'd had a wonderful evening. She blushed and laughed in agreement.

'So Conchita or mystery woman, then, Steph?' asked Bev.

'Oh, not this game, please!' replied Steph, too exhausted to enter into the 'fantasy sex league' game they played together so often.

'No, come on. Tell me.'

Steph silently blew into her coffee and enjoyed the steam on her face.

'Now let me see,' said Bev as she tried to find a couple of options. 'I'm just trying to find out who's your type. Who would you fancy . . .? OK, Angie on the post grad course or our Sarah?'

'Angie, definitely,' said Steph quickly.

'Oooh. Interesting.' Bev giggled, fascinated by the new twist their traditional pastime had taken.

'Angie or mystery woman?'

'That's not fair!' Steph smiled, entering into the spirit of the conversation.

'Right. I'm going to up the ante a little here so we're talking major league fantasy – I think this one is going to be a toughy . . .'

'Go on.'

'Catherine Keener or Sharleen Spiteri . . .?'

FOUR

Chest-touching

It was knocking thirty degrees when Alex stepped out of her front door on the most important Sunday morning of her life to date. Or at least that was how she saw it as she tried to stop herself wondering if she'd be disappointed if she only got a Golden Globe and not an Oscar for her performance.

Alex had thought very carefully about her outfit for this screen test. She had been aiming to achieve a look that was chic and sexy and her lycra-assisted, fitted black shirt, black DKNY trousers and jacket made her feel grounded and comfortable. She thought about taking the jacket back inside. The heat was a good excuse for shedding the garment she thought might de-feminise her too much, but she could see the 139 bus coming down the hill from West Hampstead and, on a Sunday morning, this was too rare an appearance to pass up.

Comforted by the fact that her favourite place on the bus – upstairs, front right – was free, she focused on keeping a lid on the excitement and nerves which were combining with the bus's lurching progress through the streets of north London to give her stomach a physicality all of its own. More good omens mounted to boost Alex's confidence as the bus went through green traffic light after green traffic light. At least the gods were smiling, thought Alex as she jumped off outside Liberty into the light

41

dusting of early morning shoppers that was already coating the West End's pavements.

There was something strangely invigorating about being in Soho on a Sunday morning. Seeing the sun on the freshly hosed-down streets through sober eyes and with coherent thoughts made Alex feel virtuous and in control. It had been her decision to give up the debauched life-style she had enjoyed when she first arrived in London as a teenager and, although the images of nights out cruising from club to club on these very streets made her feel nostalgic, she was certain she would never have been on her way to a meeting like this if she hadn't reined herself in.

Alex was buzzed into the building and made her way up to the studio on the first floor. Matt, the director, was totally absorbed in a game of *Tomb Raider* as Alex wandered into the space and Brett was sitting on the sofa flicking through a copy of *Vogue*. Neither registered her presence so Alex leaned in the doorway and waited for them to realise she was there.

'Matt, I think my character would have his hair like this in the movie – what do you reckon?' asked Brett, holding up a picture of one of the models in the magazine. As he did so he saw Alex staring at him from the doorway and leaped up out of his seat.

'Alex! Really good to see you again,' he said, practically running across the room with embarrassment at having been caught being less than butch. He kissed Alex on both cheeks and led her into the room. 'So how have you been? Good?' he chattered on.

'Fine. Thank you,' said Alex, trying hard not to show how fazed she was by the whole situation. This wasn't quite how she had expected things to pan out. Where were the casting directors, assistants, PAs . . . where were 'their people'?

'Matt! Hey! Alex is here,' shouted Brett above the high-volume sound effects that were coming out of Matt's computer.

Spotting a jug of filter coffee in the corner Alex decided to take control of the scenario. 'Coffee anyone?' she asked nonchalantly.

'Hey, Alex,' came Matt's reply although his attention didn't stray from the screen. 'Black no sac, for me, please.'

'Sure. Brett?'

'A dash of cream for me. Thanks.'

Alex went over to put the mug of coffee down next to Matt.

'Sorry, Alex. Won't be a minute. I just want to get out of this fucking room,' said Matt as his fingers moved clumsily over the keyboard.

'Yeah, me too!' said Alex daringly. 'I don't know about you boys, but I've got things to do this afternoon.' With that she leaned over Matt, positioned her fingers over the guide keys and expertly manipulated Lara around her cell and out onto the next level.

'Jesus, that was amazing!' exclaimed Matt from between Alex's breasts. Alex laughed and walked back over to Brett.

'So is that it or do you want to see what else I can do?' Alex was pleased to see that years of watching Joan Collins on TV were finally coming in useful.

'Yep. No, you're right,' mumbled Matt as he tried to collect his thoughts. They trooped into an adjoining room where a camera was set up and Matt blocked the scene they were going to do.

'OK, so let's walk it through a couple of times so you know when to hit your marks and then we'll do a take or two. Happy, Alex? Any questions?' Alex shook her head and they embarked on the scene that she had been going through in her living room only a short time before. Given the reception she had received on her arrival, she didn't find it hard to play 'Victoria', the patronising, powerful businesswoman to Brett's streetwise, bad-boy-with-heart-of-gold 'Tom'.

The challenge was the next scene.

'Yes, yes. That's absolutely perfect, sweetheart,' declared Matt from behind the lights. 'Good for you, Brett?'

'Great,' said Brett as he smiled at Alex. 'I can tell you're going to look good enough to eat,' he whispered in her ear before Matt came over.

'Now, Alex, I'm sure your agent must have said that we want to go through scene 45 too –'

'The seduction scene,' explained Brett as he shuffled around suddenly nervous again.

'Yeah. Fine,' said Alex, trying to remember the last time she had sexual contact with a man. A vague memory came to mind of some kind of laying on of hands during a play she'd done, but that had been a doctor and doctors don't really count, especially not fake ones.

'You know we're not looking for anything too heavy. I just want to get an idea of how you come across on film – so, you know, just follow my directions.' Alex nodded at Matt. 'So we'll start with a kiss in the doorway, working over to something more passionate in the middle of the room, where, Alex, you'll take off Brett's shirt and then we'll have a bit of chest-touching, blah, blah, blah. Brett, you just do the usual and then we'll end up with you both on the bed. Questions?'

Alex went over and put her jacket on a chair.

'You smell gorgeous, Alex,' said Brett as Alex moved in for the kill. 'What are you wearing?'

'Hugo Boss.' Alex always wore the men's aftershave instead of the women's version.

'My favourite.' Alex was slightly taken aback by what she took to be Brett's attempt at sarcasm and pulled away to try and read his expression a little better before moving in to kiss him. His expression was giving nothing away as she lifted her hands to stroke his face; she was pleased to feel that his skin was smooth and freshly shaven. Brett was pulling her closer into his body as they tried to work the script into their embrace.

'OK, and move into the room,' ordered Matt from behind the camera. 'Go, Alex – the shirt!' he said with mounting enthusiasm. Alex followed her director's instructions and pulled roughly at the buttons of Brett's shirt. She was impressed when she saw that underneath his body was as firm and muscular as all the posters in the teen magazines had suggested.

'Flies, Brett. Go for her flies and then move over to the bed,' barked Matt.

Alex added some heavy breathing to her performance and closed her eyes as Brett reached between their bodies to undo her flies. It was thoughts of Steph undoing her trousers in the studio at college that made Alex gasp at Brett's touch. Somehow they moved across the room and ended up with Alex straddling Brett on the bed. She was pleased, if a little surprised, to feel his erection pushing against his trousers and into her crotch and grinned at Brett who was looking shocked and flushed with embarrassment at his reaction to her. Mission accomplished, she thought as Matt called 'cut'.

'So, darling, how did it go?' asked Quentin as Alex walked into the coffee shop.

'Well, I think,' said Alex.

'Did Matt say anything?'

'He looked pleased, but you know,' said Alex, 'you can never really tell, can you?'

'What about Brett? Did he say anything?' quizzed Quentin, eager to have some sign that his cut of Alex's fee was safely in the bag.

'Brett was a sweetie,' said Alex, smiling at the thought of having simulated sex with one of the most desirable pieces of meat in Hollywood. 'He said I smelled nice.'

'Really . . .' said the portly agent sitting opposite her as he tried to fathom any possible hidden meaning in the comment. Not finding any he questioned Alex further: 'Did he give you any other sign at all that he liked you?'

'You mean apart from the fucking enormous hard-on in his pants when I was snogging him?' teased Alex.

'You're joking!' Quentin was almost foaming at the mouth with this priceless piece of information.

'Oh, Quentin, you're so gullible!' said Alex, laughing. She couldn't bare to see Quentin quite so joyous and, besides, she felt strangely drawn to Brett and didn't want to start any gossip that might backfire on her. 'Matt is going to call you on Friday to put us all out of our misery.'

'But that's practically a week away!' whined Quentin.

All Saints and Martyrs

'Three pints of Kronenbourg, two halves of dry cider and a Pernod and black, please.' Steph looked around the college local to find someone to help her carry the drinks back over to the table. 'Oi, Tina!' Steph yelled across the noisy room. Tina was enthralling the assembled company with the dance routine she had been learning for the production of *Grease* that was an inevitable part of every drama student's education. 'Tina!' Steph tried attracting her attention again and this time was successful. Putting her audience on hold, Tina step-ball-changed her way over to the bar.

'Bev, Kylie, you and Sarah,' said Steph, pointing at the drinks that were lined up on the counter.

'Ooooh. And who's the Pernod for?' mocked Tina.

'Marsha.'

'It'll take more than a Pernod and black to get her to cast you as Joan of Arc!' teased Tina as she poked Steph in the ribs. Marsha had been drafted in by the college as a guest director of *St Joan*, their next play, and Steph wanted nothing more than to dress up in some armour and fling a sword around. Tina went to take the drink from the bar when Steph intercepted her and picked up the glass herself.

'You're all right,' said Steph. 'I can manage these.'

'Cheers, Steph!' said Tina. Fortunately the drinks prevented more *Grease*-like moves being incorporated into her journey back to the group.

Steph scanned the room for Marsha. She had seen her talking to a group of first-year students earlier on and hoped she hadn't slipped out before she had a chance to collar her. She squeezed past the crowd that had enveloped the bar and was relieved to see that Marsha was standing just behind Bev and the others. Plonking Sarah's cider down on the table, Steph swung round and touched Marsha's arm.

'Hello, Marsha,' she said tentatively.

'Well, if it isn't our disappearing Rosalind,' remarked Marsha, alluding to the workshop Steph had not finished a couple of weeks ago. Steph gave Marsha the drink she had bought for her.

'To what do I owe this pleasure?' asked the tutor, flattered and intrigued by Steph's behaviour.

'I was wondering if I could have a word . . .' said Steph awkwardly.

'Of course, my dear.' Marsha separated herself from the people she was talking to and Steph followed her over to a quieter corner. 'What's on your mind?'

'Well, I never really apologised for dropping out of your workshop that time.' Steph was desperate for news of Alex, but didn't want to alert Marsha to the real purpose of their conversation. She told the older woman about having had some emotional problems which had made it difficult for her to concentrate on her work, but that it was all resolved now and she was looking forward to working on the play with her.

'. . . and I didn't even get to say goodbye to Alex,' sighed Steph. 'I really enjoyed working with her and it must have seemed a bit rude of me just to disappear like that.' Steph waited anxiously to see whether Marsha would pick up the bait and volunteer some information about their mutual friend without forcing Steph to come out and ask directly.

'As a matter of fact, luvvy, she wasn't able to make it back for the last session either, so you shouldn't feel bad about letting her down.'

'Really?' squeaked Steph, trying to contain her enthusiasm.

'Yes. She had a recall for a film she had auditioned for – a pretty big one actually – and had to rush off to read with Brett Torento.' She emphasised Brett's name in a way that was meant to impress.

'Brett Torento!' Steph was impressed. This really was a big deal. 'How did she get on?'

'Well, between you and me, she's done rather well,' hissed Marsha across the table in their booth. 'She'll know for sure in a couple of days' time.'

'Jesus! Tell her good luck from me, won't you?' said Steph politely.

'Of course, darling.' A thousand thoughts were going through Steph's mind. While she felt happy for Alex that her ambition was on the point of coming true, she knew that if she did get the part, there was no way Alex would willingly enter into the relationship Steph fantasised about having with her.

'What's Steph doing sitting nose to nose with Marsha?' asked Sarah. Sarah was a similar type to Steph – shortish, darkish and very competitive. The two had been going after the same parts

47

ever since they arrived at college and Sarah was deeply suspicious of Steph's conversation with Marsha.

'She's trying to increase her chances of getting to play "Joan", of course,' stirred Tina.

'Do you think so?' asked Sarah with a flash of anger in her eyes.

'For God's sake, Sarah. She's winding you up.' Bev didn't want her nice, quiet mid-week drinking session to turn ugly and attempted to smother Sarah's jealousy before it got out of hand.

'But . . .' stammered Sarah whose words were sticking in her throat somewhat.

'But what?' asked Kylie.

'I've heard Marsha's a dyke,' continued Sarah.

'Which means . . .?' said Bev, laughing.

'Well, I've heard some stuff about Steph recently too . . .' Sarah didn't know how to finish her sentence.

'Oh yes, about Steph being queer?' interjected Kylie.

'Precisely!' protested Sarah.

'Funky, huh?' said Kylie. The small, blonde Australian's real name was Alison, but she had earned the nickname after giving a frighteningly accurate rendition of *I Should Be So Lucky* at a karaoke night in town.

'Oh, please! Old news,' said Tina.

'So what do you think they're up to? All of a sudden Steph's the Godmother of some dyke role-stealing mafia?' Bev's sarcastic remarks made Sarah turn a sheepish shade of pink.

'OK. OK! Bygones.' Sarah went off to buy a round of McCoys as a peace-offering.

She was passing round the packets of crisps just as Steph came over to rejoin her mates and Marsha went back over to the women she had been talking to in the adjacent group. Sarah forced herself to smile at Steph in spite of her misgivings.

'So what's happening on Friday night?' asked Kylie, eager to sort out her weekend's socialising.

'Well, I'm off to Glasgow,' responded Bev.

'I didn't know you were going away,' said Tina.

'Yeah. Family duties to attend to. By the way, Steph, I was

wondering if you'd mind if a couple of friends stayed at the flat while I was away.'

''Course not. No problem.' Steph was really looking forward to having a bit of space after the emotional mind-fuck of the last few weeks, but Bev had been such a good friend to her that she felt mean saying no.

'So, Steph, what are you up to?' Kylie asked again.

'Oh, I dunno. Nothing much . . .'

'That reminds me,' said Bev and suddenly started rooting about in her bag under the table they were standing around. She dragged Steph to one side and thrust a piece of paper in Steph's hand. Steph caught Marsha's eye as she took the note Bev handed to her. She knew it was going to be a 'lifestyle-enhancing opportunity' and she was right. There was an address on it and scribbled underneath was 'women-only health club night' and a date. Steph read the words out loud – maybe louder than she realised – and this time Marsha shifted her position so she could hear Bev and Steph's conversation more clearly.

'Well, that's my Friday night sorted!' exclaimed Steph.

'It sounds fantastic, doesn't it,' encouraged Bev.

'How did you find out about this?' Steph was astounded by her friend's powers of investigation.

'I have my sources!' Bev laughed as she took in Steph's reaction. 'I don't think many people know about it, but I thought it might be something you would be interested in.'

'But I couldn't go to something like that on my own,' protested her friend although the prospect of spending a 'relaxed' evening in a sauna packed with dykes was beginning to tickle her fancy.

'I think that's exactly what you're meant to do, hen!' Bev laughed. 'I think it's meant to give people the opportunity of making new friends.'

Marsha's ears were burning by the time the women finished their drinks and headed for home.

FIVE

Touching Nerves

A lex had been on tenterhooks all week waiting for the phone call that would decide her fate. And now it was Friday morning she couldn't bear to be more than a couple of feet away from the phone. She'd had to turn the TV off as she'd already answered the phone three times that morning only to realise that it was part of some dreadful American soap that happened to be on. So when the phone did ring – in reality – she was so anxious she hardly dared pick up the receiver.

'Hello.' Her voice was breathy with anticipation.

'My, aren't we sounding sexy this morning!' came Marsha's voice through the ear-piece.

'Jesus, Marsha, I thought you were Quentin,' gasped Alex.

'Oh – no news yet?'

'No.'

'That's what I was phoning to find out really.'

'Marsha, you'll be the first to know, I assure you!' said Alex, warming to this diversion. 'So how are you?'

'Fine. I'm starting work on a play next week at the college where we did that last workshop.'

Alex found herself blushing at her memories of the last time she was there. Her thoughts turned towards Steph.

'You might be intrigued to hear that I had quite an interesting night the other night.'

'What salacious gossip have you got for me then?'

'I was having a drink with some students in the pub and overheard a conversation between that girl Steph you did your scene with and her chum.'

'Really?' Alex's flushed deepened.

'Did you know she was gay, Alex?'

'No. Not at all. Is that it? I thought it was going to be something more interesting than that!' said Alex, interested to the core in what Marsha was going to come out with next.

'She's not as delightful as you, my dear, but still rather attractive, wouldn't you say?'

'I don't know, Marsha! I don't really remember her that well. So how did you find this out?'

'Heard her talking to her friend about going to the women's health club tonight. Obviously looking for a bit of the other. Whatever you did to her during that workshop, my dear, must have hit a nerve!'

'You mean the Health Club in the City?' Alex was slightly jealous but also impressed that Steph had found out about such a coveted dyke secret haven already.

'That's the one. You've obviously driven her into the arms of a clutch of sweaty dykes, my love!'

Alex's warm, sexy feelings transformed into panic as she thought Marsha had found out what had gone on.

'Don't be ridiculous, Marsha. Whatever she's up to has nothing to do with me!'

'Don't underestimate your effect on women, Alex darling. After all, she did tell me to pass on her wishes of good luck to you for this film role.'

'Did she? Well, that's very sweet of her to think of me and obviously indicative of her developing a huge crush on me.' Alex laughed at Marsha's insatiable appetite for intrigue and innuendo. Their conversation continued in the way that it always did with Marsha coming on to Alex and Alex fielding her advances by protesting she was devoted to some boyfriend who had gone

Stateside about a year and a half ago and mysteriously couldn't bring himself to come home.

'– Marsha, I've got a call waiting,' interrupted Alex as the beeps broke into their conversation. 'I'll call you back.' She cut Marsha off and the phone rang immediately. Taking a deep breath, she composed herself before lifting the receiver again.

'Hello.'

'Alex, baby, you're on your way!' It was her agent's voice that boomed down the line. 'Matt loved you; Brett adored you. You start shooting in two weeks' time!'

Alex had never felt such intense excitement without the aid of sexual stimulation. She could hardly speak. She didn't know what to think. 'Two weeks?' was the only thing she could manage to say.

'The girls in the office think we should all go out tonight and celebrate. See you at the club tonight at 9.30 p.m. OK, luvvy? Well done, again.' Quentin blew a wet kiss down the phone and hung up. Amongst Alex's elation at having got the part was a tinge of regret that it was Steph who was going to the health club and jealousy that it was not going to be her who got to join in the fuckfest.

Steaming

Bev had left Steph with lots of advice and good wishes before heading off to Euston to begin her schlepp up to Glasgow. Among the instructions was the fact that her friends Angie and Maggie would be turning up later that evening but she didn't need to worry about being in as she'd given them a key. Steph wasn't planning on coming home any time soon, anyway. She had spent the afternoon in the shower, shaving and waxing everything that needed to be shaved and waxed in preparation for the night's activities. She had no idea what to expect but had told herself that now Alex was well and truly out of her reach, she may as well stop brooding about it and go out and enjoy herself. Turning the telly off after her weekly dose of Friday night comedy, Steph checked herself out in the mirror. She looked at her tube of mascara to make sure for the thousandth time that it was water-proof, wondered about changing out of the loose linen shirt she had on in favour of something more 'urban' before deciding that she wouldn't really have it on long enough to worry about it. She adjusted the top of the bikini she had put on – just in case she had misjudged the etiquette totally – and left the house.

By the time Steph was on the Piccadilly Line on her way into town, Alex had been at Quentin's club for at least an hour. In that time she had toasted her – and Quentin's – success several times over with Rachel and Sabrina who worked in his office, as well as with many other people she didn't really know.

'Darling, you must be sooo excited!' came yet another stranger's voice from the crowd as he made his way over to Alex. Unable to go through the whole spiel again about how fantastic the role was and how her fictitious boyfriend had sent her a dozen congratulatory roses, Alex made her excuses and ducked out to the loos. She leaned on the porcelain basin and splashed some water on her face. In the mirror she saw a woman emerge from one of the cubicles. She was gorgeous. Dark, sophisticated and incredibly sexy. Champagne always made Alex horny and she felt her body responding to the vision that stood behind her. For a second they looked at each other in the mirror and smiled. Alex finished drying her face and turned to face the woman who didn't make any move to get to the basin, but just fixed Alex with her eyes. Alex knew what was happening and as tempted as she was to accept the invitation that was being offered she knew she couldn't do it. The other woman spoke first.

'You're the one who's just got the Brett Torento movie, aren't you?'

'That's right.' Alex felt uncomfortable about all these people suddenly knowing who she was.

'Congratulations. It's a wonderful break.' The woman leaned in and gave Alex a lingering kiss on the cheek. Alex's body was saying 'What the hell?' as she put her hands on the woman's shoulders. But it was her mind that dictated the words that came out of her mouth.

'Thank you.' Another pause while Alex made up her mind for sure that she wanted to leave. 'Sorry, but I've got to get back to my agent. He must be wondering what's happened to me.'

'Shame,' said the other woman as Alex eased past her and went back into the bar. She accepted another glass of champagne and sunk back into the booth their party had commandeered and tried to wash away the feelings the woman had awakened inside her. Quentin spotted her and came over.

'All a bit hard to take in, isn't it, darling?' He breathed cigar smoke over her as he talked and put his arm round her. 'I told you it would all happen for you if you stuck with me, Alex.'

'Yes, Quentin,' said Alex curtly.

'So how are you going to say thank you to your Uncle Quentin then?'

'Jesus. You don't get it at all, do you?' Alex snapped. She was prepared to adhere to Quentin's professional demands but when he got lascivious with her, it made her stomach turn. She got up, downed the rest of her champagne and started to walk away.

'Where are you going?' Quentin shouted after her.

'Home.'

'But this is your evening!'

'Exactly and I don't want to be here any more.' The air felt cold when Alex slipped out of the club. After her encounter with the woman in the toilet, Alex didn't feel at all like going home to be on her own. She pulled a piece of paper out of her pocket. It was the address of the health club Steph was going to. Throwing caution to the wind, she hailed a cab and set off for the City.

Steph surveyed the scene she had walked into at the Health Club with trepidation. A delightful woman had given her towels, a locker key and shown her to the changing rooms. As they walked through the impeccably clean and deliciously scented corridor, Steph wanted to ask her exactly what the evening was about and whether she was going to be working all night, but didn't know how to ask either question.

'Just put your clothes in the locker and go through the door at the far end,' said the woman, as she gave Steph the once-over.

'The steam rooms, sauna and pool are all through there.' Steph lingered in the doorway of the changing rooms and the woman didn't show any signs of wanting to leave. 'OK?' asked her guide.

'Yeah. Ummm. I was just wondering. Errr . . . what do people wear in here?' stammered Steph, trying her hardest to keep her voice under control.

'Whatever you feel comfortable in,' came the reply. 'It's a very, umm, how shall I put it, "relaxed" atmosphere in here. Some women keep their swimsuits on, some don't, so it's really up to you.' Steph was intrigued by this woman, who was slightly more curvaceous than your average 'gym pilgrim'. She was wearing a crop-top and leggings that left little to the imagination, much to Steph's delight. 'So this is your first visit here?'

'Yep!'

'I'm sure you'll have a great time. It's quite busy tonight. I'm sure you'll have no trouble at all hooking up with someone.'

'Can't wait,' said Steph, thinking that as far as she was concerned it would take a lot to top the woman standing in front of her. The woman moved away reluctantly and was nearly out of the door before Steph finally plucked up the courage to ask her when she was knocking off.

'Around 11.00 p.m. I'll see you in the steam room at around ten past. OK?'

'Great!' Steph couldn't believe her luck as she abandoned her clothes – bikini 'n' all – grabbed a towel and strode off through the door at the back of the room and made straight for the sauna. The dry heat that hit her was intense as she sat down on one of the top shelves and let the atmosphere work on her tense muscles. After a few moments spent considering what was in store for her in the steam room a little later on, she had gathered her thoughts sufficiently to look around her. There were several women draped around the room in various states of undress and at various stages of sexual arousal. Steph tried not to stare as she saw the woman below her put her hand underneath her partner's towel and obviously, by the look on the other woman's face, into her fanny. They leaned forward and kissed languorously as the woman's hand undulated under the white, fluffy towel. Steph could feel her fanny responding to the scene and also to the prospect of the 'reception-ist's' invitation. The women seemed totally uninhibited as they proceeded with their love-making in front of the others in the sauna. The towel fell to the floor as the woman moved her hand away from her partner's cunt and kneeled in front of her open legs. As she thrust her tongue in the open cunt before her another woman moved across and starting kissing the lips she had left. The rest of the women in the room seemed too absorbed in their own activities to pay the emerging threesome any attention so, not wanting to assume the position of voyeuse, Steph decided she had time for a quick dip in the pool before keeping her appointment in the steam room. She felt a hand brush against her leg as if to stop her as she climbed down off her bench. She paused and let the woman run her hands gently over her buttocks before leaning down to break the news that she already had a date.

'I'm sure I'll be coming again,' said Steph as she felt blood rushing to her head and clitoris. With Crop-top Woman waiting in the steam room she didn't feel her parting statement was overly optimistic. She left the writhing women to their own devices and set off for her rendezvous.

Standing outside the health club, Alex hadn't given much thought to how she was going to conceal her identity or what she might do if she actually bumped into Steph. She gave a sigh of relief as the woman on reception seemed more preoccupied with handing over her shift to the next receptionist than with her slightly bizarre attempts at hiding her face. She scurried down the corridor with her towels and key and was pleased to see that no one else was in the changing rooms. Too much activity going on elsewhere, she remembered as she pulled off her clothes and stuffed them in her locker. The champagne had made her fearless, but hadn't dulled her senses enough to prevent her from realising that the steam room was the place to be for someone hoping not to be recognised. There she would collect her thoughts and try and formulate a plan that would enable her to scour the building for Steph. After hopping into the shower, she wound a towel round her head and another round her torso. It was a rather ineffectual disguise, but the best she could muster in the circumstances. She only hoped she would get a glimpse of Steph before the evening was out. She didn't want to speak to her, just see her, preferably naked. Preferably for long enough for her to have a wank and get back home undetected. Alex eased the door open and slipped quietly inside the large, mist-filled room. The steam was thick and, as she opened one of the bottles of mineral water provided, she lay back to enjoy the tongues of wet heat that caressed her body. Suddenly she became aware of voices.

'I thought you'd got caught up at reception,' came one voice floating through the steam.

'Someone came in while I was trying to get away,' said the other. 'I thought you might have got waylaid while I was working.'

'Well, the sauna was quite interesting but I didn't want to miss you, so I came right here.' Alex raised her head to look in the direction of the voices, but couldn't see who was there as the atmosphere was too thick. There was a pause and, as her interest subsided, Alex lay back down. Sounds of heavy breathing and mouths sucking at flesh wafted across the room. There was a pause before one of the women said: 'I don't even know your name.' The voice struck a chord in Alex's memory.

'Angela. But just call me Angie,' was the response.

'Well, Angie, you can call me Steph.' The hairs rose on Alex's neck. She was pinned to the bench with desire and anticipation of what was about to unfurl.

Angie pulled at the towel wrapped around Steph's waist and ran her hands over her moist thighs. She leaned over and guided her down so she was lying on the bench. Lowering her body down so she was lying on top of Steph she kissed her passionately and hard. Steph opened her mouth and felt Angie's probing tongue touch her own. Reaching up, she took Angie's firm breasts in her hands. She fondled Angie's breasts and caressed her nipples to make them hard. Angie gasped at her touch. Steph could feel the wetness of Angie's juices on her thigh as the woman thrust against her body and pushed her tongue deep into Steph's open mouth.

57

Manoeuvring herself out of the way, Angie's hand slipped in between Steph's legs and found her cunt. The wetness that greeted her had nothing to do with the temperature of the room. Steph's clit was already large and throbbing and Angie couldn't wait to feel it on her tongue.

'Open your legs, Steph.' Feeling Steph's body on top of her own made Angie react as if she hadn't had sex for years instead of hours. Alex twisted round so she was lying on her front, and inwardly pleaded for the density of the steam to disperse so she could get a better view of the couple she was sharing the room with.

'Anything you say,' said Steph assuredly. She swung round on the bench so Angie could get to her cunt that was aching for an orgasm.

'Christ, you're beautiful, Steph,' said the woman staring at Steph's open cunt before running her tongue over the length of Steph's hole. The steam cleared a little so Alex could see Angie's face in Steph's pussy and she remembered the time she had been in the same position. As Angie pushed Steph's legs wide apart and began licking Steph's inner thighs, the steam cleared and Alex was taken aback by the view she had of Steph's sex. Alex moved her hand down her body to touch her own cunt which was as wet and horny as Steph's. Alex took her hard clit between her fingers and rolled back the lips of her cunt so she could feel its protruding hardness more easily. Alex heard Steph gasp as Angie stuck her tongue in Steph's hole.

'Fuck, you taste good.' Angie's voice was muffled but Alex's body responded as if it had been her tongue in Steph. Alex felt her juices stream from her cunt and down her thighs.

Steph gripped the back of Angie's head and pulled her face even further between her open legs. As Angie's tongue worked her clit and her hole, Steph felt the orgasm building inside her. Alex heard Steph's breathing getting deep and fast. Alex touched her own fanny in time with Steph's moans. She wanted to come at the same time. Through the steam she saw Steph throw her head back and her hips grinding into Angie's face.

'Oh yeah!' Steph's voice through the steam was almost too

much for Alex to bear. Her fingers moved faster and faster in her cunt, from her clit to her hole until she too was on the brink of orgasm.

'Angie, you're going to make me come,' came Steph's voice across the room.

Angie flicked her tongue over Steph's clit and with a stifled 'yeess', Steph came in Angie's face. Although Steph didn't realise it, her and Alex's bodies convulsed with the intensity of simultaneous sexual satisfaction for the second time in under a month.

With the kind of clarity of thought that comes after having achieved a much needed sexual goal, Alex became all too aware of the risk she was running by staying there any longer. She grabbed her towels and bolted for the door. Steph heard the door shut. 'Oh my God, I thought we were alone!' she whispered in Angie's ear.

'You're never alone here. That's the beauty of it,' said Angie as she presented her aroused cunt to Steph.

'So? What are you going to do with that?' she asked. Steph was thrusting her fingers in and out of Angie's saturated cunt when Alex finally emerged from the shower and started to get dressed.

Angie pushed hard against Steph's body as Steph moved her fingers inside Angie's capacious cunt, twisting them around inside until she heard her partner cry out as she found 'the spot'.

'Oh yeah! Just there, babe. Just there.'

Steph massaged the inside of Angie's cunt with her fingers until she heard her groan with pleasure.

Alex was unsure whether to go home or wait for Steph to emerge from the club and confront her. She had desperately wanted to be in Angie's shoes earlier on and was being torn apart by her inability to keep her feelings under control.

'I want to take you home with me,' said Angie. 'But I'm meant to be meeting a mate at another friend's house tonight.' Suddenly the penny dropped. Steph knew that she had been set up and that Bev's match-making attempts had gone like clockwork.

'She's not called Maggie, is she?' asked Steph innocently.

59

'Yes. How did you know?'

'A little bird called Bev told me.'

'You're not *the* Steph, are you?'

'Yep. That's me!' The two women looked at each other and laughed.

'Shall we go then?' asked Angie.

The coincidence of two cabs coming along at the same time, coupled with the opportunity of saying 'follow that cab' was too much for Alex to resist. Alex got into one and Steph and Angie got into the other and off they all went to Finsbury Park.

SIX

Behind Closed Curtains

Steph and Angie arrived home to find Maggie sitting on the sofa leafing through Bev's *Hello!* magazines and listening to Steph's *Groove Armada* CD. Angie snatched the magazine out of Maggie's hands. 'This isn't a dentist's waiting room, you know!' she said, making her friend jump.

'Sodding hell! I didn't hear you come in!' exclaimed Maggie as she turned to greet her visitors. 'So you must be Steph.' Maggie got up to give Steph a kiss on the cheek as her hostess stood in her living room feeling more than a little disorientated.

'This is all a bit bizarre!' was all Steph could muster as an opening gambit.

'So, you found each other then?' The radiance of Maggie's red hair was only overshadowed by the brilliance of her American-white teeth shining through her grin.

'Boy, do I feel set up!' replied Steph.

'You should be grateful! Not many beginning dykes have great mates like Bev to help them negotiate their way along the uncharted path of lesbian sexuality,' declared Angie, demonstrating her sixth sense for scotch by making straight for its home in the cabinet.

'But at the club . . . you didn't . . . do it just because I was –'

'For fuck's sake, Steph. I fancied you the moment you came

61

through the door,' soothed Angie. 'Besides I didn't know who you were when we organised our little rendezvous, did I?'

'No, I guess not,' mumbled Steph. There was nothing worse than the thought of being the subject of a 'sympathy fuck' and there was something about Angie that Steph found really attractive. She was tall, dark and had gorgeous short, thick hair. Watching her as she swapped the evening's gossip with her friend, Steph thought Angie was the kind of person who feels good in their skin, as the French would say, and it was the relaxed confidence that surrounded her that really made her glow.

'Fancy some ice in this?' Angie asked.

'Sure,' said Steph, determined to go with the flow. 'The kitchen's at the end of the hallway.' Angie disappeared out of the door.

'So you and Angie got it together at the club, did you?' asked Maggie as she slumped back on the sofa and let the grooves from the sound system dictate the mood.

'Errr. Yeah. You could say that,' admitted Steph. She was trawling her memory for information about Bev's mates but couldn't remember her having spoken about them in any kind of 'couple' sense.

'I see,' said Maggie enviously. 'I wish I had been able to get down there too.'

'Yeah. Better than reading old copies of *Hello!* I can tell you!' Steph eased herself down onto the floor using the sofa as a back rest and waited to see how the evening was going to unfold.

Having arrived at Steph's house, Alex didn't really know what she was going to do with herself. The excitement and anticipation she had felt in the club and then in the cab as it tailed Steph through the streets and back towards her home had drained away. As had the buzz of copious amounts of champagne. No matter how much she wanted to, it would be madness to knock on the door and barge in on Steph and the woman she had picked up in the sauna. Standing on the pavement, she watched her cab disappear off into the distance and wondered where on earth she was going to get another one to take her home. The Seven Sisters Road wasn't the most salubrious area to be hanging around in the middle of the night, so she sat down on the wall outside Steph's living-room window and pulled her mobile phone out of her bag. She didn't have the number of a cab company but knew a quick flick through her address list would bring up the number of some Good Samaritan that would be all too pleased to come and pick her up. Looking through the window she could see the silhouettes of the people inside and was comforted by the sound of voices and low music.

Steph felt the cold warmth of iced scotch trickle down her throat and looked forward to the pleasant, fuzzy-limbed feeling she would soon experience as the liquid worked its way round her body. Angie had sat down next to her and they all concentrated on their drinks and the clinking of ice against glass. Maggie dropped her naked foot over the side of the sofa which Angie took between her hands and started to massage. Racking her brains and failing to find some appropriate topic of conversation, Steph filled her glass and passed the bottle round.

'Everything all right, Steph?' asked Angie.

'Absolutely fine.' She saw Angie's hand working its way up Maggie's calf muscle and wondered again exactly what the relationship was between the two women.

'We're not a couple, Steph, if that's what you're thinking,' whispered Angie, leaning over to find Steph's ear.

'Actually it was precisely what I was thinking!' Steph laughed.

'We're just mates who have sex with each other from time to time.'

'Oh. OK.' Steph thought that sounded like quite a cool arrangement to have.

'And if I'm not mistaken, I think we'd both like to have sex with you tonight.' Angie looked up at Maggie for some sign of agreement which Maggie was quick to provide.

Alex kept looking up at the window as she scrolled down the list of numbers on the screen of her mobile phone. She looked up as she heard the sound of laughter coming from the house. She saw the woman from the steam room come over to the window and thought she had been rumbled. But, instead of asking Alex what the fuck she was doing perched on the wall at the end of their garden, the figure bent down beneath the window sill and appeared to lift a bag up triumphantly. More laughter.

The cursor fell on Marsha's number. Alex knew that Marsha would do anything for her but was reluctant to call her ex-tutor. Still the cursor hovered over the number. Alex strained to see what was going on inside the house. She saw a woman bend down to put the bag back on the floor and rummage inside. The dildo that she extracted and held up for her audience stood out perfectly in the back-lit scene that Alex was observing. A wave of jealousy surged through Alex's body. There was more laughter from the house. Alex wanted nothing more than to ring the bell and join in the activities that were unfolding inside but knew she couldn't. She heard more voices and then a figure came to the window and snapped the curtains shut.

Alex felt her finger press the send key and heard the sound of Marsha's phone ringing in her ear.

Not being particularly in the mood for a game, Steph didn't really know what Maggie meant when she asked Angie to get them something to play with. She didn't need to draw on her abilities as a quick learner, however, to know what Angie had in mind when she tossed the large, multi-coloured dildo across the room to her. Steph fondled the shrink-wrapped 'toy' in her hands.

'Draw the curtains, Angie,' urged Steph, unwilling to give the neighbours the benefit of a free lesbian floor show. After shutting out the neighbours, Angie drew Maggie into an embrace in the middle of the room. They stood and watched Steph for a second.

'Just a little "thank you" present,' Maggie explained to Steph as she pulled the rubber cock out of its wrapping.

'Thank you for what?' Steph smiled.

'For having us, of course.'

Leaving Steph to bond with her new acquisition, Angie reached down for Maggie's flies and twisted her round so she was facing Steph who had climbed up onto the sofa. Maggie was small enough for Angie to wrap completely in her arms. Reaching from behind her friend, Angie undid Maggie's trousers and pulled out the strap-on that she was wearing underneath her clothes. Guiding Maggie into her body in time with the slow movement of her pelvis, she pulled on the phallus-shaped object that was poking out from her friend's trousers as they swayed to the beat of the music that filled the room. Maggie's face registered her pleasure as she felt the leather harness rub against her cunt. She reached behind her and ran her hands slowly up the inside of Angie's soft, parted thighs.

The wetness Steph felt in her fanny as she observed the two women was extreme and immediate. She watched Angie place her hands on Maggie's waist and run them up her body and over her tits. Steph slowly undid her shirt and let the material fall open. As the two women fixed her with their eyes, she pulled her bikini top off from underneath her shirt and started touching her full breasts. Steph enjoyed the fact that she was making these women so turned on.

'Take your shorts off, Steph,' said Angie who was still dragging her hands over the smaller woman's torso and pressing her aroused cunt into Maggie's arse. Steph wondered whether Angie was always the one who called the shots and felt a sudden rush of blood to her clit as she anticipated what was to come. Raising her hips off the sofa, she pulled her pants and shorts off in one movement. The white linen shirt was the only thing she wore now and the half-view of Steph's tanned body that could be seen through the near-transparent material that was draped over her breasts made her guests hotter than ever. Steph opened her legs and began to rub the head of the dildo over her fanny. Angie pulled harder on the dildo strapped onto Maggie's cunt. Steph was the most alluring woman she had met in a long time and while she was totally into having sex for sex's sake, fucking Steph wasn't just falling into the 'thrill-seeking' category.

The women continued to watch and be watched. Steph moved her legs even wider apart. She saw Angie's hand go into Maggie's pocket and pull out a condom. She squeezed the prophylactic out of its packet and positioned it at the tip of Maggie's dildo. Slowly she rolled the rubber down over Maggie's dildo, making sure to stimulate Maggie's cunt by manipulating it gently as she did so. Steph dipped her finger in her saturated fanny and licked her own juices. She watched Angie silently lift Maggie's T-shirt up and over her head.

'I think I'm ready now.' Steph's voice was monotone and controlled in spite of her excitement at the thought of being penetrated by a woman. She slumped further down on the sofa so that her cunt was positioned right on the edge. Maggie strode over to her, her thick rubber dick still poking out of the hole in her jeans. She kneeled down in between Steph's legs and slid her hands down the woman's thighs and round onto her arse. Angie was standing behind her friend, kissing and licking her neck and ears. Easing her body weight onto her arms Maggie positioned her dildo over Steph's cunt. She dragged it over Steph's large, desirous clit and heard Steph gasp. Tantalised by the pressure of Maggie's movements Steph moved her hips in an attempt to get the thing in her cunt.

'Don't play with me, Maggie.' Maggie's face was inches from her own and although she could feel the woman's breath on her face, they made no attempt to kiss. Maggie could feel Angie's hands caressing her buttocks through her jeans. Reaching past her friend, Angie ran her finger over the length of the open cunt that was before them. Maggie sucked greedily at the same finger when it was pushed against her lips.

'Think she's ready?' asked Angie.

'I guess so,' was Maggie's verdict. Angie positioned the rubber dick over Steph's hole. Maggie felt the pressure of Angie's hand on her arse increase, pushing her hips forward and her dick into Steph's cunt. Clenching her arse muscles she thrust harder and penetrated Steph in one swift movement. The shaft was thick and Steph cried out as she felt it filling her cunt.

'Are you OK?' asked Maggie. The last thing she wanted to do was to hurt the beautiful woman underneath her.

'Oh, God yeah. Maggie. Don't stop. Please don't stop.' Reassured that she was the provider of a pleasurable kind of pain, Maggie fucked Steph hard and fast. Leaning forward to build her rhythm, Maggie felt her tits brush against Steph's. She plunged her cock as far as she could into Steph's hole. Steph was revelling in the fullness she was feeling and the sensations that were being generated by the cold metallic pressure of Maggie's flies on her skin. Maggie eased the dildo out of Steph's sex until the head was almost visible, only to start pumping her cock into her again. She felt Angie's hands pulling at her jeans. She managed to let Angie pull them down and off without taking her cock out of Steph's cunt. With Angie's finger sliding in and out of her fanny and the dildo pressing against her clit every time she sank it into Steph, she knew that no matter how hard she tried to hold it back she was on the verge of coming. Angie proceeded to fuck Maggie with one hand and found Steph's clit with the other. It was large and aroused and Angie could almost see it throbbing with desire. She heard Steph's breathing getting shorter and sharper and recognised the pre-orgasm flush that had spread over Maggie's chest.

'I'm coming! I'm coming!' Maggie announced her orgasm as Angie worked Steph's clit in time with her friend's thrusts.

'Fuck me! Maggie, fuck me!' yelled Steph, her hands pulling Maggie's body into her own which was reaching out to meet her. Steph felt her cunt muscles contracting round the rubber cock inside her and her clit exploding with the force of her orgasm. Maggie's ever-increasing groans of satisfaction added to the noise of their climaxes as she lay on top of Steph's body, her dildo still filling her hole. Slowly she moved away and the women enjoyed the sight and sound of the come-saturated dildo being extracted from her sex. Maggie kissed Steph lightly on the lips. Steph's body was so alive with erotic sensations that feeling Maggie's hot lips on her own and the feel of Angie's hand resting over her fanny made her clit start to pulsate once more.

Maggie turned to Angie and kissed her friend who was now sitting patiently on the floor to the side of the women. Steph watched Maggie run her fingers through Angie's hair and push her tongue into her mouth. For the second time she thought just how much Angie looked like Alex and her desire continued to mount.

Maggie reached between her legs and pulled the condom off her dick. 'I suppose you'll be wanting some now, will you?'

Maggie teased Angie as she lowered her head to suck on her friend's breasts.

'I was hoping that Steph might want to try out her new gift.' Steph was peeling her shirt off her body and dropped the sex-drenched item on the floor as Angie looked at her and devoured Steph's naked body with her eyes. 'No offence, honey.' Maggie's feelings were far from hurt as she eagerly supplied Steph with the new harness they had bought to go with her dildo. With the length of rubber hanging between her legs, Steph suddenly realised what Marsha had been talking about in the acting workshop. She felt powerful and sexy and in control. She sat down on the floor in front of Angie who closed her hands round the shaft of her cock and pulled the slimy rubber condom down to its base. Steph's legs were either side of Angie's hips and she drew her in closer. The thought of running her tongue over Angie's pert, full breasts and nipples was driving Steph crazy. Angie's skin tasted soapy to Steph as she sucked on her nipple and was aroused by the pleasant musky scent of Angie's sex that rose up between them. Steph could feel Angie's strong fingers kneading into the muscles in her back and could hear soft moans of excitement as Steph rolled her tongue over one nipple and then the other. Steph felt Angie's hands gently pushing on her shoulders and gave in to her wordless command to fall back onto the floor. Moving up Steph's body, Angie positioned her cunt over Steph's dick. Steph could see Angie's juices glistening on her pubic hair and slid her thumbs down the side of Angie's cunt lips to make way for her cock. She guided Angie's hips so that the head of her dildo was at the entrance to her hole. Angie shut her eyes and groaned with lust and anticipation. Placing her hands on Angie's hips, Steph guided Angie down onto her cock and lifted her hips upwards to meet her. Steph gasped as she saw the large rubber object disappear with ease into Angie's pussy. With her fingers playing with Angie's clit, Angie lifted her body so Steph could pump her cunt with long, measured strokes. She allowed Angie to enjoy the full length of her dick each time, but made sure not to withdraw it completely.

'Steph, that feels so good,' exclaimed Angie as she stared down into her lover's face.

'Looks pretty fucking horny from where I'm standing too,' said Maggie who was recuperating from her exhausting shag by having a wank as she watched the two women fucking on the floor in front of her.

Maggie's comment made Angie suddenly aware of the fact that she had been totally fixated on Steph. Angie reached out for her friend, not wanting her to feel left out and, knowing exactly what Angie wanted, Maggie went over and joined the writhing couple. The sight of Maggie's open, wet sex standing over her made Steph's blood pound harder through her veins. Tilting her pelvis, Maggie presented her cunt to Angie's eager mouth. Steph's ring-side seat of Angie's hungry tongue lapping at Maggie's dripping cunt and chewing on her clit was almost too much to bear. Steph pumped her dick in and out of Angie's hole harder and harder and could hear Angie's muff-muffled moans of pleasure from above her. Maggie's orgasm was quick and quiet but left Angie drenched with her juices. Her friend pushed Angie down onto her back and, after obligingly licking her come from her face, left it to Steph to make her come. Angie abandoned herself to Steph's rhythm. Each thrust intensified the waves of orgasm that consumed her pelvis and overtook the whole of her body in waves of glorious sensation, culminating in a primal 'uuuhhh' escaping from her lips. When she opened her eyes she saw Steph's glowing face smiling down at her. She pulled Steph down on top of her and smothered her in kisses as they rolled around on the floor. For a moment Steph wondered whether Angie could be the one who would stop her thinking about Alex.

Mood Swings and Roundabouts

Alex hadn't been too open to answering Marsha's questions as they drove back to the tutor's Muswell Hill apartment.

'What in heaven's name were you doing wandering around Finsbury Park at two o'clock in the morning?' asked a bemused Marsha.

'Not now, Marsha, please,' was all Alex could reply.

'You drag me out here and you're not going to tell me why!' exclaimed her rather bedraggled-looking chauffeur.

'The friend I was meant to be visiting was out. OK?'

'Humm.' Marsha contemplated Alex's dark mood and outlandish behaviour. 'I thought this would have been the most exciting day of your life, darling.'

'It is.'

'Well, forgive me for saying so, but if this is euphoria, I dread to think what you're like when you're depressed!'

'It's late and we're both tired, Marsha. Can we talk about this in the morning?'

'As you wish.'

Marsha led Alex up the stairs of her flat and into the spare room.

'Thank you for coming, Marsha,' said Alex as the older woman bent down to kiss her gently on the cheek.

'I'm glad you felt you could call,' she said soothingly. 'Try and get some sleep and we'll sort out whatever's bothering you in the morning. All right?'

Alex could hear the sound of voices in the next room as she drew the duvet up around her and inhaled the comforting smell of fresh detergent. She hadn't banked on Marsha having company and hoped that whoever it was would be gone by the time she got up in the morning.

Disorientated, Alex looked around the room and wondered where on earth she was. The ethnic *objets* that littered the surfaces and the sound of Mahler coming from the room downstairs were good clues and prompted the events of the previous night to rush in front of her eyes like scenery from a speeding train. The dramatic music made Alex smile as she remembered the astonishment in Marsha's voice when Alex finally placed the call. Marsha did rather fancy herself as bohemian and unshockable but with a vulnerability that bordered on the dangerous. But Alex knew that, despite her desire to be seen as fey and eccentric, Marsha was as tough as old boots.

Alex was pleased to see that the sun was shining as she opened the curtains and went downstairs to say good morning to Marsha.

She knew Marsha was going to have more questions for her than Chris Tarrant had for a season's worth of would-be millionaires, but she didn't know yet quite how she was going to handle the situation.

To her delight Marsha was alone in her kitchen and enveloped in a kaftan that practically shook with colour and pattern.

'Coffee, darling?' she asked as if it were the most usual thing in the world for Alex to emerge from her spare room wrapped in her towelling robe.

'Umm. Black, please. No sugar.' Alex pulled out a chair from under the table and waited to be served.

It was practically the afternoon before the tangle of bodies on Steph's bed finally unravelled themselves and heaved their sex-weary bodies into the bathroom. Washed, scrubbed and only a little bruised they sat around the breakfast table deciding what to do with the rest of their day.

'OK. I've got it!' said Maggie. 'A turn round Safeway to pick up some food, back here, pack a picnic, grab the football and stroll down to Finsbury Park.'

'Not too sure about the football bit,' said Angie as she rubbed her groin. 'Maybe I could be the ref.'

'I never knew you were such a lightweight, Angie!' teased Maggie.

'Sounds great,' said Steph, happy to have her day mapped out for her, although she was wondering how she could engineer some time alone with Angie. She looked at Angie who was leaning back in her chair across the table from her and was pleased to find she was already returning her gaze. They smiled at each other, united by their apathy in the face of Maggie's cheeriness.

'. . . then back here, clean up, and head off into town. I've heard there's a new club that's just opened in Victoria. Maybe we could check it out?'

'For dykes?' asked Angie.

'*Mais, bien sur, chérie,*' said Maggie, smiling, pleased by the lack of resistance to her plan. 'Anything less is a waste of energy as far as I'm concerned!' The women smiled at her enthusiasm. 'Come

71

on then! What are you waiting for?' Maggie sprang into action and tried to herd the others out of the house and in the direction of the supermarket.

'I tell you what,' said Angie, making no effort to move. 'Why don't you go to the shops and we'll stay here and tidy away the breakfast things?'

'You see! Bloody lightweights, the pair of you.' Maggie grabbed her wallet and headed for the door.

'Oh, Mags! Get us a paper, will you?' shouted Angie. There was no answer but the door slamming shut.

'Good time last night, Steph?' asked Angie.

'I'm surprised you have to ask,' replied Steph. Angie was a difficult woman to read. Because so little seemed to faze her it was hard to know what was going on in her mind.

'Can't wait to do it again.' Angie smiled seductively.

'I guess you'll have to ask Maggie about that!'

'No. You know what I mean. I'd really like to get to know you, Steph.'

'Yeah. Me you too.'

'How can I tell you what's wrong if I can't get a word in edgeways!' butted in Alex. She wasn't sure how Marsha would react when she told her about the set-up she had with her agent but knew she had to tell someone, if only to safeguard her own sanity.

'So you're a dyke, but you can't have a relationship or even sex with women because you think your career will collapse if this Quentin monster finds out and withdraws his support?' clarified Marsha.

'Yes. I suppose that's about the sum of it.'

'Good God!'

'Are you shocked?'

'Shocked that you've agreed to such a thing!'

'Not that I'm gay?'

'For heaven's sake, Alex. Credit me with a bit of nouse. I knew from the moment I met you.'

'That obvious, is it?' said Alex as panic flooded her body.

'Only to the very accustomed and extremely well-trained eye, my dear.' Marsha walked past Alex and ruffled her hair as a supportive, reassuring gesture. 'So can I also presume that the house you were waiting outside last night harbours some sort of femme fatale who has had such an effect on you that you are unable to celebrate the most significant event of your career to date?'

'You could say that.' Alex peered up at Marsha and wondered what it was about her that made her the only person who could make her feel like a little kid.

'Well, Alex. I don't really know what to say. I have never been in your situation, but I think I should urge you to question your agent's motivation.'

'What do you mean?'

'Well, my dear. Are you sure that you couldn't have a perfectly happy, if private, private life and enjoy a flourishing career? I have met a lot of men in this business who get their kicks from overpowering and controlling young women. What I'm saying is, is he just saying these things because he enjoys the power he holds over you, or do you really believe that your career would suffer if you left him?' Alex pushed her hands through her hair and thought hard. She didn't like the fact that she might have been gullible and impressionable and far too eager to get on to see what was really going on. 'There are plenty of agents with far more going for them than Quentin-bloody-de-Fleur, my dear, and I assure you not all of them are manipulative control freaks.'

Alex needed space to think. What Marsha was saying was empowering, but it also made her feel sick to her stomach. She got up from the table to go upstairs and get dressed.

'By the way, you haven't signed anything, have you, Alex?' Alex turned round and grimaced.

Steph's front door opened and Maggie rustled in carrying several plastic bags.

'Jeez, guys, I thought you were going to clear away,' said Maggie when she saw the kitchen looking exactly as she'd left it but with less coffee in the cafetière. 'I don't think you deserve this now!' She flung Angie's tabloid down on the table.

Steph could feel all the colour draining slowing from her face as she looked at the inset picture of Alex on the front page. The caption read: 'British newcomer lands role in top movie'.

Angie had already read the front page and was looking at the picture of Alex. Maggie looked over her shoulder. 'She's a bit fit,' she remarked lasciviously. 'Who is she?'

'I think she looks at a bit like me.' Angie imitated Alex's pose in the publicity picture they had printed.

'You wish, sweetheart! Turn to page six, then!' Maggie tried to turn the page to find out the rest of the story. But Angie steadfastly hung on. Picking the paper up she held it up to show Steph. Striking the pose again, she said: 'What do you think Steph?, Practically twins, aren't we?' Maggie tried to grab the paper from Angie's hands, then realised Steph wasn't entering into the spirit of their horseplay.

'Jesus. Are you OK, Steph?' Angie asked anxiously. 'You look like you've seen a ghost.'

'I'm fine. Really. Just too much whisky and not enough sleep.'

'Can I get anything for you?' asked Maggie.

'No, really. I'll be OK. Why don't you two just go on out to the park and I'll call you a bit later if I'm feeling better?'

'I don't want to leave you looking like this.' Angie put her arm round Steph's shoulders. Steph could feel the tears begin to ooze out of the corners of her eyes.

'No. Please. I'll be fine on my own. Just go, yeah?'

Angie kissed Steph lightly on her forehead and brushed the hair out of her face. 'Can I call you?' she asked tentatively.

'Why don't I call you?'

'Whatever you want.' Angie looked at Maggie and pulled a face. Angie was confused by the sudden change that had come over Steph. She was disappointed not to be spending more time with her but knew it was their cue to leave.

SEVEN
Freakish Behaviour

It was probably just as well that Marsha hadn't cast Steph as the lead in *St Joan* as the events that had occurred over the last few days meant she had rarely felt less Joan-like or saint-like in her life. Consequently, for once, she was happy to let Sarah take centre stage and float around in the background in a variety of small parts for which a standard slightly quizzical expression suited every scene. Bev had been almost beside herself with curiosity when she got back from Glasgow on Monday morning. She wanted to know everything: whether she had met Angie at the health club, did she like her, what she thought of Maggie and wasn't she simply the best mate ever for orchestrating the whole thing? Steph did her utmost to make Bev think that she'd just had the best time – which she had before she'd seen Alex's picture in the paper – but she knew that once Bev had spoken to Maggie and Angie herself, she would find out about her apparently freakish behaviour.

It wasn't until the following week in rehearsals that Bev was able to confront Steph about avoiding Angie's phone calls. Bev hooched up closer to Steph as Marsha swept around the studio giving them notes after their first full run-through. Marsha was employing Joan's sword to attract the attention of those she was talking about and currently it was being used to point out how

Jason Burlington's shoulder tension was causing his epaulettes to brush the base of his ears.

'Relax, darling,' Marsha encouraged the rather frightened-looking boy. 'Generate your voice from your centre . . .' Jason's eyes registered panic as the sword was whipped away from his shoulder and made for his groin. 'We don't want to see your neck muscles bulging or your shoulders heaving ever again, do we, people?' There was a vague murmur of agreement as Marsha's sword sought out her next victim.

'Ah, Sarah . . .'

Content that Marsha's attention would be diverted from the whole group for at least five minutes, Bev turned to whisper in Steph's ear. 'Angie left another message on the machine for you today,' she said.

'Oh really?' Steph knew Bev had picked her moment carefully to bring this up. Bev had Steph cornered as this was one situation her friend couldn't get up and walk out of without causing a stir, and Bev knew it.

'She really likes you, you know. Why won't you call her back at least?'

'Look, Bev, I'm just not in the right space at the moment,' said Steph.

'But she said you had such a good time.'

'Yeah. We did. It's just that if I went out with her again, I think I would be doing it for all the wrong reasons.'

'What do you mean? You're attracted to her, aren't you?'

'Yes, but that's half the problem. I think she is really nice but, oh God, I can't really explain . . .'

'Jesus, girl! She's asking you out for a drink. It's not that heavy, you know.'

'I know that, Bev. It's just that she reminds me too much of someone else, that's all,' hissed Steph.

'Not that bleedin' woman again?' sighed Bev. 'How are we going to help you move on?'

'Beverley, my dear.' Marsha's voice interrupted their little tête-à-tête. 'If you paid more attention to my notes and less time talking to Stephanie you'd know that you're meant to set the ladder and bucket *after* the Dauphin sits down in Act One, not before. By the way, Gavin, how is your head? No harm done?'

Pole Position

Bev and Steph agreed that they would go into town that night, have a few drinks and try to find a way of snapping Steph out of what Bev had taken to calling Steph's 'bad funk' although Steph didn't know what *Shakatak* had to do with anything. Steph sat in the bar and chased the lemon round her glass with her straw. She knew something had got to give. Her graduation show was coming up quickly and at this rate she was going to have as much impact on stage as the fruit she was playing with.

Bev was already half an hour late when Steph heard her phone ring and saw the college number flash up on the screen. Plugging her free ear with one hand she tried to hear what Bev was saying to her. Steph gathered that rehearsals for the song presentation she was working on were running late. She was very sorry for letting her down, especially today, but suggested they rearranged for the following night. The new, positive-minded Steph decided it would do her no good to go home and try and sort herself out. Living at the scene of the crime didn't make for a clear thought process. She had been eyeing a poster on the wall of the bar which advertised a women's strip night at a club just down the road. Feeling in a bit of a Raymond Chandler-esque 'lone hero against the world' kind of mood, she decided to sup up and go take in some pole dancing.

Walking down the stairs she was pleased to note that the club was smoky, seedy and dark. Only a sprinkling of women populated the velour-covered room – just the sort of place where the great and the good of detective fiction would come to down scotch and do their best thinking. Steph headed straight for a stool at the bar and, after ordering her drink, turned her attention to the action on stage. Although Steph had never been to a strip club before, the place looked and felt very familiar, even down to the woman on stage – who was attractive in a 70s, long hair, Jacqueline Smith sort of way – and the slightly tinny, baseless music she was dancing to.

She felt someone sit down on the stool next to her and turned to look at her cute, male companion.

'I thought this was women's night?' said Steph, wondering how he'd slipped through the gender detector.

'Women and boyfriends of the barman.' He smiled and settled back in his stool. They sat in silence for a while, both staring at the gyrating dancer. 'Great body, huh?' he said, nodding in the direction of the stage.

'Yeah,' agreed Steph.

'Want me to introduce you? You look like you could do with some female company.'

'I'm kind of enjoying just looking at the moment,' said Steph. 'Thanks anyway – sorry, what's your name?'

'Brian.'

'Thanks anyway, Brian.' Steph hadn't meant to tell a stranger her life story that night but seeing as Brian had the time and Steph the inclination, that's what ended up happening. 'I'm totally infatuated with her, Brian,' said Steph as she came to the end of her story. 'I know she liked me or she wouldn't have come over to my place that evening.'

'You mean, after you'd got it together at this acting class thing?' Brian was kind and interested in Steph's story, but was finding it hard to keep up with her garbled interpretation of events.

'Yeah. I know it's absolutely fucking mad. I mean I know that she might not want the whole world to know that she's a dyke, but, Jesus, it's a bit extreme, don't you think?' Steph banged on, enjoying the freedom of being able to talk about her problem with someone who knew nothing whatsoever about her and wouldn't have a clue she was talking about Alex.

'So would I know her then?' Brian was thoroughly enjoying the drama in Steph's account and was egging her on to tell her who she was. 'Is she on telly?'

'I'm not telling!' Steph laughed at Brian's attempts to lighten the mood. He shouted over the bar to his boyfriend and together they dredged the depths of their imagination to come up with more and more ludicrous suggestions for who Steph's lover might have been.

'Why don't you just bloody go round to her house and tell her how you feel!' Brian loved an unrequited love story and his Blitz spirit was really helping to give Steph some hope.

'Do you know what, Brian? You're right!' agreed Steph. 'I should find out where she lives and go round and tell her how I feel and she can like it or lump it!'

'If she's so famous, you know what you should really do, don't you?' chipped in Brian's boyfriend from behind the bar. 'Tell her if she doesn't pick up where you left off, you'll sell your story to the papers!'

'Oh, yeah,' agreed Brian. 'Everyone adores a good kiss 'n' tell!'

'Jesus, guys! What kind of girl do you think I am?' said Steph with mock indignation.

'The kind who comes to a women's strip joint and spends all night talking with a couple of poofs which is pretty bloody strange as far as I can see!'

Brian was right. She wasn't making the most of the situation at all and, armed with a plan and feeling lighter than she had for a long time, thought a little fun might be just the right way to finish off the evening.

'Maybe I'm ready for that introduction now, Brian.' Brian reached for the internal phone and spoke to someone for a few minutes.

'She's going clubbing but said she wouldn't mind some company,' reported Brian. 'I told her you're as cute as a button and she's waiting at the front door. She doesn't do this for just anyone, you know!'

'What's her name?'

'Ally.'

'Laters, boys!' said Steph as she moved towards the exit. 'And cheers for everything!'

Uncomplicated Moments

The club had been fun. Spending a Tuesday night in a packed, sweaty, loved-up venue was just the ticket as far as Steph was concerned. And Ally had turned out to be a scream. Steph had wondered just what kind of arrangement she had with the boys at the bar, but soon discovered why they were so keen to fix her up. The dancer was pretty much in a similar situation to her own. Ally was 33, just split up from her girlfriend and was suffering from the aching clit as well as the aching heart that went with that scenario. She was studying to be a lawyer, hence the nights raking in the cash at the strip club.

Steph looked around Ally's flat and out of the window onto the streets below. 'Steph – aren't you going to come to bed?' Ally's voice came from the bedroom. Steph was expecting it to be some kind of red PVC, leather-lined boudoir and was a little disappointed to see that the walls weren't adorned with whips, seven-inch stilettos and handcuffs. Ally was lying on the futon and had lit incense and several candles. The lights were low and the sultry air of the spring night wafted in through the muslin-covered window carrying the night's noise with it. Ally came over and started undressing Steph, slowly and carefully. Her touch was soft and sensual and lingering and Steph abandoned herself to it completely. Pushing her silk robe off her shoulders and onto the floor, Ally moved closer to Steph until her visitor could feel her smooth olive skin and tight dancer's body against the length of her own. Ally kissed Steph lightly on the neck and moved Steph over to the bed.

'Don't be tense, Steph,' said Ally as she ran her hands over Steph's back, working at the knots as she went. The two women let their hands explore the newness of the other's body. Ally's kiss felt soft, sensual and erotic on Steph's lips and she willingly opened her mouth to take the woman's tongue inside. Their tongues sensuously entwining inside the other's mouth, Steph drew Ally's body closer into her. The feeling of her naked thighs against her own was comforting and enticing. The way Ally curled herself around Steph's body in slow, languid movements made the younger woman feel as if they were making love under water. If anyone could feel relaxed and stimulated at the same time, this was what Steph was experiencing and enjoying every uncomplicated moment. Ally's movements were painstaking and precise but incredibly sexy in a controlled, knowing way. Steph felt Ally's pubic hair moving against her own and parted her legs to allow her inside. The pressure of Ally's thigh against her cunt was delicious. In no hurry to bring their lovemaking to a climax before having devoured every inch of the other's body, the two women writhed and wound their way over the bed. Steph felt Ally's hands massaging the bottom of her feet and groaned as she pressed a spot that seemed to release the ball of tension that had been in her neck for weeks.

'Christ, that feels good,' Steph said to the woman making love to her. Ally looked up and smiled at her as she continued to kiss, lick and stroke her way up the inside of Steph's calves and thighs. With her mouth getting nearer to Steph's throbbing cunt, Ally climbed on top of Steph, swinging round as she did so, in order that Steph could get the full impact of her aroused and saturated cunt. Putting her hands on Ally's hips, she drew her partner up further still until both their mouths were only inches away from the other's cunt. Steph could feel Ally's tongue tantalisingly lick the very top of her thigh, but the open fanny above her, with its hanging labia swollen with desire, looked too appetising for her to tease in the same way. The sudden flick of Steph's tongue on her clit made Ally groan with pleasure. She dragged her tongue back and forth over Ally's wet sex, lapping up her juices and inhaling the smell of her aroused cunt. As Steph stuck her tongue in her hole, she felt the warmth of Ally's mouth on her own clit. As she ate the pussy that was sliding backwards and forwards across her mouth, she could feel Ally biting, licking, stroking and sucking at her clit and felt like she had the biggest hard-on in the world – the sensation of eating cunt and being eaten was exquisite. Steph continued to tongue Ally's hole but it was when she started flicking her clit with her finger that she knew Ally was close to coming. The sound of Ally's deep, throaty moans turned Steph on even more. The feeling of Ally's tongue on her clit and her finger sliding in and out of her drenched hole was more than she could bare. Both women found it hard to hold onto the other as their hips jerked in simultaneous orgasm. Ally turned and took Steph in her arms.

'Thank you,' she said softly.

'Thank *you*,' Steph replied.

'Forgotten about your girlfriend problems?' asked Ally.

'What girlfriend problems?' Steph smiled at the dreamy woman she was lying next to and slept more soundly than she had for weeks.

Plans and Persistence

Steph wasn't on the call sheet for rehearsals the next day but was going to be very busy nevertheless; she had a plan to execute. 'OK. Now think. How would VI Warshawski go about finding someone in a city like this?' she murmured to herself as she contemplated her first move. Donning bad clothes, devouring home-made pasta and embarking on marathon jogging sessions were the major things Steph remembered from her favourite novels, all of which were out of the question, so she reached for the phonebook instead. Start with the basics. Flicking through the pages, she knew it would be a long-shot but had to try anyway. 'Alexandra Dechy, Alexandra Dechy . . .' Steph repeated the name over and over as she scanned the pages of the directory. No luck. Maybe she's just moved in, thought Steph, pleased that her analytical skills were warming up somewhat. Dialling directory enquiries she was told that there was a number registered under that name in St John's Wood, but they couldn't give it to her as it was ex-directory. No, they really couldn't give it to her. Not even if she was the person's long-lost sister just returned from Australia and had only three days to live. As she put the phone down, Steph knew she'd overplayed the thing about being her sister, but, hey, desperate times and all that. OK, next step: call her agent. Would have to find a better story than the sister thing. Steph picked up the phone and dialled Quentin de Fleur's agency.

'Oh hello, can I speak to the person who represents Alexandra Dechy, please?' Steph asked the upper-class voice that answered the phone. Fortunately it was only a brief snatch of Tom Jones that came down the line before someone else came on the line.

'Sabrina speaking, can I help you?' came a new voice.

'Do you look after Alexandra Dechy?' asked Steph.

'I am Quentin de Fleur's assistant, yes.'

'Oh, great, hi. My name's Sophie, I've been asked to make a comprehensive contact list for everyone working on the shoot and need you to give me Alex's home number, fax, address, email – you know, all the essentials, just in case of emergency. You know how unpredictable these sorts of things can be!' Steph was surprised at actually how efficient she sounded.

'Can you hold just a second?' Sabrina asked.

'Yes,' said Steph as Sabrina put her hand over the receiver and spoke to someone nearby.

'What did you say your name was?' she asked again.

'Sophie. Sophie Brooks,' said Steph after peering down at the phonebook for inspiration. Steph heard what she presumed to be Quentin's voice before Sabrina came back on the line. 'Mr de Fleur says he's got a copy of the up-to-date contact list in front of him; can I ask which department you're calling from?'

'Oh, OK. There must have been some kind of misunderstanding. Sorry to have bothered you.' Steph quickly put the phone down before Sabrina could ask any more awkward questions. She had just blown her best shot at getting an easy result and was a little frustrated by how difficult it was becoming to find out such a simple fact. Marsha had to be the next port of call, but Steph knew she was going to have to be very subtle about the way she handled the guest director – she didn't want her running off to blab about her to Alex before she'd had a chance to speak to Alex herself. There is always a feasible reason for wanting to contact anyone, as long as you have enough time and imagination to think of it and Steph had both. She cleared her head and lay down on her bed to think. What would Marsha think was a legitimate reason for her wanting to get in touch with Alex? She tossed various ideas around in her head. It had to be something to do with the film role she'd landed, but just wanting to say congratulations wasn't good enough. It had to be about someone that she wasn't directly involved with, like she was doing someone else a favour. She flicked through one of the ubiquitous *Hello!*s looking for inspiration. It was pictures of the airbrushed stars draped around their homes that finally gave her the idea. She would have a really good friend – maybe even relative – who was just starting out as a journalist and was looking for her break into the world of women's glossies. An interview with Alex would be just the thing.

'. . . I know, it's a little unorthodox to go through you, Marsha, but, as you're always telling us, contacts aren't contacts unless you contact them, are they?' Steph had managed to drag Marsha out of the staff room to speak to her on the phone in the college office.

'True, very true. What magazine is this friend hoping to place the piece with?' asked Marsha.

'Oh right, yeah. You know, one of the top ones, definitely.' Steph sensed that Marsha was breaking. 'I tell you what. Why don't you give me her address and I'll pop a copy of her work in the post to Alex tonight?' Steph continued to plug away.

'She so busy at present, Steph, I don't know . . .' Steph was almost holding her breath in anticipation as Marsha weighed up the pros and cons. 'Right – this is what we'll do. Get your friend to fax some information and a contact number over to me at the college and then I'll pass it on to Alex. How's that for a plan?'

'Great. Yeah. I'll mention that to her. Thanks for your help, Marsha.' Three ideas, three dead ends. Then an even more daring idea sprang into her mind. The records at Alex's old drama school. They were bound to have her address. All she would have to do was wheedle her way into the office of the School of Performing Doo-daas or wherever it was that she trained, have a flick through the files and Bob would be her uncle.

It was one thing to try and fool people on the phone but quite another to actually go through an organisation's confidential records, however. Steph wiped her sweaty palms on her trousers as she waited outside the secretary's office at Alex's old drama school. She hadn't wanted to risk not being given an appointment that day, so simply turned up unannounced declaring that she was interested in auditioning for a place at the school and was hoping to pick up an application form.

'Sophie?' A woman emerged from the office she was sitting outside. 'Sophie Brooks?'

'Yes. That's me,' said Steph who nearly hadn't recognised her new name.

'Come in, won't you?' Steph followed the neat, tailored woman into the old-fashioned office that creaked with filing cabinets and piles of papers. Steph's heart sank. How was she going to find what she wanted in this chaos? The woman didn't even have a computer.

'So you're interested in studying with us here, are you?' asked the woman as she plonked another pile of papers down at the foot of her desk.

'Absolutely. I was wondering when your auditions are and whether I'm too late for next year's intake?' Steph was trying to look keen and focused, but her eyes were flicking manically around the room looking for some hint of a filing system, duodecimal or otherwise.

'I'm afraid to say, Sophie, that you are technically a little late for next year's intake.' There was a pause as the woman scrabbled around in a drawer and pulled out an old, battered book. 'Have you done much acting before?' she asked.

'Yes. I've done a lot of amateur theatre at home in Bradford and was an extra on TV once.'

'That's lovely.' The woman pushed the book she'd taken out of her drawer over towards Steph. 'Put your name and address in there, my dear, so we can send you some more information about our courses. But I'll just nip next door to ask the registrar if we do have any more spaces for next year. You do seem enormously keen.'

'Thank you,' said Steph smiling sweetly. The door was hardly shut before Steph was round the other side of the desk rooting around in the secretary's drawers. She found an old bag of pineapple chunks, a Silver Jubilee commemorative coin and a £20 voucher for Anne Summers but, as interesting as these objects were, they weren't what she wanted. Then her eyes fell on the circular address carousel that was nestling underneath a cardboard file. Glancing towards the door, she pulled it out of its hiding place and flipped through the alphabet to the letter 'D'. The words 'DECHY, Alexandra' leaped off the card. Steph's eyes practically burned the address off the paper and into her mind. She had just memorised the address and phone number when the secretary came back into the room followed by an old gimmer who couldn't have been a day younger than 104.

'What absolute luck, Sophie! Mr Reginald can see you now!'

'What are you going to do for us, my dear?' growled Mr Reginald, as if he were halfway through Richard III's 'Now is the winter . . .' speech on the main stage at the Barbican. Steph smiled politely and wondered what to do. As they looked at her expectantly, she realised her slightly quizzical *St Joan* expression wasn't quite going to cut the mustard in this situation.

When she finally made it out of the school and back into the twenty-first century, Steph didn't know what to do first. Should she go home and clean up or go straight to Alex's and stake out her flat? Time was getting on and Steph didn't want to miss Alex if she was going out for the evening, so she decided to head for the tube and go straight up to St John's Wood.

Dear Stalker

Alex's flat looked pretty ordinary from the outside, but it was the thought that Alex might at any moment come to the window, open the door or even pull up in a cab that generated the butterflies in Steph's stomach. There had been no reply when she rang the buzzer the first time, so Steph had decided to wait around for a bit. Excited at first by the thought of being on the verge of completing her mission successfully, Steph soon learned the importance of having a car during a stake-out. Consequently she only managed about half an hour of hiding behind trees and sauntering up and down the road before the sight of people drinking nice, cold beer in the pub on the corner weakened her resolve. She was just downing the last of her London Pride when she saw a car draw up outside Alex's house. It was black and shiny. Alex got out and leaped up the steps to the door before Steph got close enough to speak to her. There was a bloke in the car but instead of driving off, he turned the engine off and waited. Steph took her place behind her tree once again. One good thing about stalking a posh bird was the fact that there were more trees to skulk behind than in the rougher areas of town. A couple of minutes later, Alex re-emerged from her flat. She was wearing a stunning, sheer, black dress, and shoes that accentuated the elegant muscles of her calves. A bloke got out of the car to meet her. They stood next to the car talking. Now was the moment Steph should have been running across the road to confront Alex but, feeling, looking and smelling more like an urban warrior than a potential lover, Steph suddenly decided to let them go off wherever they were going. Declaring her undying love for Alex in the street in front of some strange man wasn't really how Steph had imagined the evening panning out. At least now she knew where Alex lived and that made it easier to put her feelings on hold.

EIGHT
Family Ties

After the initial celebration, Alex's feet hadn't really touched the ground since the moment she got the part of 'Victoria' in the film. It had been one long round of read-throughs, costume fittings, interviews and line learning. Although Marsha's words had stuck with her, she hadn't had a chance to spend much time thinking about what she was going to do about her situation, if anything. Suddenly being in demand, being made to feel special by the attention of friends, colleagues and complete strangers was exhilarating and not something that she would find easy to let go of, if it came to it. Although she had felt the buzz that came with getting breaks before, her first theatre role and then her first television role, this was different. The more time she spent with everyone to do with the movie the more she realised that she was playing in a different league now.

Having been cast and now coveted by people who had the power to get a multi-million-dollar movie off the ground Alex shouldn't have been surprised that a car was put at her disposal for the duration of the project, but she was nevertheless. Taking the only opportunity she would have for the next couple of months to go home and share her excitement with her mother, Alex had no qualms about getting her driver to take her to her family home in the Cotswolds.

'Alex, you look lovely!' Laughing, her mother greeted her daughter at the door of her picture-postcard cottage. Alex was pleased by her mother's reaction. She didn't often go back to visit her family. Her decision to go to London and train to be an actress hadn't been an easy one for her upper-middle-class parents to understand and whenever she had gone back there in the past the underlying question of when was she going to get a proper job had always lain heavy in the air. Nothing was ever openly articulated in Alex's family and she found it hard to find a way of justifying her career decision within the given family code and, as a result, found it easier just to avoid the situation. Now, however, she couldn't resist returning to enjoy what she thought was sure to be an explicit congratulation of her achievement.

'Hello, Mum!' said Alex as she walked up the gravel path to the door. 'Sorry I'm late. I hope we haven't lost the table at the restaurant.'

'No. I called ahead because your father has been called out on an emergency at the hospital, so I thought I'd try and hold it until ten o'clock.'

'So how are you?' asked Alex.

'Fine. Absolutely fine. But what about you, Alex darling? We're so proud of you.' Alex's mum – who was called Kate in an existence where she wasn't defined as 'Mum' – opened her arms and Alex was surprised to be embraced in a full hug instead of the touchless peck on either cheek that was her usual greeting. It's surprising what a touch of success does for you, she thought, as her mother led her into the house. The open fire was burning in spite of the warm weather and Alex was pleased of its heat to thaw her body that was cold with nerves. Kate busied herself with getting them some drinks.

'I'm so pleased you were able to come down,' said Kate as she sunk onto the understuffed, velvet cushions of the sofa next to her daughter.

'Yes. I'm pleased too.' Alex looked around at the house she had grown up in. Memories of her childhood spent with her older brother, Mark, were everywhere.

'So how's Mark?' asked Alex, comforted by the knowledge that for once there was nothing he could possibly be doing that would overshadow her own news.

'He sends his best wishes. He's working on a research project in a hospital in Chicago at the moment – don't ask me what it's all about though!'

'Dad must be wetting his knickers at the thought of Mark following in his footsteps like that!'

'Yes, he was rather excited when Mark was invited over . . . but we're all so pleased that you're getting on at last, Alex.' Kate's comment was meant to be reassuring but it only served to reaffirm to Alex everything that she had to live up to.

'You must send him my love,' said Alex reluctantly. The thick tick of the clock on the mantelpiece drew Alex's attention to the time. It was approaching ten o'clock. 'Shouldn't we get going?' said Alex.

'Damn your father!' said Kate as she looked towards the door, hoping that Alex's dad would enter and all would go as planned.

'Look, Mum. It's never going to happen. He's not going to come back on time. Why don't we just cancel and spend the evening here?' asked Alex, for once feeling able to take control of the situation.

'But we had it all planned . . .' Kate was at once drawn to Alex's willingness to abandon 'a plan' and worried about her husband. 'What if he decides to go straight to the restaurant and we're not there?'

'Then he'll either eat and come home or just come home. For heaven's sake, Mum, you shouldn't let him rule your life like that,' burst out Alex. Alex hadn't meant her words to sound so harsh, but her father's absenteeism and her mother's disproportionate devotion were things that had always got Alex's goat and she found it hard to hide her disdain. Kate gave her daughter the look which meant a change of subject was needed. 'I don't need you to take me to some fancy restaurant, you know, Mum. In fact, a meal on a tray in front of the fire would be absolutely perfect as far as I'm concerned.'

'Are you sure, darling? I just remembered that when Mark got his residency we took him out to –'

'Mark, SchMark, mother! This is me.'

'Right you are then. Fisherman's pie and oven chips all right?'

'Sounds great.' Kate went off into the kitchen and Alex could hear the sound of the fan oven being turned on and frozen food being flung inside.

'So what's this Brett chap I've been hearing so much about like then?' asked Kate as she reappeared in the doorway. 'Everyone round here seems to think he's a bit of all right!'

Hold on a Minute, Sunshine

Steph had tried Alex's number several times since the afternoon she'd spent hanging around outside her flat. All she got was the answer machine, which was pleasurable in a way, but not quite what Steph wanted to hear. Finally giving in to the idea that Alex had gone away for a few days, Steph was able to get down to some work and by the time the production was due to open, she had even mastered three new facial expressions to supplement her staple 'slightly quizzical' look.

'Good God! You look pleased with yourself,' commented Bev as they queued up at the canteen.

'I know, I've been working on it. It's rather convincing, don't you think?' replied Steph.

'Oh, I don't know. It's a bit frightening if you ask me!'

'A strawberry Slimfast and a packet of cheese and onion crisps, please,' said Steph to the man behind the counter.

'No! No, hold on a minute – if you're back on the Slimfasts it can only mean one thing!' joked Bev. 'You haven't gone and got a life at last, have you, Stephanie?'

'No, I've got a plan.'

'I hear you – cheese and tomato toastie, please – but I'm not sure I'm with you.' Bev was wondering what Steph was going to announce and kept her fingers crossed that it wasn't anything too extreme.

'I've decided, Bev, that it's no good sitting around angsting about someone I think I can't have, so I'm just going to confront her about it. Tell her how I feel and do everything I can to make her realise that we should give it a go and see what she says.' The matter-of-fact tone with which Steph divulged this information slightly worried Bev.

'And if this woman tells you to take your compulsive-obsessive arse elsewhere, what will you do then?' asked Bev, who thought that Steph was looking as structurally unsound as all the British millennium projects put together.

'Call Angie.'

'Hold on a minute, sunshine, that's my mate you're planning on using!' Bev could see it all going horribly wrong which would mean she'd be left to pick up everyone's broken bits.

'I'm seeing her this afternoon in fact. I feel dreadful about that morning when she and Maggie were round and, you know, some sorts of behaviour deserve an explanation, don't you think?'

'Don't *I* think? That's what I've been saying all along!' Bev was pleasantly surprised at Steph's sudden change of heart and rationality and hoped it would last.

Steph had suggested meeting Angie in town as she wasn't sure whether she would want to come to the house, but, in the end, it had been Angie's decision to get together at Steph's flat. Having made coffee and gone through the pleasantries of enquiring after each other's health, there was no way of skirting the issue any more.

'I'm sorry I've been so bad at returning your calls, Angie,' Steph began.

'Hey, you know, we're all busy people,' said Angie, who was more intent on seeing what the future held than getting bogged down in what was past. 'So what have you been up to? Anything exciting?'

'Yeah. This and that. Mostly that!' said Steph, going along with Angie's attempts at easing the atmosphere.

'I hear from Bev you've got a production coming up soon,' said Angie, picking up the chit-chat baton.

'That's right.'

'You must tell me when it is. I'd love –'

'Look, Angie, I've really got to say this. I'm sorry about what happened when you and Maggie were over that Friday. I had a really good time and didn't want it to end as crappily as it did,' blurted out Steph.

'Steph, I was just a bit confused. I really thought you liked me and, well, was kind of hoping that we might be able to get together again.'

'I do like you. I really do. It's just that I've got a few things going on at the moment that I need to sort out and, to be honest, I'm not really in the right space to embark on a relationship at the moment.'

'A relationship?' Angie smiled at Steph's earnest face. 'Who said anything about a relationship?' Steph could feel the flush of embarrassment creep out from her hair line and spread over her face.

'Oh, I . . . I don't really know what to say,' Steph stammered. 'I just got the impression from what Bev was saying that you were looking for something a little more, well, a little more . . .'

'Serious than we had the other night?' Angie finished her sentence for her.

'Yes.'

'Jesus, Steph!' exclaimed Angie. 'I did really want to see you but I wasn't about to say to my straight mate, "You know, Steph is just the best shag and I can't get the image of her fucking me with a dildo out of my mind, so would you encourage her to call me so she can fuck me senseless again, please," was I? She's straight, for Christ's sake; all straight women think about is romance and marriage and babies – they don't do the sex thing like we do and I don't think she'd really understand.'

'Put like that . . .' mused Steph.

'Look. I don't know what sort of stuff you've got going on, but it sounds like there's someone else who's on your mind –'

'You could say that.'

'But, Steph, I'm not talking about love and commitment. Sex can have so many different meanings; there's the "love" kind, which is great if you can get it, the functional "I need a fuck and I need one now" kind, and the uncomplicated "I really like the way this person makes me feel" kind. You're a really beautiful person, Steph. We had great sex and I'd like to do it again – end of story.'

'I must sound really conceited,' said Steph. Angie's words made a lot of sense and although Steph wanted to experience what Angie called 'the love kind' of sex with Alex, on reflection she didn't think that should necessarily preclude her from enjoying 'the uncomplicated kind' in the meantime.

'Why don't we go in the other room?' asked Angie, who didn't wait to be shown the way. Steph got up and followed her. Angie made straight for the bed and propped herself up against the wall at the end. Her flimsy summer skirt rose up her thighs and Steph remembered lying between them the other night. Angie opened her legs and gesticulated that she wanted Steph to come and sit in the space in between. Pushing her arse right up against Angie's cunt, Steph felt Angie's breasts on her back and relaxed into the arms that embraced her and the kisses that she felt on her neck. Angie's hands were on Steph's naked thighs, delving underneath the short skirt that Steph had on to reach the sensitive area just at the top of her legs. Steph leaned back and enjoyed the feeling of Angie's hands running over her body and her breath on the back of her neck. She felt Angie's fingers brush against the crotch of her pants and sighed with delight and anticipation. Pulling Steph's knickers to one side, Angie finally slid her fingers into Steph's hole. Steph's first orgasm was gentle and warming, but there were plenty more where that came from.

Please Yourself

Alex and her mother had sat up for hours. Ostensibly they were chatting but they both knew they were really waiting for Alex's father to come home. He didn't. And he wasn't even at the breakfast table the following morning. The inevitable subject of Alex's love life came round and for once Alex actually contemplated telling her mother the truth when her mum asked if she was seeing anyone.

'There is someone I've met but I'm not really sure how it's all going to work out,' explained Alex.

'I thought there was something that wasn't quite right about you, Alex,' Kate probed. 'You seem a little preoccupied.'

'Sorry.'

'Don't be, darling. I'm just pleased that there's someone on the scene at last! I do worry about you being lonely, Alex. Your father and I were beginning to wonder if you were ever going to find the right man to settle down with.' Alex looked at her mother. She was the epitome of your kind, conventional, flower-arranging, coffee-morning-organising suburban wife. Alex often wondered how such straight-laced parents could have produced an attention-seeking, sex-obsessed dyke like herself and thought that now probably wasn't the best time to try and find out. There was a crunch of gravel on the drive and then a key turned in the front door. It was a noise that triggered a response that had been repeated many times over the years. Kate jumped off the sofa and trotted into the hallway to meet her husband.

'Michael, darling! I thought you were never coming home!' exclaimed Kate, visibly relieved that her household was more or less complete. Alex could hear the sound of lowered voices as her parents spoke in the hallway and waited to be greeted by her father.

'There's plenty of time, Kate. I'll just go upstairs and get changed and then I'll come and say hello. Besides, before I do anything I've got to ring Mark. He needs my help with some research material . . .' Alex heard the familiar irritability in her father's voice as it faded away and was hurt but not shocked that he thought it more important to telephone her brother before coming in to say hello to her. She had hoped that this would be the moment when her father would actually be able to take an interest in her and her success in her work, but she was wrong. She slipped up the narrow stairs to her room at the back of the cottage and started to put her things in her bag. It had been really nice spending time with her mother, but as far as her career was concerned, she had finally realised that it was not the way she was going to impress her parents or win their approval. All they wanted her to do was get married and up the duff. She knew that if she was putting so much energy into her career to please anyone, it had to be herself.

Her car had been quick to arrive and whisk Alex back to the security of her home ground. Spending time with her parents was always rather sobering, but this time it had been even more so. Cocooned in the car, she allowed herself to think about the feelings that had led her to go and seek out Steph at the health club and then, even more extreme, follow her home. She couldn't put her finger on exactly what it was about the young woman. She was absolutely gorgeous, of course, but there was something more that had really struck a chord with her. Maybe it was Steph's openness and passion and perhaps her unpredictability that had captured Alex's imagination. Whatever it was, Alex still felt her body tingle whenever she thought about making love with her and was a little surprised that she hadn't heard from Steph. She had seemed very into her at the time and the bottom line was that Alex was more than a little disappointed that she hadn't at least tried to get in touch with her. She pushed aside her mother's worries about her loneliness that had suddenly popped into her mind and concentrated on the concrete of London that had all but devoured the countryside.

'Thank you, Tony,' Alex said to her driver as he carried her bags up the steps to her flat. Lingering in the doorway, Alex wasn't sure whether he was waiting for a tip or to be asked in for a cup of tea. 'Do you want to come in?' she asked tentatively.

'No. I was just wondering what time would you like me to bring Mr Torento round tonight? The party starts at 8.30 in W1. I need to know what time you would like to get there?'

'Good God, I'd forgotten about that completely.' Alex could hear the phone ringing in the hall and talked to Tony as she backed into her flat. 'Well, why don't you pass by around 8.15 and we'll take it from there?'

'Right you are, Ms Dechy.' Alex managed to snatch the phone off its cradle just in time. She said hello, hoping it was going to be some friendly voice to welcome her home but heard nothing at the other end. She urged the other person to speak but after a couple of seconds the line went dead.

Tunnel Vision

Steph had been so used to hearing the answer-machine message, that she had been totally flummoxed when Alex had actually picked up. Taken aback and totally tongue-tied she put the phone down, disgusted with her silence. Steph's mind was racing. She now knew Alex was at home. This was her perfect opportunity to go and carry out her plan. She looked at her watch. It was 7.30 p.m. If she was quick she might still be there by the time she arrived at Alex's home. There was no time to change or shower or do any of the things she would usually do before going to meet someone she was desperate to impress, so she sprayed on some perfume, gave herself the once-over in the mirror, and practically ran out of the door and down to the tube. The platform at Finsbury Park tube was packed and hot and there was no message on the LCD display informing her how long the next train would be. Steph began to feel agitated. When she read that the next southbound wasn't for fifteen minutes, she started to pace.

Alex hadn't given any thought to what she should wear for this party in town. Shooting started on Monday and it was an occasion the producers had laid on to bring all the cast and director together for one final 'bonding' session before the camera started to roll and their money really started to drip steadily away. Given the amount of Suits around it wouldn't be hard to look stylish and hip, but Alex wanted to really stand out and finally went for the 'Neal Street' end of her wardrobe – tasteful, striking and just a little bit 'edgy'. She had just begun to panic slightly at the thought of having a famous movie star in her home when the doorbell rang.

'Hey you!' said Brett as Alex opened the door and invited him in. 'How are you doing?'

'Fine, thanks,' said Alex, who was always a little taken aback by the way he treated her like they'd been friends for years.

'Great place you've got here,' he said, scanning the room.

97

Brett's superb body, LA tan and sun-bleached hair meant he would always have a hard time looking anything other than fantastic, and this occasion was no exception.

'Fancy a G&T before we go?' asked Alex, wanting to savour the moment so many other women would have died for.

'That is just so English!' Brett laughed in delight. 'I would love a "G&T".' His attempt at mimicking Alex's accent fell way short of the mark and they both laughed in recognition of the fact.

Having experienced delays, trains stopping in tunnels and packed carriages, Steph was almost beside herself as she finally emerged at St John's Wood tube. She looked at her watch. It was getting on for 8.30 p.m. now. She knew she would be lucky to find Alex still in.

'I don't suppose we could get away with just staying here for the evening?' Brett asked as he tossed back the last of his drink.

'I think you might be missed.' Alex smiled. 'Why don't you want to go?'

'Just not my scene really.'

'And this is?' Alex was amazed that Brett would rather spend an evening at her house than lord it around town.

'More so.' He smiled. 'Oh, well. I guess we can't put it off then.' He stuck his arm out for Alex to slot hers through and they headed for the door. Brett turned to look at Alex as she paused to double lock the door. 'What on earth are these things you're almost wearing?' He went to slap Alex on the bum to indicate that he was talking about her trousers that were so low-slung they only just covered her pubic hair, but she spun round just in time to catch his hand. They both started laughing as Brett continued to try and get at Alex's arse while Alex fought him off. They chased each other down the steps of Alex's flat and towards their waiting car.

Nothing could have prepared Steph for the sight of Alex and Brett fooling around together in the street, laughing and shrieking and seemingly all over one another. She stopped dead in her tracks. She didn't know what emotion hit her first, but it was a heady cocktail of anger, disappointment, jealousy and grief that finally knocked her for six.

An Educated Guess

Everyone was at the party. Alex had spent a lot of time mingling and was relieved when she spotted that one of the bar's plumptious sofas had become free. From this viewpoint she surveyed the bevy of beautiful people who occupied the room and, drawing on her vodka Martini, started counting her lucky stars – literally. She was in the process of comparing the image of being on the point of shooting a movie that she had had in her mind since the year dot with the reality of the situation, when she sensed someone standing behind her. She turned round and saw it was Brett who was sneaking up behind her.

'Jesus, Brett! What are you doing?'

Brett leaned down so that his mouth was hovering over her ear. She could feel his alcohol-heavy breath on her skin. 'I have come over as I have a proposition for you, Ms Dechy,' he said in his intense 'love scene' voice.

'You're not still fixating about my arse, are you, poppet?' Alex enquired. His manner was making her a little nervous. She didn't know what she would do if he wanted to sleep with her. She hadn't been fucked by a man for donkey's years and the thought of even the lovely Brett slipping her a length didn't exactly make her any more open to it.

'So, I'm a sucker for a cute, tight arse! What can I say?' he went on.

'So what's this proposition then?' Alex was keen to get to the point.

'I was wondering if you might like to come to a different club with me.' Brett came and sat on the arm of the sofa and looked down at Alex expectantly.

'Who else is going?'

'No one,' said Brett enigmatically. 'I don't think it's really their kind of thing.'

'And what makes you think it'll be mine?' asked Alex who was finding his manner intriguing and infuriating.

'Educated guess.' Brett smiled. 'Alex, listen. I can only take so much of this deathly boring polite conversation. I'm just proposing that we go somewhere where we can both have a little more fun. Are you up for it?' Alex was finding Brett hard to fathom. He was an outrageous flirt and from the look on his face she knew he was talking about going to find sex from somewhere, but she didn't feel threatened at all. Once again she felt more like his partner in crime rather than his partner in sex. Never one to knowingly pass up new experiences, Alex thought she may as well just go with the flow.

'How could I refuse?'

Brett gave the taxi driver directions and they headed towards Chelsea. After a short walk through the district's winding streets Brett led her to what looked like a private house. He buzzed the intercom and after a brief exchange the door opened. Brett and Alex went into a dark room where they were presented with a glass of champagne. There was music playing but the atmosphere was low-key and there were only a few people sitting at the tables that were dotted around the room.

'Nice, huh?'

'Very,' said Alex as she scanned the room. 'Not quite what I was expecting.'

'Really?' Brett was interested to hear what Alex had been expecting.

'I was thinking we'd end up somewhere a little livelier, I suppose,' she replied.

'Well, this is just the first bar,' explained Brett. 'Think of it as a bit of a chill-out room.'

'OK . . .'

'I didn't want to take you straight through because I just wanted to make absolutely sure you're cool about it before we go in.'

'About what?' As soon as the words came out of Alex's mouth it dawned on her that none of the other people in the room were sitting in mixed groups. Brett saw the expression on Alex's face change as she finally realised that they were in some kind of posh, gay pick-up joint.

'Get it?' he asked.

'Got it!' Alex laughed. She was taken aback by what Brett was trying to tell her. 'Your fixation with my arse is all falling into place now!' Brett just grinned and topped up their glasses. 'So why did you think I might have a good time here?'

'Intuition, I guess,' he said. 'Plus the fact that you've never spoken about your private life, haven't tried to jump me –'

'You arrogant sod!'

'– well, it's true! – and you have rather an impressive array of lesbian literature on the shelves in your living room. Oh and that photo in the bathroom of you with your tongue down some babe's throat was a bit of a pointer . . .'

'Jesus! I knew there was something I forgot to put away!' Instead of being terrified at having her sexuality exposed, Alex felt relieved.

'You've just been looking a little up-tight, Alex, and to be honest I thought you might find someone here who could make you more relaxed.'

'Did you indeed?' The man's audacity was refreshing and entertaining. 'So are you gay as well or do you just like a bit of cock from time to time?' It was Alex's turn to push the boundaries.

'I'm more than a "from time to time" kinda guy, if that answers your question?'

'Pretty much.' Alex thought about the situation. 'Don't you worry about getting found out?'

'Alex, darling,' said Brett. 'I think you take life a little too seriously. You know I have a fantastic time making movies and I can be anything people want me to be but I'm not going to let that kind of attitude stop me enjoying myself. Hell, life's too short and I've managed up to now, haven't I? So why worry!' It took Alex a couple of seconds to digest what Brett was saying.

'But you had a bloody great hard-on when we did that scene in the audition!' Alex was finding the new Brett that was sitting opposite her difficult to get a handle on.

'Yeah. Sorry about that. I think my memory recall of my last fuck was a little too vivid. He was a Hugo Boss guy too! What's a man to do?' Alex leaned back in her chair, and looked at Brett until she felt accustomed to this new image of him.

'So, shall I go introduce you to some of the women in here?'

'Since you've obviously gone to so much effort to make me happy, it would be a little churlish to say no.'

'Let's go have some fun then, yeah?'

Alex looked at Brett. He was gorgeous and relaxed and totally in control of his life and she realised that there was no reason why she couldn't be the same. The prospect of a long, slow fuck with some woman that night meant that her cunt had started to throb already, but she made a pact with herself that first thing in the morning she would end this nonsense. She'd call Steph, apologise and ask her to come over to the flat so they could talk.

NINE

Now or Never

The inner sanctum of the club that Brett had lead Alex into wasn't so much a 'back room' but the intentions of the people who were there wouldn't have been out of place in some small, dark, lust-laden room. Brett soon disappeared with a beautiful, floppy-haired public schoolboy type and Alex was left to her own devices. Brett had gone to great lengths to let her know that there was an unspoken pact between the people who came to the club that the liaisons that happened there were never spoken about outside those four walls, but by the time Alex was standing at the bar looking at the array of desirable women that surrounded her, she didn't really care. For the first time in a long time she felt able to have nameless, guiltless sex.

In fact Alex did manage to find out that the woman she invited into one of the upstairs rooms was called Jen, but that was as far as the small talk went. Jen had been wearing an Armani suit to die for but hadn't given a second thought about leaving it in a crumpled heap at the side of the waterbed they had sex on. Lying in her earth-bound bed at home, Alex recalled how she had abandoned herself to the rhythm of the water and Jen's movement on top of her as the woman fucked, licked and caressed her sex-deprived body. She also remembered being surprised that such a small Prada bag was capable of containing such a large dildo.

With these thoughts ruminating at the back of her mind she turned her attention to formulating a plan that would help get her real life back under control. She knew she had to call Steph. She didn't know what she was going to say after everything that had happened between them, but the woman had consumed her thoughts to such an extent that she had to give it a go. If she wasn't interested, she wasn't interested and she would have to deal with that if it happened. She had lived her life for too long thinking 'what if' and 'if only' and decided it was time to put her feelings on the line. It was now or never. Alex reached for her address book, looked up Steph's number and dialled it.

'Hello,' came a voice Alex didn't recognise down the line. It was broad Scottish and definitely not Steph.

'Oh, hi,' said Alex, remembering to breathe from her diaphragm to make her voice sound controlled. 'Is Steph there, please?'

'No. You've just missed her,' said Bev.

'Oh, OK.'

'She's out this morning, but should be back later on. Can I take a message?' Bev was intrigued as to who the mystery caller was and was keen to get some more information.

'Errr. No, that's all right.' Alex hadn't considered the possibility that Steph wouldn't be there.

'Are you sure?' Bev probed some more.

'No. I'll call another time.'

'OK. Bye.'

'Goodbye.' Alex put the phone down, disgruntled that her bravery had reaped no reward.

Bev was on the phone when Steph came in. She had been out to play some Sunday morning football with the lads from college. It had seemed like a good way of getting the image of Brett and Alex out of her mind at the time, but she returned home no less preoccupied. Bev eventually finished her conversation and went into Steph's room to see how she was. Wrapped in post-shower towels around her head and body, Steph was not in the mood for a heart to heart. She had already made up her mind that she had to go back to Alex's house to confront her about her feelings.

Drastic action needed to be taken. It was Sunday night; she was bound to be in.

'Good game?' asked Bev who, fortunately, was too young to remember Bruce Forsyth.

'Yeah. You know. William was his usual fucking annoying self. I mean who gives a shit about the off-side trap when you're playing in the park?'

'Umm.' Bev wasn't really into football.

'What have you been up to?'

'Been on the phone most of the morning. Mum called. Said she really liked the present I gave them when I was up there last time.'

'Really.' Steph was too intent on towelling herself dry to pay much attention.

'Oh and someone called for you earlier but they wouldn't leave a message.'

'Male or female?'

'Female. Nice voice.'

'Could be fucking anyone,' said Steph annoyed that her preparations were being impeded by Bev's presence. 'Did you do 1471?'

'Christ, Steph! I'm not "manic stalker woman" like you!'

'Oh well, if she's that bothered she'll call back.'

'Shall I leave you to get on then?' Bev realised she was surplus to requirements and wasn't too keen to pursue a conversation when Steph was in this kind of single-minded mood.

'Yeah, OK.'

'Going out?'

'Yeah.'

Well, This Is a Surprise!

Alex was trying to relax when the doorbell rang. She had lit some candles and was thinking about whether she should call Steph again, but thought it would be better left to later in the week when she had got the first few days of shooting over with. The phone had gone earlier in the afternoon, but it was a hang-up. Obviously a wrong number. So she'd settled down with a bottle of Medoc, the script and her notebook that contained the ideas she had jotted down about her character's scene to scene development. Not that there was much there to write. 'Hard bitch turns into soft sexual pushover at the sight of gorgeous man' was the thrust of it, but she wanted to make the most of what she had been given. She was still repeating the line 'But, Tom, I'm a woman, not a machine!' over and over in her head to make sure she had the action behind the thought thoroughly programmed in her mind as she went to pick up the entry phone.

Steph's heart was racing as she stood on Alex's doorstep waiting for her to respond to the buzzer. After all the time she'd spent thinking about Alex, wondering what she was doing and wanting so much to be able to see her, suddenly she didn't know whether being on her doorstep was such a good idea. Then she remembered how she felt when she'd seen Alex and Brett together the night before and realised that she had to tell her how she felt for the sake of her own mental health.

'Hello.' Hearing the sound of Alex's voice made Steph's mouth instantaneously dehydrate.

'Hi,' she squeaked into the microphone. 'It's Steph.'

'Who, sorry?' Alex was tired of her neighbour's guests buzzing her flat simply because they were too lazy to get their entry phone mechanism fixed and the frustration showed in her voice.

Pulling herself together and finding a bigger voice Steph said: 'It's Steph.' Still there was no positive response. 'You know, Steph, as in . . .?' Steph didn't really know what she could say as an appropriate aide-mémoire and her voice tailed off just as Alex realised who it was knocking on her door. Alex was shocked into silence until eventually Steph asked: 'Can I come in?'

'Yes. Yes. Of course.' Alex pushed the button that opened the outer door and paused briefly to check herself in the hall mirror before opening the door to her flat. Alex was intrigued and excited by her unexpected visitor and had to remind herself that Steph didn't know just how much she had been thinking about her – she was determined to let Steph take the lead and just play it cool.

Alex opened the door. 'Well, this is a surprise!' she said as she stood aside for Steph to walk in. Both women took a second or two to take in the other's appearance. Both heaved a silent sigh of relief that the attraction was as intense as the moment they kissed in the acting class. They stood awkwardly in Alex's small hall, not knowing quite what to say or whether to proffer a kiss by way of a greeting.

'Nice place,' said Steph, deciding to follow her nose and make for what she guessed would be the living room.

'Thank you.' Alex smiled at Steph as she plonked herself down on the sofa. 'Drink?'

'Yes, please.'

'Wine or gin?'

'Gin. Thanks.'

Alex bent down to pick up the empty that was at the side of the sofa and Steph couldn't help but feel a surge of lust rise up through her body as she looked at her gorgeous arse encased in perfect-fitting, faded denim jeans. With Alex safely in the kitchen fixing their drinks, Steph looked round the room. It was pretty much as she had imagined – stripped floor-boards, thick pile, deep red rug, open fire, light walls and books, newspapers and magazines everywhere. Steph picked up the script that Alex had left on the sofa and flicked through it.

'It's hardly *Uncle Vanya*,' said Alex as she handed a chunky tumbler full of gin and tonic to Steph.

'Thank God for that!' Steph laughed. She still had bad memories of being told that her 'Sonia' was more 'Mary Tyler Moore' than 'deranged Russian aristocrat'.

'Is it going well?'

'Rehearsals have been good. I shoot my first scene tomorrow.' Alex was beginning to wonder whether Steph would ever get round to coming out with the point of her visit. She wanted to tell her that she hadn't stopped thinking about her since they last made love and that seeing her with that other woman in the health club had just been excruciating. She wanted to tell her about how she'd decided to scrap the stupid deal she had with her agent and that she was having a hard time controlling her instinct to make a pass at her. Alex wanted to do all those things but somehow managed for once to keep control of her tongue and proceed with

107

caution. She didn't know why Steph was there and until she did she thought it was better to keep quiet.

'You must be very excited,' said Steph.

'What? Sorry?' For a moment Alex thought Steph had read her mind.

'About the shoot tomorrow,' explained Steph. She hadn't expected Alex to be quite so quiet and guessed that she was probably freaked out by the fact that Steph had found out where she lived and was wondering what she was going to do. 'I suppose I couldn't have chosen a more inappropriate time to come over really, could I?' Steph went on.

'What do you mean?' Alex was pleased that Steph was finally starting to say something, however obscure.

'Well, you know. Illicit, lesbian lover turns up on doorstep of woman who's signed a "no sex" bargain on the eve of your first day of shooting. Kind of ironic, don't you think?' Alex didn't know how to respond so didn't say anything. She was a little taken aback by the intensity in Steph's voice, but was beginning to get an inkling that Steph wasn't there just to wish her good luck and go. 'Alex, I'm sorry for barging in on you like this, I really am, but I thought I was going to go off my head if I didn't see you again.'

'I see.' Alex was interested to note that the trace of anger in Steph's voice had faded and that her tone was now more desperate than accusatory.

'You see, the truth is that I haven't been able to get you out of my mind, Alex. That night we spent together . . . Just walking past Studio B makes me want to cry! I can't forget the way you touched me, the way you made me feel and I just had to come over to tell you that I just can't stop thinking about you.'

'But I thought you were going to go out and have some fun, Steph, not stay in pining over someone like me.'

'Yeah. And I did. But everyone I've been with –'

'Everyone?' exclaimed Alex. Obviously the woman at the health club was just the tip of the iceberg regarding Steph's sexual exploits, and Alex began to feel even more turned on by the fact that Steph had taken her mission so seriously.

'Well, yeah. You know, there have been a couple,' justified Steph. 'But none of them even came close to what I felt when we made love.'

'Oh, so we "made love", now did we?' Alex was enjoying Steph's earnest and passionate declaration and decided to let her talk while she thought about how she was going to handle the situation.

'It might have just been a quick fucking blip in your master plan for cinematic domination for you, Alex, but you really touched me and I don't know what to do about it . . .'

'Listen, Steph. Do you remember what I said to you that morning –' Alex could see that Steph was getting agitated and knew this was not the time to start playing games with one another.

'Do I remember it? It's etched on my brain! All that crap about being a dyke through and through and then I go and see you practically fucking that stupid Chuck guy in the street!'

'You mean Brett?'

'Chuck, Brett, what the fuck does it matter? You were all over him and it made me want to throw up. Just how far are you able to go to prostitute yourself for the sake of realising your ambition, Alex?'

'You were here before?' Alex was shocked that Steph had seen her together with Brett.

'Yes. Yesterday night.' Steph had got up off the sofa and was pacing around the room. She had been thinking about the moment she would finally speak to Alex for weeks and this was unlike any of the dry-runs she'd had in her mind. She could feel herself verging on the hysterical but was desperate not to make a fool of herself.

'So how *did* you get my address?' Alex had not been prepared for the depth of feeling Steph was showing and although she wanted to go over to her, take her in her arms and tell her it would be OK, she was a bit wary of Steph's anger.

'I stole it!'

'Good God! Where from?' Alex realised her mad, stalking episode was nothing compared to what Steph had been up to.

'Your old drama school.' Alex didn't know whether to laugh or be very, very disturbed.

'You really went down there and went through their records just to find out where I live?'

'I know it sounds mad, Alex, but I couldn't think of any other way.' Alex was now standing next to Steph who was getting more and more upset. She wanted to tell her about her new-found sexual liberation and the desire she felt for Steph, but something stopped her from saying the words. 'Alex, I adore you. I fancy you something rotten and I can't stop thinking about you.' Steph moved in closer to Alex and took her face in her hands. She ran her thumbs over Alex's full, red lips and kissed her passionately.

'No, Steph. Listen!' Alex tried to get herself out of Steph's embrace but her words were blurred by Steph's kiss. She had to put a stop to this and find a way of making Steph listen to her before it all got out of hand. 'I've got to tell you something –'

'I know you want me, Alex. I can see it in the way you look at me.' Steph had pinned Alex's hands against the wall with the precise amount of pressure that made Alex feel excited but not threatened. Alex felt her cunt start to throb as Steph's mood changed and instead of being tearful and upset, she started to dominate her. 'But just how far are you prepared to go in order to safeguard your precious career?'

'What do you mean?' asked Alex as she searched Steph's face for some clue regarding her intention.

'What if I told you that unless you do exactly what I say, I will take my story to the papers?' Steph couldn't really believe the words that were coming out of her mouth, let alone the fact that she was holding Alex hostage against her own living-room wall. The women's faces were so close to each other that their noses were almost touching. Alex felt Steph increase the pressure slightly on her wrists and felt the throbbing in her cunt intensify. Alex knew it was wrong not to tell Steph the truth. But as she stood there at the mercy of the woman she had spent the last few weeks fantasising about, the idea of being sexually dominated by her was far too appealing to resist. The possibilities were endless and Alex hoped Steph would be daring enough to wield the power she was about to give her imaginatively.

'Weighing up your options, Alex, or just lost for words?'

'I am considering the situation you have put me in, yes,' replied Alex.

'I mean what I say,' confirmed Steph. She didn't really know where she was getting the confidence and bravado to behave in such a way, and was a little surprised by how turned on she was becoming by having so much power over Alex, but went with the feeling all the same.

'I believe you, Steph. I believe you.' Alex could see that Steph was finding the scenario as erotic as she was and didn't want anything to undermine her perceived reality.

'I also know that you find me as horny as I find you –'

'Do you really?' challenged Alex even though she knew Steph would only have to put her hand in her pants to find out for sure that she was right.

'Yes,' confirmed Steph. 'So why take the risk?'

'You do realise that what you're saying is tantamount to blackmail?' Alex's voice was low and serious.

'Well, I like to think of it as being more along the lines of helping someone out of a ridiculous hole they've managed to dig for themselves,' explained Steph as she leaned closer into Alex's body.

'But, Steph, I've got so much to lose right now.' However titillated she was at the prospect, Alex didn't want to appear to take this ultimatum lying down and felt obliged to add a little colour to the proceedings.

'Don't worry,' Steph replied, 'nothing bad's going to happen . . . as long as you do everything I tell you.' Alex could feel Steph releasing her wrists and running her hands down her bare arms. 'So what's it going to be?'

Steph could hardly bear to hear Alex's reply. In spite of all the threats she had issued she knew that, deep down, if Alex had called her bluff, she would have just gone home with her tail between her legs and that would have been the end of it.

'It doesn't look like I have much choice really, does it?' whispered Alex meekly in Steph's ear.

'So you're going to do whatever I say?' This situation was so surreal and so totally unpremeditated that Steph wasn't really ready for Alex to agree to her demands. But with the power cards firmly in her hand, she thought she had better start acting as if she knew how to use them.

'I suppose I'll have to.' It occurred to Alex that hiding her willingness to play the game would be more of an acting challenge than her part in the movie would ever be.

Cool as a Cucumber

'Where's your bedroom?' asked Steph and moved away from Alex so she could lead the way. Alex led Steph into her room at the back of the house. It was tidy, sparse and warm. Alex looked at Steph and wondered what she was thinking. She had a suspicion by the look in her eyes that she was unsure about what to do next, but wasn't about to help her out. It was up to Steph to dictate what happened and Alex could only hope that Steph had picked up how turned on she had been when she had pinned her against the wall.

Standing in the half light, Steph went up to Alex and slowly unbuttoned the shirt she had on. Alex was practically holding her breath in anticipation as she felt Steph's fingers brushing against her chest and stomach. Standing motionless in the middle of the room, she let Steph complete her task. Steph discarded Alex's shirt. Alex could see Steph's eyes wandering all over her body and was excited by the depth of Steph's desire. Steph turned her attention to Alex's jeans and she started to unbutton them. Her movements were slow and purposeful. Alex looked down at Steph's face and smiled. The absolute attention Steph was giving her was really turning her on, but her hands remained at her sides. She felt her clit pulsating with desire and anticipation at what Steph might have in store for her. She stepped out of her jeans and Steph reached behind her to unfasten the clip on her bra. Their mouths were close, but Steph made no move to kiss her.

Steph wasn't too sure how long she would be able to keep up the charade she had set up on impulse so had decided to take things slowly so as to savour every moment. Alex's body was every bit as delicious as she remembered it. Steph ran her hands up and down Alex's back; the pressure of her fingers on her tight muscles made Alex moan softly as she felt the tension slipping away. Letting her smooth, black bra fall to the floor, she looked Alex straight in the eye as her hands moved round Alex's torso and found her partner's breasts. Alex's face remained expressionless, but Steph noted that her pupils were dilated with desire. Steph reached further down and slipped her hand inside Alex's pants. Her fingers found their way into Alex's wet cunt. Steph pulled her knickers down roughly and Alex stepped out of them.

'Get on the bed,' ordered Steph. Alex obliged and automatically reached up to hold onto the metal frame at the head of the bed, in a gesture that offered Steph her body on a plate.

'Open your legs.' Steph's voice was heavy and her throat dry. Alex did as she was told. All she could do was wait for Steph to make her come and she was so turned on that she knew it wouldn't take much effort on the part of her lover. Steph moved onto the bed, fully clothed, and positioned herself in between Alex's legs. Alex was desperate for Steph to tie her up so she could experience that delicious sensation that came with abandoning control of your body to someone who was intent on giving you pleasure. She knew Steph would never suggest this on her own so had to make it seem like it was her tormentor's idea.

Alex could feel the touch of Steph's hands as she ran them over her parted thighs. She was inching her way towards Alex's cunt, but Alex wanted to be penetrated by more than this young woman's gaze. Alex started to move her hips.

'Touch my clit, Steph!' said Alex in a half-pleading whisper. Steph ignored her demands. 'Fuck me, or something, please!' Again no response. Alex released her grip on the metal frame, parted her swollen labia and plunged her fingers into her hole.

'Jesus, Alex!' said Steph. 'I thought I was meant to be telling you what to do!'

'If you won't fuck me, then I'm going to have to do it myself!' retorted Alex.

'For fuck's sake!' said Steph. She climbed off the bed and went over to Alex's chest of drawers. Flinging some drawers open, she finally found what she wanted, a stash of scarves. Pulling them out of the drawer she was intrigued to find they already had loops tied into them. She looked over at her lover who was lying on the bed and smiled, reassured that this was what Alex wanted. Sitting astride her body, Steph tied Alex's hands to the frame she had been holding onto. She ran her hands through her thick black curls and was suffused with love and desire for her.

'I'm not scaring you, am I?'

'I'd call out "Brett" if you were.' Alex tried hard to sound defiant but knew that they were both as into what was happening as the other. Steph had never tied anyone up in her life before, but had an idea that her partner had just given her her 'word'. Wrapping a scarf round Alex's ankle, she spread her legs and proceeded to tie her feet and then her hands to the bed. Steph lowered her head to inhale the delicious muskiness of Alex's sex. Alex's movements were inhibited by the restraints but it didn't stop her trying to get Steph to put her tongue in her cunt. Steph ran her tongue lightly over Alex's inner thighs, pausing fleetingly to wet her engorged clitoris then disappeared out of the room.

'Where are you going?' There was no reply but Alex could hear the fridge door being opened and shut and the water running and then being shut off. Alex couldn't see what Steph had in her hand when she came back in the room, but gasped when she felt ice cubes being rubbed over her nipples that were so erect they ached. The ice soon turned into water which ran over her breasts and trickled down onto her stomach.

'If I had known, I would have brought something better to fuck you with, but I guess this will have to do.' Steph was lying alongside Alex when she said this, and was keeping whatever was in her hand well out of view. Steph moved down Alex's body that was taut with anticipation and, licking Alex's juices, parted her lover's cunt lips with her tongue. The cold cucumber that Steph eased into Alex's hot, wet cunt made Alex scream with surprise and pleasure. Waves of her first orgasm rushed through her body as Steph pumped it in and out of her pussy.

'Don't stop, Steph, don't stop!' Steph continued to fuck Alex as her lover moved her hips in time with her thrusts. Alex's second orgasm was even more intense than the first and was accompanied by cries of pleasure. Pulling the improvised dildo out of her cunt, Steph climbed in between Alex's legs and, pushing her partner's bucking hips into the mattress, sucked and licked her clit, determined to draw a third orgasm from her. Alex had put so much pressure on her restraints that she had broken free. Sitting up she pushed Steph's face harder into her crotch.

'That's so good! Oh, Jesus, Steph, that feels good,' she gasped, as Steph felt a jet of watery come shoot into her mouth and down her throat.

Alex had been more than happy to reciprocate the passion Steph had shown. It had been very late by the time Steph was pulling on her clothes and getting ready to leave.

'That wasn't so bad, now was it?' smiled Steph as she pulled on her T-shirt.

'I think the word "bad" can have many meanings!' said Alex, trying to hide her disappointment that Steph was going. 'So what happens now?' she asked.

'I go home and you get some sleep.'

'You know what I mean,' replied Alex. 'Are you planning on coming round and forcing yourself on me again, or have you got what you wanted?' Alex looked at Steph expectantly, hoping against hope that she would say she was going to be spending many more evenings with her in the near future.

'Well, you know, Alex, this was very nice –'

'Nice, isn't quite the word I'd use, but still!' Alex laughed.

'But I think me coming round here all the time could get a bit safe, if you know what I mean?' Steph's imagination had been stirred into action by the sex they'd had.

'What do you mean "safe"?' Alex was fascinated by Steph's attitude and was eager to find out more.

'Well, you know, me coming round here and us shagging –

that's nice and everything, but I don't think you're really finding this much of a challenge, are you?'

'Good grief, Steph, I've already shown you how much power you're holding over me . . .'

'Yeah. But I've been wondering just how far you'd be prepared to go. How many risks you would take just to stop me from blowing the whistle.'

'What are you saying?' Alex tried to turn the excitement in her voice into something that sounded a little more apprehensive but wasn't too sure whether she succeeded or not.

'Well, I was thinking that maybe we should up the stakes a little.' Steph kissed Alex gently on the cheek. 'I'll be in touch with your instructions,' she said and then left.

TEN
Play It Again

A s she hopped into a solitary cab that was meandering down the Finchley Road, Steph went back over the events of the evening in her mind. She was shocked at how her jealousy and desire had combined to bring out a side of her character she had never really seen before. She felt guilty about accusing Alex of prostituting herself, but rationalised her feelings by concluding that if Alex would rather go along with her scheme than call her bluff, then she deserved everything she got. And she had got quite a lot. An image of Alex spreadeagled on the bed with her hands and feet bound to the bedstead flashed through Steph's mind and left a tingling feeling in her stomach. The few men Steph had slept with in the past had favoured the missionary position, and it was only now that she was beginning to realise that the message they had been preaching was dull, dull, dull. Her imagination was starting to stir. Although Alex hadn't necessarily chosen to have sex with her she had definitely enjoyed it and Steph was wondering what to do with her next. Her plan was to just try and keep this charade going for however long it took to make Alex realise that she couldn't live without her. She remembered the touch of Alex's lips on hers and felt that pleasant, fuzzy feeling ping round her body again. Alex had the most gorgeous kiss in the world.

The cab pulled up outside her flat and Steph paid up and went inside. She was absolutely knackered but thoughts were going round and round in her mind. As she lay in bed she raised her hand to push her hair from her face. Her fingers still smelled of Alex's sex and she inhaled the comforting aroma deeply before drifting off to sleep.

Steph's parting comment about instructions, demands, dares and rules was exactly the kind of thing that turned Alex on the most and the effort of wondering what Steph had in store for her kept her awake for a good few hours after her unexpected visitor had gone. Alex had thought Steph might have had some kind of crush on her after meeting her at the acting class, but had been surprised and pleased by exactly how strongly Steph felt. She smiled at the naive way Steph had tried to manipulate her into sleeping with her when it was obvious by the look in Steph's eyes that she would never do anything to hurt her. She wondered why she hadn't just told Steph there and then how she felt about her and got it all out in the open. It didn't take much psychological digging, however, for her to admit to herself that she thrived on complex scenarios like this. Letting Steph believe she had all the power was obviously going to lead to some exciting times, however, and Alex was more than happy to go with the flow. Gradually she slid into a deep, if relatively brief, sleep.

If Tony, her driver, hadn't rung to say he was stuck in traffic on the Westway, Alex would never have been ready in time. Having slept through the alarm, she had about twenty minutes to get up and at 'em – it was just about doable.

Reeling Her In

The interminable hanging around that goes hand in hand with filming gave Alex far too much time to monitor all the means of communication by which Steph might possibly try and get in touch with her. She left her mobile phone on while she surfed the net in her trailer. Occasionally, it would beep to tell her a text message had arrived and her heart would leap. Most of the messages were from Brett, however, who was in a bigger, better trailer positioned nearer the set, but a couple were from other friends who were bored at work and just wanted to say hi. So, apart from a couple of hours spent in hair and make-up, Alex's morning had been one long round of checking her email, voice mail, text message inbox and answer-machine messages to no avail. When the third assistant came to say she was needed on set, it almost seemed like an intrusion.

'Didn't hear you come in last night,' said Bev as she made her way into college with her flatmate.

'Didn't you?' mumbled Steph.

'Where did you get to? Anywhere nice?'

'Oh, you know. Just out.'

Bev looked at her friend. Steph had been so preoccupied over the last few weeks that she was really beginning to worry about her. They used to be able to talk about their problems, no matter what it was, but this time it was different. Steph was quiet and being downright cagey.

'You are OK, aren't you, Steph?' asked Bev. 'You know you can always tell me if there's something bothering you.'

'Yeah. I know, Bev.' Steph knew she had been treating her friend badly and wanted to tell her what was going on in her life but this was not the right moment.

'You're not worrying about the production, are you?' persisted Bev.

'Hell no!' Steph laughed at what was the least of her worries.

'OK. Well, what I'm probably really trying to say is that our graduation show is in a month or so and, well, you know . . . it would be a shame to throw three years' hard work down the drain just because of some woman you've met.' Bev wasn't really the lecturing kind but she felt obliged to do something to bring her friend back down to earth.

'I know you mean well, Bev, but I think I've got it all under control now,' reassured Steph. 'I know it may not seem like it but things are different now and I'm sure in a couple of weeks or so, I'll be totally sorted, one way or another, and back on track.'

'So you're saying I should just let you get on with it?'

'Pretty much, yes.' Steph felt dreadful about making Bev so concerned but knew there was nothing more she could say to put her friend's mind at ease.

On arriving at college Steph thought how ironic it was that their voice class had been transferred to Studio B. As she lay on her back directing long vowel sounds towards a certain point on the ceiling, the 'mmmm', 'aahhh' and 'ooohhh' sounds that began to fill the room reminded her of the first time she had made Alex come, right there in that very room. She remembered how exciting it had been to be making love somewhere that was so out of bounds. Her mind turned to the night Alex had spent with her and how her behaviour didn't really match up with the type of person who is trying to keep their sexuality a secret. Alex's explanation floated back into her mind: *'I just find the idea of having sex in unusual places really horny, that's all.'* That was the moment when it finally dawned on Steph exactly what she had to do to reel Alex in. She would have to dream up a scenario that pandered to the exhibitionist side of Alex's personality as well as her penchant for putting herself in risky positions. Once she presented a challenge like that to Alex she knew she wouldn't be able to say no. Blackmail or no blackmail, she would be just too tempted. It was a win-win situation.

Throughout the day, Steph dredged her memory for something that would inspire Alex's first test. For some unknown reason that scene in *Risky Business* where Tom Cruise shags some bird on a subway train sprang into her mind. But sex on the germy, smelly, old underground was not really a turn-on, especially as you'd have to travel around on it for hours just waiting to get a carriage to yourself. She remembered one of her brother's mates telling her how he'd once 'knobbed' his girlfriend (his term not hers) on the roof of the family caravan while it was parked in the driveway of her house, but fortunately that image quickly passed. She also remembered reading about a couple who had been fined for having sex in the loo on a plane. That was more like it – the fuck, not the fine. The Mile High Club was glamorous and sexy, but too expensive for Steph at that moment. Her thoughts turned to loos in general and then loos in hotels. Posh hotels with huge rooms where ladies went to powder their noses as opposed to the type of place with pits where women went to have a slash. She thought it sounded a little tame, but for a first go it would have to do. She would go into town after college and check out a few possible venues.

Steph had a picture in her mind of the type of place she was looking for but surprisingly few of the hotels she knew had the kind of sumptuous surroundings she was after. It had to be a place that was busy but not bustling, up-market but not overly exclusive; somewhere where they would be noticed but not hassled by ridiculously old and ugly businessmen who thought they stood a chance.

Finally, after a couple of hours tramping the streets, she found what she was looking for. It was very Mayfair, very classy and absolutely perfect. Now all Steph had to figure out was when this particular gauntlet was going to be flung down. She wanted to see Alex again soon, but didn't want to look 'out-of-control-eager' so she decided to give Alex her instructions that day with a view to meeting at the end of the week. Sitting in the bar of the hotel Steph ordered a drink and pulled out her mobile phone. She thought a text message would be the best way to contact her – it was intimate, instant but non-confrontational. She punched in the name and the address of the hotel and then said, 'Be in the bar, Friday, 9.30 p.m.' She selected Alex's mobile number that she had stored in her phone, pressed 'send' and watched the little letter icon fold up and fly off the screen.

A man in an impossibly immaculate uniform came over and presented her with the coffee she had ordered and a bill in a little leather folder which he left on the side of the table in front of her. The sudden rush of caffeine got her reaching for her cigarettes. She felt so relaxed as she sat there watching people coming and going that she was reluctant to leave the sanctuary she'd found and re-enter the real world. After spending an hour or so drinking one cup of coffee, she had to bite the bullet and head for home. Even though it took twice as long to get home by bus than tube, Steph opted for the former simply because it meant she would be able to hear if Alex replied to her text message.

The bus was plodding up Camden Road when Steph heard her phone beep. It was a message from Alex which read: 'Need to know more about Friday – call me tonight. A.' Steph smiled and willed the bus to go faster.

Steph had taken the phone into her room to call Alex. Lying on her bed she dialled the number that she now knew by heart and waited for Alex to pick up.

After everything that had gone on between them Steph found it difficult to know what to say to her. What she really wanted to say was that she missed Alex dreadfully and couldn't wait to see her again but they weren't the words of a person in control of either their emotions or the situation.

'So what's up?' asked Steph as Alex picked up the phone.

'I just need to know what I'm letting myself in for, that's all,' replied Alex. She'd had a long tiring day, but still managed to feel excited at the sound of Steph's voice.

'Now, where's the fun in telling you what I've got planned?' Steph was slipping into her role relatively easily.

Alex could tell by the tone Steph was adopting that she wouldn't be able to wriggle out of meeting her at this hotel that easily. 'Why don't you just come round here? I'll even cook you dinner, if you like,' said Alex.

'Like I said, Alex. I think you're the kind of woman who would enjoy something a little more, what's the word . . . exotic.' Alex knew what she was getting at. Seducing Steph in a drama studio hadn't actually presented an image of someone who shied away from taking a risk or two. Her mouth was watering as she anticipated the kind of scenario Steph might have dreamed up, but to go along with it really was pushing it too far. Sex at home was fine, but sex somewhere public at this stage of the game could make everything go horribly wrong.

'Are you still there?' asked Steph after giving Alex a little thinking time.

'Yes. I'm just thinking about what you've said.'

'And what have you concluded?' Steph was getting slightly anxious that Alex wasn't going to take the bait.

'So what if I say no?'

'I think we went over that last night, didn't we?' Steph tried to keep the quaver out of her voice.

'And you'd really do that?'

'Only one way to find out.' Steph's optimism was fading fast. Alex, on the other hand, was very keen to play the game Steph was proposing but was anxious about the contract she had signed with her agent. If by some quirk of fate they were discovered doing something they shouldn't and it all turned ugly, how would that impact on her? Her cunt and her head were telling her mouth to say totally different things, until finally she ended up saying yes. 'OK. I'll meet you there at 9.30 p.m. on Friday,' said Alex. She wasn't absolutely sure that Steph wouldn't carry out her threat – or so she told herself – so really it was best all round to go along with her plan. At least if she did get caught she would have had some fun in the process.

'Don't be late,' said Steph and put the phone down.

Alex put the phone down slowly and wondered what on earth she had got herself into. She glanced at the clock and realised she just had time to call Marsha before going out to meet friends for dinner. She dialled her number and after a few rings it clicked into the answer-machine message. Alex had really wanted to speak to her, but had to be content with leaving a message. 'Hello, Marsha, it's Alex,' she said, trying to sound as upbeat as possible. 'I was wondering if I could buy you dinner tomorrow night as a kind of thank-you for coming to pick me up the other night? Leave me a message if you get in early tonight, or call me tomorrow on my mobile. Bye for now.'

Old Dogs and Englishwomen

Alex had been pleased to see the light flashing on her answer machine when she got home the night before and pleased also that Marsha was a ready and willing dinner guest.

'Tony, if you drop me off outside Budgens on the Broadway,

I'll be fine,' Alex said to her driver as they made their way to the restaurant in Crouch End Marsha had chosen. She went in and saw that Marsha was sitting at the bar already, drinking wine and digging into some olives.

'My dear, how sweet of you to call!' said Marsha as she kissed Alex solidly on both cheeks.

'It's the least I could do, really,' replied Alex. The waiter came over and led them to a table. Food and drink were served and Marsha devoured the innocuous titbits of showbiz gossip Alex had to offer as hungrily as she tucked into her meal.

'So you're having a good time then, darling?' asked Marsha.

'Well, I've only done two days shooting, but, you know, so far so good.'

'I'm so pleased that it's all turning out so well for you, Alex,' said Marsha fondly. There was a natural lull in the conversation and Alex knew that this was the time to ask Marsha for some more advice. She was just searching for the right way to introduce her agent into the conversation when Marsha saved her the trouble. 'Have you decided, then, what you're going to do with that old dog of an agent of yours?'

'Yes –' said Alex assertively.

'Excellent!' Marsha clapped her hands in delight.

'. . . and no.'

'Oh. I had thought the decision would have been an easy one,' said Marsha, who looked a little disappointed by Alex's uncertainty.

'I just need to know where I stand, that's all,' began Alex and explained that she had met someone she was really taken with. She told her how her contract was coming up for renewal pretty soon and wondered what might happen if she did anything that broke it in the meantime.

'You're worried that he'd sue you for breach of contract if he found out you were having an affair with a woman, you mean?' Marsha, once again, was finding it hard to keep up.

'Well, yeah. Could he sue me? Would he sue me? And if he did, would he win?' Alex looked into Marsha's eyes, willing her to come up with the definitive answer.

'Petal, you have got yourself in a bit of a pickle, haven't you?' Marsha reached across the table and took Alex's hand in hers. 'Well, it seems to me that he would do more harm than good to his reputation by making an issue of you breaking such a ridiculous agreement. I mean what sort of person wants that kind of business practice to be on public record? But my advice to you would be to keep it low-key with this young woman you're obviously so keen on and once your term is up, that's the time for you to go public, if that's really what you want to do.'

Alex looked down at her empty plate and contemplated what Marsha had said. 'So you don't know for sure what might happen?'

'Of course not, darling!' Marsha laughed. 'I'm no legal expert but I can't really see you marching into a lawyer's office and telling them what you've just told me, so it looks like you're just going to have to sit tight.' Alex pulled a face. 'Oh, come on, Alex,' chivvied Marsha. 'I'm sure Stephanie will understand.'

Alex looked up at Marsha in amazement. She had no idea that her friend had worked out who she had become involved with and it shocked her to hear Marsha say her name. 'How do you know?'

'I'm not blind, Alex. So come on, chin up. A couple more weeks can't hurt!'

But it did. That was the trouble.

Nothing to Lose

For Steph the week couldn't go quickly enough but seemed to be interminable. For Alex the week flashed by but there was barely a minute when she wasn't thinking about her meeting with Steph and barely two consecutive minutes when she managed to stick to a decision about whether to go through with it or bottle out. It was only when she found herself walking around Mayfair with her A-Z in one hand searching for the address Steph had given her that she had to acknowledge the fact that Steph's invitation had just been too seductive to resist. And besides, she was a grown adult in control of her body – she could leave at whatever point she wanted to.

Alex arrived at 9.30 p.m. on the dot. She walked into the lobby of the hotel and was impressed by Steph's choice. The hotel was old but well kept and tasteful. She made her way through to the bar. Alex looked round the room and was studying the crowd of people who had gathered for pre- or post-dinner drinks when she saw Steph sitting at a table in the corner. She was wearing a little black dress and looked absolutely awesome. Alex took a moment to catch her breath before going over to her.

'How's that for time-keeping?' she joked as she bent down to kiss Steph on the cheek. Steph blushed as Alex sat down next to her and fixed her with her gaze.

'Well, I'm impressed so far,' Steph said, holding the eye contact Alex was offering her as long as she could. The waiter brought a bottle of champagne over in a silver wine cooler and placed it at the side of their table. He popped the cork and poured two glasses.

'Now it's my turn to be impressed,' said Alex, wondering how on earth Steph could afford to buy champagne in a place like that.

Steph picked up her glass. 'To living on the edge,' she said.

'You can say that again!' exclaimed Alex and brushed her glass against the one that was offered. Suddenly she knew that all her apprehension had been misplaced. The woman she was sitting with was obviously as smitten with Alex as she was with her. Once again Alex knew that she should tell Steph exactly how she felt, but the dynamic that had been created was one she was reluctant to destroy before seeing how the evening was going to evolve.

They sat and chatted whilst they drank the champagne. Alex regaled Steph with the same kind of movie stories she had told Marsha earlier in the week and Steph told her about the work she was doing at college. For a while, they almost forgot about the reason why they were at the hotel in the first place and concentrated on finding out more about each other. The champagne was doing its work, however, and as the evening drew on and they got nearer and nearer to each other, the desire for the other's body that first drew them together took the place of conversation. When Alex leaned forward to put her empty glass on the table, Steph ran her hand down her back and let it rest on her arse. Alex moved back to cover her action from the view of the others in the bar but instead of withdrawing her hand, Steph simply moved round in her seat and placed her other hand on Alex's crossed legs. She started to reach underneath the material that covered her legs. Alex's cunt reacted instantly to the feeling of Steph's hand on her bare leg and wondered what she was going to do next.

Steph leaned into Alex and kissed her gently on the neck. She could feel how turned on Alex was and couldn't wait to execute the final stage of her plan.

'Not here, Steph, please,' urged Alex who was a little concerned about how far Steph was prepared to go.

'Follow me,' said Steph and got up from the table. Alex was feeling nervous and excited as she followed Steph across the bar and into an area at the back of the hotel. She almost felt relieved when Steph took her hand and led her into the women's loos. It was a large room that was done up in the same manner as the rest of the hotel with a couple of large armchairs in the mirrored antechamber with half a dozen cubicles in the adjoining room. There were some women touching up their make-up at the mirror, but otherwise the rooms were empty. Steph went over to the basin to wash her hands while Alex sat down in one of the armchairs and watched Steph as she went and stood next to the other women at the mirror, marvelling at the simultaneous view it gave her of Steph's breasts and arse. She saw Steph's reflection looking back at her and felt her fanny getting moist with antici-pation. Both of them willed the women to leave before someone else could come in and spoil their fun. Finally they finished their rituals and left.

As soon as the door swung shut Steph bent down and reached for the doorstop that was lying beside it and wedged it firmly underneath. Her heart was beating wildly as she went over to where Alex was sitting and kissed her softly on the lips. Kneeling in between Alex's parted legs Steph kissed her harder and pushed her tongue into her lover's open mouth. Steph ran her hands down Alex's body and lingered on her breasts. She could feel Alex's erect nipples underneath her top pressing into her palms. Steph felt Alex's hands reach up to her face and then felt them running through her hair, pulling her in closer. Both women knew they didn't have much time so Steph reached underneath Alex's skirt and tugged at her knickers. Alex readily shifted her weight to allow Steph to pull them down so that they were hanging round one ankle. The noises of the hotel filtered through the door and over the Muzak that was being piped into the room. Steph knew it wouldn't take much pressure for the doorstop to give way which also meant that they wouldn't have much time between someone trying to get in and the door being forced open. The thought of being so vulnerable made her movements more urgent. Steph pushed Alex's skirt up so that it was bunched around the top of her firm, slender thighs. Alex slid down in the chair so that her arse was just on the edge and opened her legs to expose her naked cunt.

A sharp clatter of falling crockery outside the door suddenly diverted Steph's attention. Both women froze as they listened to the men's voices outside debating whether or not to get a cloth from the women's toilets to clean up whatever mess they had made in the doorway. The women held their breath as the door handle started to dip. Neither wanted to show that they might lose their nerve but Steph didn't know where to look – at Alex's beautiful, needy cunt that was displayed before her or at the moving door handle.

'You're not really going in there, are you, you big poof?' The man doing the talking must have pushed his mate because there was a thud as someone stumbled into the door. Another voice protested and then both voices began to fade. Both Alex's and Steph's eyes fell on the doorstop which had been dislodged slightly but neither woman was prepared to waste any more time. There was a moment of eye contact between them before Steph plunged her tongue into Alex's open, aching cunt and ran her hands up Alex's body until her hands found her lover's breasts. Alex groaned at Steph's touch and thrust her hips up to meet Steph's probing tongue. Alex could see their reflection in the mirrors opposite. The anticipation of being discovered and the reflection of Steph tonguing her cunt in this public place was more erotic than any of her fantasies. It made her more turned on than ever. She wanted and needed to come. It needed to be quick so she put her hands behind Steph's head and gently guided her mouth towards her clit. Steph flicked Alex's clit with the tip of her tongue and stroked her engorged cunt lips with her fingers until Alex felt the waves of her climax building inside her. She gripped the arms of the chair and let her orgasm flood through her body and into Steph's mouth. With no time to bask in her climax, she got off the chair, kicked her knickers off completely and pulled Steph to her feet. Alex kissed Steph hard on the mouth. The smell and taste of her own come tasted good on Steph's lips and whetted her appetite even more. Unable to keep their hands off each other, they stumbled around the room until Alex pushed Steph backwards towards the wash area. Steph readily helped Alex manoeuvre her onto the unit that housed the basins and allowed Alex to pull her dress up and her pants off. She felt the harshness of the cold, metallic taps digging into her as she leaned back to open her legs and winced with pleasure. Getting straight down to business, Alex dropped to her knees and buried her face in Steph's sex. Alex looked up at Steph's come-covered face and licked her clit harder and faster. Although she was enjoying the most extreme pleasure, the effort Steph was making not to make a sound meant her face looked more like she was in pain. Alex was licking her swollen clit when they heard someone trying to get in the door.

'I think it's locked,' came a posh, pissed voice from the other side of the door.

'Oh, for pity's sake, Flicky, it can't be locked; it's probably just stuck,' came another posh, pissed voice. 'Let me have a go.'

Steph was on the verge of coming. 'Don't stop,' she mouthed to Alex who had stopped what she was doing and was looking towards the door. Just as a broad, horsey shoulder heaved against the flimsy door, Alex grabbed Steph and hauled her into a cubicle. The outer door swung wide open just as the door to the cubicle swung shut with Alex and Steph inside.

'You're such a bloody wimp, Flick,' said the shoulder heaver and they came into the room and each chose a cubicle, oblivious to the fact that a woman in the adjacent stall was about to have the orgasm they had nearly denied her. In spite of the scant protection between them and the pissed, posh people, Alex quickly took up where she had so violently left off. She rammed her finger into Steph's cunt and massaged her hard clit with her other hand. Just as Steph was about to come Alex covered Steph's mouth with her juice-soaked hand. Flicky and friend were washing their hands when they heard Steph's stifled orgasmic groan. They looked at each other in the mirror, both a little puzzled. Then the penny dropped. Horsey leaned into her companion and whispered to Flick, 'There are people having sex in there!'

'What a bloody cheek, bringing a man into the women's lav!' mouthed Flick, nodding in the direction of the now silent cubicle. It was then that their eyes fell on the two pairs of women's knickers that were still lying on the floor of the hotel's powder room. Aghast, they looked at each other, looked towards the occupied cubicle and practically ran over to the exit.

A few seconds later, Steph and Alex walked out of the toilet. Their palpitations and a slight glow surrounding them was the only physical evidence of what had gone on. That and a couple of pairs of knickers in the hotel bin.

ELEVEN

A Compliment Here and There

'You nearly got us caught in there, Steph!' chastised Alex as they walked briskly out of the hotel and into the cool night air.

'I know! Wasn't it fantastic? I wish I could have seen the look on their faces when they realised what was going on!' Steph was walking quickly and Alex had to make an effort to keep up with her exhilarated companion.

'But, Steph, you're going to have to learn how to control yourself a little.'

'I don't think you're in a position to make any sort of demands, are you, Alex? Or have you forgotten that it's my game we're playing and, as the person in control of the concept, it's me who says what can and can't happen?'

Looking at the monster she had created, Alex suddenly realised what it must have been like to be Dr Frankenstein. Steph turned round to see where Alex had got to. 'Come on, Alex, keep up!'

'Where are we going?'

'Fancy a turn round the Serpentine?'

'Well, coming from anyone else that could almost be romantic!' Alex laughed as she picked up the pace and caught up with Steph. After the frenetic activity earlier in the evening, Hyde Park seemed quite serene. For a while the two women just lay on the grass next to the lake, listened to the water's easy movement and enjoyed the brightness of the moon in the spring sky. Alex looked across at Steph and smiled at the thought of the things this angelic-looking person was capable of doing to her. She was trying to decide what was going on behind Steph's warm, brown eyes, when Steph turned on her side to return her gaze.

'You did enjoy it, though, didn't you, Alex?' asked Steph seriously. She had been wondering what to do next and was worried that Alex would have had her fill and break off the deal.

'Couldn't you tell?'

'Well, yeah. I guess.' They both silently searched each other's face for clues as to how to move on. Alex reached out and brushed Steph's jaw line with the back of her fingers. 'You really are beautiful, Steph,' she said quietly.

'You can't get round me like that, you know, Dechy!' answered Steph, laughing.

'Like what?' exclaimed Alex.

'You know, a bit of flattery, a compliment here and there to weaken my resolve!' said Steph.

'What do you mean?'

'You can't wriggle out of our little deal that easily. Especially as now I'm just beginning to enjoy myself!' explained Steph. Alex had got so caught up in the moment that she had all but forgotten about 'the deal' they had supposedly struck.

'So you're still determined to continue with this game we're playing?' probed Alex who was interested to see that Steph was going to persist with the charade.

'You've paid your money and taken your choice, Alex,' replied Steph. 'I don't think it would show much strength of character on my part if I let you get off the hook that easily, do you?' Whether or not Alex was into having sex with her wasn't really the issue. Steph was aware that Alex was enjoying every minute of their affair, but she didn't want to risk her calling time on their relationship. They'd had a wonderful evening, but then they'd had a wonderful evening when they first met. Alex had walked away then and given half the chance she might do so again.

'OK, so we've established that you have complete control over me and my body,' Alex said as she moved her hand down Steph's torso and let it rest on her waist. 'What are you going to put me through next?'

'That's for me to think of and you to find out,' teased Steph as she removed Alex's hand from her waist and got to her feet.

'We're off now then, are we?' asked Alex sarcastically as she stood up too.

'You can walk me to the tube if you like,' said Steph as she started walking over to the park gates.

'Thanks!' Alex brushed off her skirt, put on her shoes and chased after Steph. They walked in silence a lot of the way. It was only when they reached the entrance to the tube that Steph turned round and kissed Alex awkwardly on the cheek.

'I'll call you,' she said and disappeared down the steps.

Buck-a-roo

Although Alex had a pretty packed weekend ahead of her, she managed to weave her message-checking schedule into her shooting and social commitments. Fortunately Saturday and Sunday were night shoots, so she had been able to have a lie-in and collect her thoughts before being whisked off to the location the following evening.

She had hardly managed to climb into the negligée that she was wearing in the next scene when her phone beeped. It was Brett. They had discovered they had a mutual love of kids' games. Brett was boasting about a recent visit to Hamley's and was trying to entice her into his trailer with offers of being the first to play with his new Buck-a-roo. An invitation she obviously couldn't refuse. Alex was up 25/22 in their Trailer Games Championships and was eager to consolidate and build on her lead. Alex flung on a robe and dashed down to Brett's place. She was dismayed to find him practising already.

'You bloody cheat!' she yelled making him jump, the horse buck and the pieces fly everywhere. 'I thought we had agreed, no warming up on new acquisitions.'

'Chill out, will you, Alex. I was just testing the mechanism,' he said as he grovelled around on the floor to retrieve the horse's baggage. 'Where's that fucking cowboy hat?'

'How long have we got?' asked Alex as she surveyed the game and trawled her childhood memories for tips on technique.

'Jeff said we're on set in about twenty minutes, so we've got time for a quickie.' Brett placed the last piece on the horse and cracked his knuckles. 'Shall we play?'

True to form Alex wiped the floor with him and also introduced the rule that the loser re-sets the game, so was looking more than a little smug by the time their session ended.

'Something tells me that dreadful grin which has taken over your face isn't just due to a winning run at this piss-stupid game,' observed Brett as he leaned back on his chair and took a swig of his beer.

'Sounds like sour grapes to me. But, hey, winning games/having sex with a gorgeous woman in a hotel loo – what would you say was more exciting?' Alex's grin got even wider.

'Are you trying to tell me that . . .' Brett was genuinely surprised at what Alex had just revealed.

'Yep!'

'With who?' Details, Brett wanted details.

'With this woman I've met.'

'Jeez, Alex! Don't you know what happened to George Michael?'

'It wasn't like that, honest,' justified Alex.

'What do you mean? You didn't get caught or this woman you picked up wasn't a cop?' Brett leaned back in his chair and started laughing.

'I didn't just "pick her up"!' said Alex. 'I've known her for a while and actually no, she's not in the police force.' As Alex told Brett all about Steph his eyes got wider and wider and Alex's heart felt lighter and lighter. She didn't realise how hard it had been for her to keep all her emotions inside and it felt good to unload to such a receptive, sympathetic and, by the end, envious, audience.

'So how long are you going to keep this poor woman in the dark about your feelings, Alex?' Brett asked.

'I don't think "poor woman" is necessarily an accurate description of her, but I know what you're saying. It's just that it's all so exciting like this. I mean, if I'd told her how I felt that first day when she came round, I don't think we would have had quite so much . . . fun.' All of a sudden Alex felt a little coy about explaining to her colleague exactly how she liked to get her kicks.

'Yeah, but she's probably thinking that you're only doing it for the sex and a bit of a laugh. She could be thinking that this is the only way she can hold on to you. I bet you a thousand pounds that if you told her, she'd still want to fuck you in hotel johns, but if you don't she could just end up getting really mad at you.' There was a knock at the door and a male voice called out: 'Hey Brett, you're on, mate! Any idea where Alex is? She's not in her trailer.'

'It's OK,' replied Brett. 'She's with me.'

The voice said: 'Right you are!' and in those three words the deliverer managed to imply 'we all know you're poling her, now put your dick away and get some work done, you lucky bastard'.

When Steph woke up the following Thursday, she looked out of the window and turned on the TV to check the weather forecast. She wasn't usually that anal about the weather but today she had a reason to hope that it would be fine, dry and hot.

'The south and south east of England will get the best of the weather today. It will be fine, dry and hot with temperatures up in the low seventies . . .' said the intelligent yet friendly BBC announcer. Steph looked at her watch. It was 8.00 a.m. Bev popped her head round the door.

'You nearly ready? We'd better get going soon.'

'Yeah. I'll be two seconds.' Steph scanned her room for her phone. She had to call Alex before she went to college but couldn't find her sodding phone anywhere. In the end she had to make do with the land-line. Alex's phone rang and rang until the answer machine cut in and played the message.

'Hi, Alex, it's me. Meet me tonight, 10.30 p.m. outside Bar All Fun on the High Street.'

★

Alex was beginning to think that Steph wasn't going to contact her. It had been four days since Steph's last text message and even that hadn't told her when they were going to get together next. She had been on set since 7.30 a.m. that morning and three hours later was still sitting in the offices where they were filming the 'corporate scenes', all dressed up and nowhere to go. There was some problem with the amount of chrome in the conference room where they were shooting. Frustrated, bored and a bit lonely, Alex called her answer machine. She heard Steph's message and, with her mind occupied with trying to guess what Steph had come up with this time, suddenly the wait wasn't so bad. She leaned back in her leather chair and let images of Steph making love to her fill her mind and affect her body. She could feel blood rushing to her clit making it hard and aroused as the tingling in her crotch grew more intense. There is a fine line between being pleasantly turned on and downright uncomfortable and it was a memory of making love with Steph on the first night they had spent together that tipped her over the edge. She made her way into the conference room that was heaving with designers, electricians and lighting people. Matt, the director, was the only person she recognised. He was looking through a telescope kind of thing when Alex touched his arm to get his attention.

'Is it OK if I nip back to my trailer for a half hour?' she asked discreetly.

'Sure. We're waiting for some new furniture here – we won't need you for ages yet, darling.'

Alex made her way back to her trailer as fast as her narrow skirt and high heels would take her. Flipping the lock down on the door, she stepped out of her knickers, slipped off her skirt, opened her stockinged legs and plunged her vibrator into her wet, welcoming pussy. She came almost immediately.

Park Life

Steph looked at herself in the mirror. Turning sideways and then straight on she changed the jumper she had put on for a slightly longer, baggier version. Going through the same checking procedure once again, she was finally satisfied that the dildo she was wearing under her jeans would not be seen by the general tube-using public as she travelled out west for her date with Alex. As she walked down to the tube she could feel the base of the rubber appendage pressing into her clit and hoped that her clothes weren't as transparent as her mood. Steph finally arrived at the bar a little early and decided to go in for a pint. She looked at her watch. She had fifteen minutes to kill.

Matt was determined not to let the day be wasted completely. At 8.30 p.m. Alex was still walking into the conference room, throwing a file down on the polished table in front of an old geezer who was playing the company president and saying: 'Mr Henderson, your figures are ridiculous and frankly I find your offer insulting!' Now this sounded easy enough, but Matt wanted to do opening-door shots, leg shots, wide-shots, mid-shots, close-ups and reverse shots of the whole lot.

Alex had finished her bit on camera and had managed to rush downstairs for a shower while the lights were repositioned for the old bloke's bits. Just before they started on the final set-up she asked Tony to turn the car round and wait behind the wheel. Alex held her breath as she waited to hear that there had been no hairs in gates or whatever they check for every time.

'OK, people, that's a wrap,' announced Matt. Alex was practi-cally in the car by the time the last word had left his mouth. She had little over half an hour to get home and then down to meet Steph. Fortunately the City was deserted and the usual snarl-ups on the Marylebone Road weren't even in evidence, so they made it home in good time.

'Cheers, Tony!' called out Alex as she leaped out of the car and up the steps to her house. 'See you in a couple of days!' Alex pulled off the clothes she had worn to work and changed into something fresher and more accessible. She had no idea where Steph was going to take her but figured that a skirt was always going to be the best policy, even though it went against her usual sartorial preference. Grabbing the keys to her car, she got behind the wheel and raced down the road to the high street bar Steph had mentioned. She was only ten minutes late when she arrived and saw Steph sitting at one of the tables outside with an empty pint glass in front of her. She honked the horn and leaned over to unlock the door for her.

'You said outside, so I guessed you didn't want to stay here,' said Alex as Steph got into the passenger seat. 'Sorry I'm late, Steph.'

'I was beginning to wonder if you were going to turn up.'

'How could I not turn up?' Alex didn't want Steph to start a sulk that would drag on and spoil their evening. She reached over and put her hand on Steph's leg. 'So now you've got me here, what's the plan?'

'Well, I had thought we could walk there, but seeing as you've got the car, we may as well drive. Turn right at the end of the street and I'll tell you where to go from there.' Steph felt Alex move her hand further up her thigh and Steph had to stop it before it worked its way up to her crotch and spoiled the surprise. It wasn't long before they arrived at the park and Steph told Alex to pull up just down the road from the gates. It was getting darker by the minute and Steph was pleased to see that there wasn't much traffic around, stationary or on the move. They got out of the car and walked down to the gates.

'You seemed to like spending time in the park, so I thought I'd take you to a different one.' Alex could see Steph's eyes glinting in the moonlight.

'I thought they locked the gates here at night,' said Alex, wondering what Steph was up to.

'They do.' Steph eyed up the gate. 'Think you can get over there if I give you a hand?' she asked.

'Can you do it?'

'Yep.'

'Well, given my height advantage, I think the old lady might be able it make it too!' The gate and surrounding iron bars weren't high and it didn't take too much effort to climb over them and get into the park.

'It's not very secluded, is it?' remarked Alex as Steph took her hand and led her over to the lake.

'It'll be fine. We're not there yet.' They walked past the lake and got to a little bridge that led to a picnic area which was cut off from the rest of the park by a border of trees and shrubs. There were a few tables in the small space but mostly it was grass and a few flowerbeds. Steph led Alex into the darkest corner of the clearing. As her eyes adjusted to the dark, Alex saw that a blanket was already lying out on the ground and there was a bottle of wine, a candle and two glasses lying next to it. She smiled. 'Either someone else has beaten us to it or you've been here already this evening,' she said, impressed by the effort Steph had obviously gone to.

'Just because we're outside, it doesn't mean we can't be civilised,' responded Steph as she sat down on the blanket and pulled out a lighter to light the candle she'd stuck into the grass. 'Last time was so rushed, I thought we deserved something a little more relaxed this time,' Steph explained.

'So you've given the park keepers the night off, have you?'

'You don't really believe they have keepers, do you?' Steph laughed. 'They are just figments of the imagination to keep scaredy cats like you out at night!'

'Whatever,' said Alex as she reached for the glass Steph was offering her. A swig of the mellow, red liquid was enough to take the edge of her nerves. She lay down on the blanket next to Steph. The night was beginning to get cooler and she was grateful for the warmth of Steph's body next to her. Steph leaned over her and kissed her on the lips.

'So how've you been?' she asked as she pulled back to look Alex in the eye.

'Good.' There was a slight pause before Alex continued, 'Anxious. A little anxious, to tell you the truth.' She had been anxious when Steph had left it so long to call her; she was anxious about what Brett had said about Steph getting angry with her and now about the possibility of getting caught.

'Because of this?' Steph questioned.

'Yeah. Kind of.'

Steph didn't have any reply to this. If she told Alex she had nothing to worry about then everything would change and she didn't really want anything to change but she didn't feel good that she was making her feel nervous either. The only response Steph could think of was to light a joint and offer it to her. Alex pulled long and hard on the spliff and passed it back to Steph.

'You think of everything, don't you?' Alex let the words escape from her body along with the smoke she'd been holding in her lungs. A couple more tokes and she no longer gave a toss about park keepers or anyone else finding them.

'I was at work when I got your message today.' Alex giggled.

'And that's funny, why?' asked Steph, who was lying on her back trying to make shapes out of the few stars she could see.

'I got so turned on at the thought of being with you again, I had to excuse myself to go off to have a wank.' This time Steph joined in with the spluttered laughter.

'Really?'

'Yes, really!'

'Wow. What did you do?' Steph stubbed out the joint in the grass and turned to Alex.

'I went back to my trailer and took off my pants and skirt – I have to wear this blue, linen thing and it creases really easily, you see – and fucked myself with my vibrator!'

'Bloody hell, that's a horny thought,' said Steph softly as she let the image consume her. 'You have a vibrator at work?'

'Yes, doesn't everyone?' They chortled together as they devised an alternative version of the Diet Coke ad that did away with men and Diet Coke altogether. 'So that's how you've been affecting me!' whispered Alex in Steph's ear as she reached out for her lover and rolled over so she was on top of her. Astride Steph's torso, Alex felt the rubber dick her partner was wearing underneath her trousers push up into her crotch immediately and she let out a small gasp of delight. Her half-stoned eyes opened wide with surprise and excitement. 'We've been lying here for God knows how long; I've been telling you all about how horny I've been all day and you've been wearing this all the time!' scolded Alex. She reached down and pulled at the strap-on Steph was wearing. Steph groaned as she felt it press into her clit even more. 'I wondered why you were wearing a frigging great jumper on a night like this.' Sliding down so she was sitting on Steph's legs, Alex began to undo the buttons on Steph's jeans. She pulled the fabric open and, free of its restraint, Steph's dick sprang out. Alex was pleased to see that it was large and thick without being a complete monster. Steph felt the rough fabric of the picnic blanket on her arse as she manoeuvred Alex onto the rug beside her and finished taking her trousers off. Alex had already undone her shirt and taken her pants off by the time Steph pushed her skirt up and got in between Alex's legs. Steph kissed her hard on the mouth. The sensations that took over her body as she felt her cock nudging against Alex's cunt lips were extreme and she couldn't wait to sink it deep inside her lover. Alex pulled Steph's jumper off and opened her shirt so she could feel Steph's tits against her chest.

'Fuck me, Steph,' Alex said softly into the ear she was caressing with her tongue. Steph moved away slightly. Shifting her weight onto one hand, she used the other to part Alex's swollen labia. She ran her finger around Alex's hole and up onto her clit and felt her juices ooze out and cover her hand. Steph placed her dildo over her wet hole as Alex opened her legs even wider. With Alex's mouth sucking at her nipple and her hands massaging her arse, Steph pushed her hips forward and watched her cock sink into Alex's cunt. The sound of Alex's dripping cunt opening to take in Steph's dick and her groan as she felt it stretching and filling up her cunt were so erotic that Steph came with her first thrust. She felt her come trickle down her legs as she moved the dildo in and out of Alex's squirming body. Just when she thought Alex was about to come, Steph stopped.

'What are you doing?' gasped Alex.

'Just go with me,' said Steph as she rolled Alex over onto her front. Alex went with the movements Steph was orchestrating and was soon on her hands and knees on the rug. Positioned behind Alex's arse, Steph reached round and massaged her lover's clit as she slipped her cock into her hole once more. Alex's cunt was so wet that it slid in easily. She pushed her arse backwards into Steph as Steph continued to pump her pussy from behind as well as work on her taut, engorged clit. She could see the sweat glistening on Alex's back as she thrust her cock in and out of Alex's fanny. She could feel and hear the short, sharp breaths and gasps that she now knew were a signifier of Alex's impending orgasm and pushed her cock as far into Alex as she could. With every thrust, Alex could feel Steph's dildo rubbing against the sensitive place deep inside her that was guaranteed to make her come. The waves of pleasure Alex felt as she finally allowed the orgasm she had been holding back since Steph first penetrated her were violent and staccato. Drained of energy, her legs gave way and she collapsed onto the blanket with Steph on top of her. Alex moaned quietly as Steph eased her dick out of her cunt – the feeling of Steph's pubic hair and the wet dildo on her buttocks was comforting.

They lay in each other's arms enjoying the stillness and calm of the night air before Alex started undoing the harness that Steph was wearing.

'What are you doing?' asked Steph.

'I can't get at you with that on, can I?' she said in reply to Steph's protestations. Alex was just running her fingers over the red lips of Steph's cunt when they both became aware of some voices. They looked at each other with panic and fear in their eyes. Steph reached over and snuffed out the candle as Alex sat up next to her on the rug.

'No, it was definitely coming from over here,' said a man's voice. 'Where that light is.'

'I think we'd better get dressed,' said Alex calmly.

'I don't see any light,' came a woman's voice. 'It was probably just some ducks or something.'

'You stay here if you want to, but I want to go and check it out.' The woman was obviously not keen as it was only one set of footsteps that Steph and Alex heard coming towards them.

'Let's go and hide in the bushes at the entrance and when he comes in we'll leg it,' planned Alex. As predicted the man came into the picnic area and flashed his torch ahead of him. Seeing the bottle and the blanket, he moved further into the clearing.

'Is anyone there?' he asked. Just as he was in the furthest corner Alex and Steph ran out of the picnic area in the direction of the bridge and straight into the man's colleague. She grabbed hold of Steph by the jumper and had Alex by the arm. Releasing her grip on Steph she shone her torch in Alex's face. Alex instinctively put her hand up to her face to protect her eyes against the bright light. Switching the beam to Steph she realised that her prisoners were both women. She trailed the light over Steph's body to check if she had any weapon but when the beam fell upon the dildo in Steph's hand, she realised what was going on.

'See to your girlfriend at home next time, young lady,' she said wearily. 'He gets all antsy if he thinks people are using his park as a knocking shop.' She heard her colleague reappearing from the clearing and let go of Alex's arm. They ran off towards the gate.

'Oi, Brenda,' shouted the colleague, 'there they are! Get after them.' All it took was for Brenda to stick her foot out innocently as the man came pelting down the path for the chase to be over.

Oblivious to the advantage Brenda had given them, Alex and Steph continued to sprint back down the side of the boating lake and they practically vaulted over the gate in one movement. It was only when they slammed the doors of Alex's car with themselves safely inside that they allowed themselves to relax.

'Just my fucking luck!' gasped Steph as she struggled to get her breath back.

'Jesus, Steph! We could have been carted off to the police station and all you can think about is missing out on an orgasm!' Alex was amused by and in awe of Steph's reaction. Steph considered this for a moment as Alex remained speechless. The look in Steph's eyes told Alex that this was exactly what she meant, so not wanting to disappoint, Alex leaned over her passenger to the lever that controlled the seat's position. A sharp tug and Steph's seat was practically horizontal. Pulling her trousers off again Steph opened her legs. Alex could see that her large clit was erect and her labia were saturated with her juices. With the hand brake digging in her ribs, and the gear lever jabbing in her back, Alex buried her face in Steph's cunt. She teased her hole with the tip of her tongue and then licked her from her arse to clit with long, flat movements. Steph started to moan loudly as Alex began sucking and licking her clit and swirling her tongue over its purple, sensitive tip. Steph's orgasm was loud and Alex could feel her lover's body jerking with pleasure as she allowed the feeling to undulate through her. Alex sat up and looked out of the window to make sure they hadn't attracted another audience. The coast was clear. Steph pulled the seat back into an upright position as Alex went to start the engine.

'Are you sure you're OK to drive?' Steph asked as she did up her trousers.

Alex thought for a second and then decided it wasn't worth the risk. They walked back down to Baker Street and both caught a cab back to Alex's place.

TWELVE

Wake Up and Smell the Coffee

It was still only just gone midnight when Alex and Steph arrived back at Alex's flat. Alex walked up to the door and turned round to see that Steph was hovering at the gate at the bottom of the steps.

'Aren't you coming in?' asked Alex, a little worried that Steph was just going to disappear off into the night.

'Do you really want me to?' asked Steph meekly. 'You did get a bit upset back there.' Alex went down to where Steph was standing. She touched her arm and searched for some eye contact.

'I'm sorry about that, honey,' soothed Alex. 'It wasn't your fault. I know I'm as much to blame.'

'But if I hadn't forced you into it . . .' Steph's comment sent a surge of guilt rushing round Alex's body.

'Look, Steph, we need to talk,' whispered Alex in the darkness. 'Why don't you come in? There's something I need to tell you.'

'Sounds heavy,' said Steph, suddenly more anxious than regretful.

Steph was ensconced on the sofa when Alex brought the coffee through. If she was going to be dumped, she may as well make herself comfortable during the process. The hot, black coffee slid down a treat but the caffeine didn't do anything for the palpitations she was already having.

Alex sipped at her drink and looked at Steph from the armchair across the room. She pulled her feet up underneath her and remembered Brett's prediction that Steph would be mad when she found out that Alex had been duping her. She looked around the living room. There was nothing in her surroundings that gave her any idea about how to open the conversation they had to have.

In the end it was Steph who forced the issue. 'So what's so startling that you have to tell me about it now?' asked Steph even though she didn't really want to hear the answer.

'Steph, you know that I have really enjoyed being with you these last few of weeks . . .' said Alex hesitantly.

'What makes me think that there's a huge great "but" about to come?' Steph was rapidly descending into a slough of despond because, as far as she was concerned, the end of her relationship with Alex and, come to that, the end of the world, was nigh.

'You're right: there is a "but".'

'For Christ's sake, Alex, spit it out, will you!' Steph's heart was in her mouth and her body was suffering as a consequence.

Alex took a deep breath and came out with it. 'I have to admit, Steph, that I haven't been totally honest with you.'

'Don't tell me. You're really a bored, Surrey housewife with three kids, a very vivid imagination and a doppelgänger who's a successful actress!'

'You're not making this very easy, Steph.' Her reaction was uncalled for but Steph wasn't at all sure she wanted to hear the rest of what Alex had to say.

'You remember that night when you first came round here?'

'Yes . . .'

'Well, I had called you during the day . . .' Alex had thought it best to start at the beginning.

'At home?'

'Yes.'

'Why did you do that?' Steph didn't have a clue where this was going but was trying desperately to figure it out. Alex put her coffee down on the table and moved over onto the sofa in an effort to bridge the physical gap between them.

'You see the truth is that I . . . I was calling you because I . . .' Alex couldn't quite decide on the right words.

'Because what?'

'Because I really missed you and I was going to ask you if you would like to go out on a date with me.' The words tumbled out of Alex's mouth at speed and it was more by luck than judgement that they happened to be in the right order.

'A date . . .?' Whatever it was that Steph had constructed in her mind as a worst-case scenario, this statement had not even entered her mind as a possible option. 'But I thought . . . You know, you had that thing with your agent?'

'Yeah. I did.'

'So what happened? I don't understand.'

'I came to my senses.'

'How? Why?' Steph was finding it difficult to digest what Alex was trying to say to her.

'Well, I'll just say that I met someone who made me realise that I wasn't really very happy with my life and that I had the power to change it if I wanted to.'

'So when did this happen?'

'Literally the night before you knocked on my door.'

'And you let me believe all this time that you were only going along with me under sufferance?'

'I don't think I ever gave you the impression that I was suffering!'

'That's not what sufferance means, you idiot!' Steph didn't really know whether to be outraged and angry by what Alex had just revealed or flattered and deliriously happy. What she ended up feeling was mildly cheesed off that she felt so foolish and extraordinarily relieved.

'God, I'm really sorry, Steph. It wasn't my intention to mislead you; it just sort of happened . . .'

'But why did you do it? I've spent the last few weeks believing that the only reason you were seeing me was because of this ridiculous charade –'

'You really thought I believed that thing about you going to the press about us?'

147

'I didn't know what you thought. I was just scared that it would all turn out like the first time.'

'Steph, I never thought you would be capable of doing anything to hurt me. I sort of thought we had some kind of "understanding" . . .' Alex reached over and gently put her hand on Steph's leg. It was meant as a conciliatory gesture and she was relieved when Steph didn't move away from her touch.

'But, Alex, what I don't understand is why you let it happen? That night when I was round here, you could have just said that you felt the same and we could have been sending each other chocolates and roses instead of dares and hollow threats for the last few weeks!'

'Exactly.'

'Exactly what?'

'I thought you would have realised by now that I'm not a chocolates and roses kinda girl!'

Steph turned to look at Alex. She felt Alex's hand squeeze her thigh and then brush stray hair away from her face. 'So this has been all about you satisfying your penchant for a particular kind of sex?'

'No!' Alex knew the indignation in her voice was unjustified as soon as she said the word.

'Are you sure?'

'Well, maybe. Yes and no. It was just a way of having it all. I got to see you – the woman I had been thinking of ever since I met you at college that day – and have some guaranteed wild times too.'

'So you've been feeling the same as me all along?'

Alex nodded sheepishly. Steph shook her head in disbelief. She was having difficulty trying to make sense of the situation. Alex slipped her arm around Steph's shoulders and drew her into her body so that her head was resting on her chest. 'I never wanted to upset you, Steph, and I knew I should have stopped it sooner. I suppose I just got a little carried away . . .' Alex figured the more information she gave Steph about how she was feeling, the easier it would be for her to understand and forgive her. She stroked Steph's hair as she continued to speak. 'I suppose it started when you were here on that first night. When you pinned me against the wall, I was just so turned on that I thought it would be fun to see where it went. I really thought you had guessed how I felt. If I'd known you were feeling so insecure, I would have said something sooner, but I thought you were getting off on it as much as I was.' Her voice trailed off into a pause. 'Steph? Steph, what are you thinking?' Steph pulled away from Alex and looked her straight in the eye.

'What I'm really thinking?'

'Yes.' Alex realised she was holding her breath in anticipation of her lover's response. She couldn't blame her if she decided to leave and never come back.

'OK. I'm thinking about how much energy I wasted worrying about how to hold onto you and that I'm absolutely knackered because of it. I'm thinking that you're right. I was "getting off on it" as much as you and that pisses me off. I'm realising you're totally fucking fucked up and I'm wondering why I adore you so much!' Steph smiled at Alex in disbelief and saw the anxiety draining from her face.

'You do? In spite of . . . everything?' Alex smiled back at Steph and felt the heavy atmosphere in the room begin to melt away.

'Don't get me wrong: I still think you're an absolute selfish bastard!' exclaimed Steph as she pushed Alex down on the sofa. 'You could have just told me that you wanted to do the stuff that we've done, you know. It wouldn't have changed anything.'

'Yes, it would! I bet you a thousand pounds you wouldn't have behaved in quite the same way,' said Alex as she struggled to get out from underneath Steph.

'A thousand pounds, eh? That's quite a lot of money for a poor drama student like me!' Steph caught hold of Alex's arms and kissed her hard on the mouth. She felt the fight disappear from Alex's body as she gave in to Steph's kiss. Alex parted her lips to allow Steph's tongue to explore her mouth. Steph had kissed this woman what felt like a million times before, but this time it felt like they were doing it for the first time. Alex pulled her arms free and caressed the nape of Steph's neck, pulling her into a deeper, slower, more sensual embrace. Steph finally pulled away and stared down at the baffling woman beneath her. She examined Alex's face and traced the line of her slender nose with her finger as she gazed into her enquiring deep blue eyes. She saw a smile begin to unfurl on Alex's face.

'Does that mean we can still play the game?' asked Alex optimistically.

It had felt good to be able to share Alex's bed that night and it was an altogether more relaxed Steph who woke up the following morning. Sitting at Alex's kitchen table drinking juice and eating toast whilst wearing one of her lover's T-shirts had previously been something Steph had only been able to dream about and she was finding it hard to grasp that it was now a reality.

'What are you doing today?' asked Alex as she offered Steph a slice of the orange she was eating.

'I'm meant to be having a session with a guy who's directing our graduation show, but I wasn't planning on going.' Steph bit into the segment that was offered and wiped the juice from her chin.

'You weren't going to go?' Alex was amazed at Steph's attitude. 'Steph, you do realise how important the graduation show is, don't you?'

'Yes, it's just that I haven't really been able to concentrate recently.' Alex knew what she was saying and felt guilty for not realising before just how she had been affecting Steph.

'Well, you're going today, OK? What are you working on for it?'

'Something from *As You Like It*, funnily enough!' was Steph's response. 'A scene from *Separation* and a song in the musical segment as well.'

'And when exactly is the show?'

'Two weeks' time.'

'Well, that's it then. When you've had a shower, I'll drive you up there.' Alex's concern made Steph feel warm inside.

'What have you got planned for today?'

'I'm going to have a word with Marsha.'

'Marsha?'

'Yep. My contract with Quentin is up for renewal soon and I was thinking of asking Marsha if she would represent me.'

'Well, aren't we getting our house in order!' teased Steph.

'Get your lazy arse in that shower then!'

For the first time in ages Steph was actually early for a rehearsal. As they drew up outside the college in Alex's car, Steph leaned over and gave her a thank-you peck on the cheek.

'I could come and pick you up later on, if you like,' offered Alex who was basking in the sudden turn towards the normal their relationship had taken.

'That's OK,' replied Steph as she reached for the handle.

'But you are coming over tonight, aren't you?' asked Alex.

'Hey, babe, I've got one thousand pounds to win! I'll call you, OK.' Steph slid out of the car and left Alex to bang her head against the steering wheel in frustration.

A Very Interesting Idea

Alex headed for the West End in search of some retail therapy. It had been a long time since she had had anyone to think about other than herself and, as she wandered around the shops, she realised that she had bought loads of stuff for Steph and nothing for herself. She also was aware of how happy it was making her and that she could make Steph happy too. As she arrived home and deposited her purchases in her living room, she wondered what Steph had meant when she said she'd call her. Did she mean that night or just sometime? She would have been more than content to have a quiet night in with Steph that night and realised that the gauntlet that she had so cavalierly thrown down was now leaping up and slapping her round the face. She'd made her bed, however, and would have to lie in it until her presence was requested. Alex's thoughts turned to Marsha. She had to get her life back on track and, for the time being, this was the one area she could take control of. She picked up her phone, dialled Marsha's number and was thankful that it was the woman and not the answer machine that took the call.

'Alex, how lovely to hear from you!' exclaimed Marsha. 'How are you?'

'I'm fine, Marsha. Very well, in fact. Look, I was wondering what you were doing this afternoon. Would you like to get together for a coffee or something? I'd really like to run an idea by you.' As usual, Marsha couldn't resist an invitation from Alex and readily agreed to meet her in a coffee shop in West Hampstead.

Marsha was sitting at a table in the window of the café smoking a cheroot when Alex arrived.

'Alex, darling! How gorgeous you look!' Marsha stood up in a cloud of smoke and perfume and kissed Alex noisily on both cheeks. They engaged in some chit-chat for some minutes until Marsha's curiosity got the better of her.

'As lovely as it is to see you, my dear, I have been more than a little intrigued by your phone call. What is this idea you've had?'

'Well, I know this might appear slightly odd at first but I hope you'll hear me out.' For the second time in less than twenty-four hours Alex was finding it hard to broach a delicate subject. She didn't know how Marsha would react to her request, but ploughed ahead anyway. 'You know my relationship with Quentin has been a little problematic –'

'That's an interesting way of putting it, petal, but I know what you're trying to say,' encouraged Marsha.

'Well, I was wondering, when my contract with him expires whether you would consider representing me?' Alex leaned back in her chair and watched her ex-tutor pull on her cheroot as she considered the proposition. Marsha was not the sort of woman who could be thrown off-guard easily and this time was no exception. Alex watched the smoke stream out of Marsha's nostril and waited for some kind of response.

'I see,' was Marsha's eventual reaction. There was another pause and more funnels of smoke before she continued. 'You realise that I haven't looked after anyone before, my dear.'

'Yes.'

'I'm just wondering why you would want me to do it?'

'Isn't it obvious?'

'Humour me, Alex.'

'OK. It's just that I feel like I've really been stung by this experience with Quentin and really need someone who knows me and is happy with that. Someone I can trust. Someone new but connected but most importantly someone who believes in me.' There was a pause as Marsha considered what Alex had said. 'I really think we could work well as a team. It could be the making of both of us . . .' continued Alex. 'What do you think?'

'I think that it's a very interesting idea. Very interesting.' Marsha stubbed out her cheroot and adjusted her neck scarf as she ruminated some more. 'It would have to be on a professional basis though, Alex. We'd have to work out percentages and all that dreadful business because I wouldn't want anything to come between our friendship.'

'Of course. It need only be for a little while, if you're not sure. A three-month trial period, if you like.'

'In that case, my dear, I think we deserve to toast our new arrangement with something stronger than a latte, don't you?' Alex agreed and ticked one box on her mental 'to do' list.

When Steph got home after her rehearsal, she picked up the phone several times with the intention of dialling Alex's number but never quite got past the first five digits. As much as she wanted to see Alex she knew that she had to prove she was capable of winning the bet. It hurt like hell, but she wasn't going to let Alex down.

When Alex got home she sat by the phone, her address book open at the page with Steph's number on it. She thought about dialling the number but didn't. This time she knew she had to let Steph call the shots – properly. It was the least she could do, wasn't it? She nearly jumped out of her skin when it actually rang.

'Is that a Ms Dechy?' came a strange accent down the phone.

'Yes. Who is this?' replied Alex.

'I'm calling from the Metropolitan Police. We've had some complaints recently about your behaviour in a certain hotel in London and I'm just making a few enquiries.'

'Brett! It's you, isn't it, you idiot! You're not that good an actor, you know!' Brett dissolved into giggles on the other end of the phone. 'That's not funny, you sod!'

'Sorry, mate!'

'Dick Van Dyke has nothing on you, does he?'

'You should know, darling!'

'Ha-bloody-ha! What do you want anyway?'

'Just catching up. Wondering if you wanted a night on the tiles with my gorgeous self.'

'Can't. I'm waiting in for someone.'

'Jeez. Like that, is it? Shame.'

'Does it have to be tonight?'

'No. It's just that I've heard that the rumours on set are that we're going at it like rabbits, so I thought we could have some fun fuelling some imaginations, that's all.'

'Really? Well, I suppose I have been whipping your arse, but I doubt that anyone would believe that it was only at Cluedo!' Alex chuntered away with Brett, happy in the knowledge that BT's call waiting service would alert her if someone else was trying to get through. The all-important beep on the line didn't materialise, however.

THIRTEEN

Dinner at Nine

Steph held out as long as she could before phoning Alex. It wasn't until she got back from football on Sunday afternoon and was showered and dressed before she got itchy fingers again.

'Hi, Alex?'

'Steph! I was about to give up on you!' Alex was relieved to hear her voice at last. 'How are you?'

'Good. Are you working Wednesday night?'

'I've got an early call tomorrow, but I should be finished by about midday. Why?'

'Well, I thought I might take you out to dinner.'

'Sounds nice.'

'I hope it will be.' Steph told her the name of a busy, desirable restaurant in Soho and said she'd book a table for 9.00 p.m. There was a pause as both suddenly felt awkward about chatting on the phone.

'I've been doing some shopping for you,' said Alex as she looked at the posh cardboard carrier bags that were still lining her living room.

'Yeah. Me you too,' replied Steph.

'Shall we exchange gifts in the restaurant then?' asked Alex, eager to see Steph's face when she saw the shower of presents she'd impulse-bought.

'That's what I had in mind.' With that the phones were put down and the anticipation began.

'What the fuck's got into you?' demanded Bev the following evening. 'Showing up in class and now you look like the cat who's got the cream! Something's up.' Steph was looking great. She had dressed up for her meal with Alex and had an undeniable glow about her.

'Look, Bev. It's too late now to go into details, but you know that woman that I've been in a stew about?'

'Yes . . .'

'Well, it's Alex. You know, Alex from the acting class?'

'I think what you mean to say is potential fucking film star, Alex, but yes, I remember her . . .' said an incredulous Bev.

'Well, I guess so, yes. It's her that I've been so cut up about but we've talked it all out and I'm going out with her tonight. I think we're having a relationship, but I'm not too sure.'

'You're doing what?' exclaimed an even more incredulous Bev.

'Please don't tell anyone though. It's really low-key at the moment, yeah?' Steph brushed past her friend and was opening the door as Bev was calling out to her, 'Have a good time!'

Alex had got to the restaurant early. She'd managed to decant all the books and garments she'd bought for Steph into two discreet bags and was looking forward to seeing what Steph had bought for her. The restaurant was full of people and the noise was bouncing off the glass tables and wooden floor. She'd already seen a couple of famous faces she recognised and the thought of being with Steph in such a glamorous place was adding to her excitement. When she saw Steph, she felt her heart leap as if they were on their first date. It was the first time in a long time that she'd allowed herself to feel such a thing and she enjoyed the sensation for a second or so before attracting Steph's attention. Alex stood up and they kissed each other on the lips before Steph sat down in the seat opposite her.

'I've missed you,' ventured Alex.

'Ditto,' replied Steph, feeling a little like Lord Patrick of Swayze in *Ghost*. A man came over to ask what they wanted to drink and without paying much attention they ordered a bottle of white wine.

'How did your rehearsal go?' asked Alex tentatively.

'Yes. It was good. I really feel like I'm making some headway.'

'Well, maybe this would help.' Alex produced the first of her purchases and gave Steph a stack of books about playing/studying/researching Shakespeare. Steph was a little taken aback by her generosity.

'Thank you! They look really good. That's really thoughtful of you, Alex.' Steph smiled at her while the waiter opened and poured their wine in silence. 'I have something for you too,' Steph said once the waiter had gone. 'But you're going to have to come to the loo with me and I'll give it to you there.'

'Oh, no! We can't do anything here, Steph. It's too busy!'

'No, come on. It's nothing like that.' Steph got up from the table and waited for Alex to follow. They made their way through the tables and into the women's toilets. Steph took Alex's hand and guided her into a cubicle.

'I've been thinking about you so much,' said Alex. She slipped her arm round Steph's waist and pulled her into her body.

'I've thought of nothing else,' replied Steph as she gave Alex the kiss she had been waiting for for what seemed like an eternity. 'You turn me on so much, Alex.'

'Ditto,' said Alex facetiously and ran her hand over Steph's breasts. 'So what have you got for me?' Steph didn't need asking twice and produced her present.

'You want me to put this on now?' asked Alex as she looked at the item at the bottom of the little bag.

'Of course. There's a thousand pounds riding on this!' whispered Steph with a glint in her eye. Alex looked at the jelly moulded 'thing' that was in her hand and laughed.

'It's state of the art,' explained Steph.

'I can see that!' exclaimed Alex as she surveyed the mini dildo with integral clit stimulator that was in her hand.

'You strap it on so the dildo bit goes inside –'

'I can see where it goes!' Alex laughed.

'. . . and I control the intensity of the vibrations,' explained Steph, wielding a remote control triumphantly.

'So you're planning to make me come in this restaurant?' enquired Alex.

'Got it in one!' said Steph, pleased that her plan was having an impact. 'Get your knickers off then.' It was Alex's turn to shake her head in disbelief, but it didn't stop her from complying with the request. She slipped the straps round her thighs and the tiny dildo slid into her already wet fanny with ease. Steph flicked the switch to make sure it was working OK and Alex gasped with surprise as she felt the vibrations on her clit and in her cunt.

'Ready?'

'I hope you're not too hungry because I don't think I'm going to be able to take this for very long!' said Alex as she adjusted the toy so that its protruding tip was positioned right over her clit.

'Let's just see how it goes,' said Steph as she opened the door and headed back to the table with her friend with the strange gait following her.

A different waiter came to take their food order. Alex went for a goat's cheese salad followed by some sort of fish-type dish and Steph ordered another Cal-Ital kind of thing. Alex didn't really have her mind on the food or what Steph was saying to her about her work at college. Steph's hand had gone in her pocket and had activated the stimulant in Alex's crotch so that it was slowly grinding and vibrating in between her legs. It made conversation difficult but Steph's talk of working on her scenes and her activities on the football field wasn't designed to engage. She let the words spill out of her mouth but was watching Alex squirm in the seat opposite her. To anyone else who was watching she would have looked like someone who desperately wanted to go to the loo, but Steph knew different. Steph saw their starters appearing from across the room and quickly turned the toy off. She didn't want any overly attentive waiters enquiring whether that strange buzzing sound was annoying them or not.

'This is too cruel,' hissed Alex across the table as soon as the waiter had gone. 'I'm so wet. I want to feel you touch me, Steph.

I feel like I've been about to come for the last twenty minutes and it's driving me crazy!'

'I aim to please!' retorted Steph as she picked at the food in front of her. Steph reached into her pocket again and the toy between Alex's legs came to life once again. Alex felt the vibrations on her clit again and found herself rolling her pelvis forward in her seat to intensify the feeling.

'Can't we go back to the loo?' asked Alex.

'Aren't you enjoying your meal?'

'I don't think I want to come here!' said Alex, realising Steph had seen her and raised her in the risk-taking stakes. The thing that was vibrating in her cunt was well on its way to making an orgasm inevitable but Alex didn't want to have to stifle her pleasure.

'Alex, I seem to remember that this is exactly the kind of thing that you didn't want to give up,' said Steph reasonably. 'Now, just relax: go with the feeling and try not to be too loud.' Steph was amazed at her own control. All she wanted to do was to get her face in Alex's fanny and lick her until she screamed, but there was pride and money at stake so she stuck with her plan.

Their plates were cleared and they sat back and waited for their main course, Steph's hand still on the control.

'Give me some more,' demanded Alex as she adjusted her position so that the thing in her cunt was pressing on her clit in exactly the right way.

'But, Alex, we haven't had our main course yet,' replied Steph as she flicked the control in her pocket and watched Alex's face contort with desire.

'I see why you chose this restaurant now!' Alex laughed as she gave into the feelings that were building from her crotch. 'Nice and busy with enough noise that we wouldn't easily draw attention to ourselves!'

'It's all in the planning,' said Steph, who was beginning to feel a little uncomfortable herself. Their main courses arrived quickly. Obviously there was another sitting after them. Steph hoped there would be for her too. They ate their food as if they hadn't eaten for weeks.

'Jesus, Steph, you've got to bring me off,' whispered Alex across the table. 'I can't stand it.' Steph reached into her pocket and flipped the dial. She saw tiny beads of sweat appear on Alex's forehead and small, round patches of red appear on her cheeks. Steph smiled as she watched Alex trying not to signal to all and sundry that she was having an earth-shaking orgasm. The waves of her orgasm were still coursing through her body when the waiter came over to clear their plates away and she tried to mask what was going on with a coughing fit.

'Was everything all right, ladies?' he asked politely.

'Absolutely wonderful,' replied a red-faced Alex. Steph placed the remote control on the table triumphantly.

'Steph, you have to be one of the most –'

'Alex, it is you, isn't it?' asked a woman who had suddenly appeared at their table.

'Yes,' said Alex, trying to collect herself.

'Are you all right? I was watching you from across the room and thought you looked as if you were in some distress.'

'I'm really sorry, you are . . .?'

'Rachel, Quentin's new assistant.'

'Oh, of course, Rachel! No, I'm totally fine. Just a bit of indigestion, that's all.'

'That's all right then,' said Rachel who made no move to leave, but just stood and looked at Alex and Steph.

'This is my friend, Steph,' introduced Alex.

'Hello, Steph, I'm from Quent–'

'Yes. You just said,' said Steph curtly.

'So you're all right then?' enquired Rachel.

'Yes. No problems at all.' Rachel lingered for a second or two longer and suddenly her eyes fell on the control Steph had forgotten was on the table. Before Steph could scoop it up, Rachel had it in her hand. 'Oooh, what's this?' she said in a girlie 'I-know-nothing-about-gadgets' voice that was just a little too fake as she set about examining the buttons.

'It's a –' replied Steph anxiously.

'What does this do?' asked Rachel. She flicked the switch up to high and Alex's face crumpled as a result of the sudden, intense

160

vibrations on her post-orgasm, hyper-sensitive clitoris. Steph lunged across the table, trying to make as much noise as possible to cover up the sound of the toy and wrestled the control from Rachel's freakishly strong, manicured hand.

'Please, you mustn't touch that!' exclaimed Steph as she finally regained possession of the device. 'Thank you.' Steph settled back down in her seat and tried to beat Rachel off with her stare. After a couple more seconds Rachel finally understood that she wasn't going to get any more information out of the pair and flounced off, only turning back once to throw a suspicious glance in their direction.

'You all right down there?' Steph giggled.

'Just about intact! Would you believe it? It would have to be her, wouldn't it? That's all I fucking need!' said Alex. At that moment the waiter came over with the bill. He handed it over to Steph.

'I think the lady's paying,' Steph said patronisingly.

'Excuse me?' said Alex.

'You can take it off the thousand pounds you owe me if you like. I take it that counts as a win?' Alex knew she couldn't do anything but fling her card on the table.

'Come on, let's go,' said Steph as Alex finished signing the receipt. 'I think I've got a bit of indigestion coming on.'

FOURTEEN
Bloody Rachel

Steph glanced at the clock on Alex's mantelpiece. It was coming up to noon and she knew she would have to be leaving for college pretty soon but Alex still hadn't finished showing her all the stuff she'd bought for her. When they got back to Alex's the night before, opening presents hadn't been uppermost in their thoughts.

'. . . I just thought it would look really good with those black trousers you've got.' Alex was talking about the top she had in her hand and went over to Steph to hold it up against her. 'It looks perfect. Why don't you go and try it on?'

Steph took hold of Alex's hands and massaged her palms with her thumbs. 'I don't want to appear ungrateful, sweetheart, but I'm going to be late for rehearsal if I don't go soon. Why don't I try everything on this evening?'

'I'd forgotten all about college. Sorry.'

Steph went into the kitchen to get her bag. She was just coming back into the room to make arrangements for the evening before leaving when the phone went. Alex picked it up.

'Quentin! Hello! Well, this is a surprise!' exclaimed Alex. She listened to Quentin's voice and mouthed to Steph, 'It's Quentin.' Steph mouthed, 'I know' in reply.

'No, you're right, I guess you are my agent, after all.' Alex

162

pulled a face at Steph that conveyed her confusion over the nature of his call. Steph slipped up behind Alex as she spoke and tried to distract her by pushing her hands underneath the T-shirt Alex had on. Her smooth skin felt so soft as she started gently caressing Alex's breasts and touching her erect nipples. Alex smiled and enjoyed the feeling of Steph's hands on her body as she let Quentin rattle on in his pompous, egocentric way.

'I really have to go soon,' whispered Steph in Alex's free ear. Alex nodded.

'So, Quentin, was this just a "touching base" call or –' asked Alex. Suddenly Steph felt Alex's body tense up and then she pushed Steph away and squirmed out of her embrace.

'So you've been talking to Rachel . . .?' repeated a rather green-looking Alex for the benefit of a rather put-out-looking Steph. 'You want to see me this week?' . . . 'Well, I am pretty busy, Quentin, unless you've got some time free this afternoon, that is' . . . 'OK, I'll be at your office at 4.00 p.m. this afternoon' . . . 'Was there anything in particular you wanted to talk about?' . . . 'Well, put like that I suppose I've got no choice but to wait and see, have I?' . . . 'See you later then, and say hello to Rachel from me, won't you,' Alex said pointedly as she put the phone back on the hook. 'Fucking hell, Steph, I think I've been found out!'

As Alex made her way into the West End to meet Quentin in his office, she went over the advice Steph had given her earlier that day – 'Go straight for his dick, Alex. If he starts trying to threaten you then lead him on; play him at his own game. Make him think that he's got all the cards and that you need him more than ever. You can't dump him in private; this sort of humiliation has to be done in public and with panache. I think our combined imaginations can come up with something suitable, don't you?' It was all very well for Steph to play the tough guy, but she wasn't going to be the one playing out the scenario. Alex felt slightly sick at the thought of how Quentin could possibly use whatever information Rachel might have given him. She couldn't work out whether Rachel was really incredibly thick or very perceptive and it worried her.

It had to be Rachel who buzzed her into the building and opened the door to Quentin's old-fashioned offices and, sure enough, it was. 'Enjoy the rest of your meal, last night, Rachel?' Alex asked as she stepped inside.

'It was very pleasant, thank you, Alex,' said Rachel and smiled. Alex cursed the witch for being so bland and unreadable. 'Mr de Fleur is waiting for you, if you'd like to go through,' she continued. 'Can I get you anything to drink?' Alex felt like a Bloody Mary but settled for a glass of water. She noticed Rachel stop off to whisper something to Sabrina before making her way over to the water cooler. She heard some snorting and giggling and turned to see what they were up to. Was it her imagination or was Sabrina looking at her differently too?

An over-stuffed Quentin was sitting in his over-stuffed chair when Alex entered the room.

'Alex, my darling!' he bellowed and heaved his feet off his over-large desk in order to approach and embrace Alex. Alex stood stock-still as the greeting ritual took place. It wasn't the reaction she had been expecting and it threw her a bit.

'So what's so important that you had to talk to me today, Quentin?' challenged Alex. At that moment Rachel came in with her glass of water and provided the perfect excuse for Quentin to ignore the question totally.

'I hear you two bumped into each other last night,' said Quentin. Alex nodded her thank-you to Rachel, confirmed that they had indeed encountered each other the previous evening and braced herself for what was to come. She reminded herself that she had to go straight for his dick, but the thought just made her feel queasy. There was a brief hiatus while Rachel finished depositing drinks and left the room.

'So how's filming going, then, luvvy?' he rumbled on. 'Are you making the most of your experience?'

'Absolutely,' said Alex, even though his decision not to question her further about her dinner date coupled with his sudden interest in whether she was enjoying herself was still more baffling. 'Everyone is so friendly and the crew have been really kind.'

'So making new friends, then?'

'Yes. I suppose. A couple.'

'And you're getting on well with young Brett?' Quentin's sudden willingness to indulge in small talk was a little disarming, but Alex decided to go with it for the time being.

'Brett is fantastic. He's been wonderful to work with and we've been having really good fun together too,' said Alex honestly.

'All that hanging around, you've got to amuse yourselves somehow, haven't you?'

'Absolutely. He's been my saviour.'

'Really? Well, that's excellent.'

Alex leaned back in her chair and sipped her glass of water. Quentin shuffled some papers around on his desk and cleared his throat as if he didn't quite know how to draw their meeting round to the matter that was really on his mind. Alex wasn't going to make it easy for him by asking him again, so she sat and waited for him to collect himself.

'So, Alex, I suppose you've realised our contract is coming up for renewal very soon.'

'Is it really?' said Alex, feigning surprise. 'Hasn't time flown?'

'And, well, I've drawn up another contract for you to sign as I thought we might as well get it out of the way before filming moves to the States. It's going to be a dreadfully busy time for you, and I think we should get any outstanding business out of the way before you leave, don't you think?'

Alex's mind was whirring. Her expectations about the meeting were hardly matching up to what was happening and she was desperately trying to figure out why there was a slight film of sweat above Quentin's top lip.

'I think that's a very good idea, Quentin. Is the contract exactly the same as the previous one?' she asked tentatively, hoping that his reaction would give some clue to his motivation.

'Pretty much. You know, the odd clause here or there, but, you know me, I'm always open to discussing changes,' he said as he loosened his tie. The problem was, however, that Alex did know him and her experience had been that he hadn't been up to discussing very much at all in the past. Her thoughts were interrupted by a beep coming from her phone.

'Sorry,' she said politely as she read Brett's text message and laughed.

'Anything important?'

'No. Just Brett fooling around.' It was the grin that crept over Quentin's face that made everything suddenly fall into place. He wanted to keep her on because he thought she'd done a U-turn on the road to Dykesville and was currently dating one of the hottest young actors in Hollywood and, as such, would be a veritable money-magnet.

'I tell you what, Quentin, why don't I take the contract away with me, have a read – maybe show it to my solicitor and then get back to you? How does that sound?' Alex smiled sweetly at the man who was shifting uncomfortably in his chair.

'If you really want to, Alex, but as I said, there's nothing really out of the ordinary in it. It would only take you a moment to have a skim through now. At least, then, it would be all out of the way.' Alex marvelled at the way Quentin had the waxy, slightly bloated look of someone whose blood pressure was far too high, but his voice didn't hint at his lack of composure.

'It's very kind of you to worry about me, Quentin, but I'm in no hurry, really.' Alex gathered up the sheaf of papers that Quentin had pushed over to her. She put the cap back on the pen he had set down alongside them, handed it back to him and said, 'I'll be in touch,' as she strode out of his office.

Quentin pulled out the handkerchief from his top pocket and dabbed his face. He realised that all was not lost, but he had to do something to try and persuade Alex to sign the contract sooner rather than later. The gossip he'd heard about Alex and Brett's affair was obviously correct – Alex was radiant. More radiant than he'd ever seen her. It wouldn't take long for the papers to get hold of the story and, once that happened, she'd have a million different people sniffing around her offering their services and that was something he wanted to avoid at all costs. He concentrated on folding up his handkerchief neatly and precisely while he decided on a strategy. Seeing as it was inevitable that some happy snapper would soon catch them together, why not engineer it himself? At least that way he would be in control of the situation. He leaned back in his chair, shut his eyes and let his mind develop the idea. Maybe, just maybe, if the woman felt really hounded she would also feel vulnerable and in this vulnerable state would seek security in the familiar practices, familiar faces; faces she could depend on. It was the perfect plan. He reached for his address book and flicked to 'F' for freelance, subsection 'P' for photographer and dialled a number. 'Hello, Rob? It's Quentin here, Quentin de Fleur. Are you working at the moment . . .?'

Getting Away with It

Steph had hurried back to Alex's after college to find out what had happened in Alex's meeting with Quentin and thought the whole misunderstanding was a hoot. 'If you got Brett on side, there could be a lot of mileage in this,' said Steph, laughing as Alex explained in greater detail what had gone on.

'I think you're right. There must be a million ways we could stitch Quentin up well and truly.' Alex was beginning to enter into the spirit of things. 'I know you're really busy at the moment, but what are you doing on Saturday?'

'We're having a run-through of the whole show in the rehearsal studio on Friday so I think Saturday's a day off. Why? What have you got in mind?'

'We're starting the Brighton scenes on Saturday and I was wondering if you might fancy a day out by the sea? You could meet Brett. He's really lovely; I'm sure you'd like him.'

'Sounds like fun! I've never been in a chauffeur-driven car before!'

'Well, I was thinking it would be even more fun if I drove. As nice as he is, I don't really want Tony to have to traipse round with us wherever we go, if you know what I mean.'

Steph knew her well enough by now to have an inkling.

Saturday was bright and sunny which also meant that the roads out of town were congested and smoggy, in spite of their early start. Armed with a stack of CDs, papers and snacks the crawl through south London wasn't so bad, but it was a relief to get out onto the quieter roads.

'I've missed you this week, Steph,' said Alex as they whistled through the countryside.

'Yeah. I had to spend some time with Bev, though. She's a great mate and I've been treating her pretty badly recently. You'll have to come round sometime and meet her again – properly this time!'

'I'd love to come over again. I have fond memories of Finsbury Park.'

Alex took Steph's hand and slipped it inside the rip of her jeans. Steph's hand felt warm against her knee.

'Like that, is it?' said Steph as she laughed at Alex who was trying hard to keep her attention on the road in front of her.

'I guess there's just something about travelling in cars that just makes me horny as hell!' Alex moved her leg so Steph could move her hand more freely.

'Oh, please!' mocked Steph. 'You'd have sex on the steps of St Paul's if you thought you could get away with it!' The car swerved slightly as Steph's hand brushed Alex's inner thigh. The women looked at each other knowing that this could all go horribly wrong but neither was prepared to stop.

'I would like to get to Brighton in one piece, Alex!'

'Why don't you leave the driving to me and undo my jeans?'

'Only if you slow down and pull over into the inside lane.' Alex took her foot off the accelerator and did as she was told. Focusing on the white lines that were keeping the car on course, Alex could feel the button of her jeans being undone and her flies being popped open. Steph wasn't surprised to see Alex's dark pubic hair pushing through the opening but was immediately turned on by the thought of Alex's naked fanny rubbing against the seam of denim that ran between her legs. The car ground to a halt and Steph looked around. They were all alone on the road at some traffic lights.

'Take your trousers off,' urged Steph, making the most of the red traffic light. Alex didn't need asking twice and when they pulled away she opened her legs to make it easier for her lover to get to her cunt. Alex's lips were swollen with desire and her juices had already started to seep onto her thighs. Steph knew that foreplay wasn't what was needed here. She parted her lips with one hand and started to massage Alex's clit while she thrust her finger deep into her hole.

Steph could hear the noise of cars rushing by in the fast lane, but continued to pump her fingers in and out of Alex's pussy. They couldn't have been going more than 30 mph but Alex was finding it hard to concentrate on her driving and was relieved to see another set of lights in the distance.

'Touch my clit, Steph!' Alex didn't think she'd be able to hold her orgasm back much longer and prayed for the lights to be red. Steph did as Alex said and started to flick, pinch and stroke Alex's hard, throbbing clit. She looked up as she felt the car slow and then stop. Alex threw her head back in pleasure as she bucked her hips off the seat so that Steph's fingers hit that place inside her cunt that produced such explosive pleasure. Letting her orgasm shudder through her body, she screamed with delight, blissfully unaware of the lorry that had pulled up next to them.

'I think we have company.' Steph smiled at the astonished dyke behind the wheel who was looking down into the car and could not believe what she was seeing. She licked Alex's juices from her fingers and winked at the woman as Alex slipped the car into gear and sped off down the road.

After showering, Alex left Steph in the hotel room examining the shower caps and flicking through the stations on the TV looking for the porn channel but with strict instructions to find somewhere fantastic for them to eat and somewhere exciting for them to go afterwards. It was a beautiful day so Steph decided to take her books and go down to the beach for a while before completing her tasks. The first one was easy anyway; she'd discovered a great fish restaurant in Hove when she and Bev had come down on the train last summer so she didn't have to worry about that. Clubs were probably two a penny, she thought, as she sank into her deck chair and went over her monologue in her mind.

★

Alex called at around 6.00 p.m. to say she'd finished shooting for the day.

'Brett said he'd like to come out to dinner with us too. Is that OK?' asked Alex, mindful of having left Steph on her own pretty much all day and not wanting to spoil any 'quiet meal for two' type plans Steph had made.

'Of course it's OK. Bev's been looking forward to me meeting him!' replied Steph. 'Can't not have a story for her when I get back, can I?'

'Shall I tell him to come to our room at nine-ish?'

'Perfect.'

Putting on a Show

Steph suddenly knew exactly what the expression 'star-struck' meant when she opened the door to their hotel room and saw Brett standing there.

'Hi. You must be Steph?'

Brett was every bit as beautiful as his nine-foot celluloid image and Steph found that she had a stupid grin spreading over her face and that she had lost the ability to speak. She nodded instead.

'I'm Brett,' he said needlessly. Still they remained in the doorway. 'Shall I come in or are you guys ready?'

'It's OK, Brett. We're ready.' Alex appeared at the door, thrust Steph's bag in her hand and they walked down the hallway. Alex pushed Steph into the backseat of the car and chatted away to Brett as they drove the short way down the coast to Hove, hoping that her lover's personality would soon re-engage. Walking, Alex had learned, would have been far too problematic. They pulled up and Alex made to get out of the car.

'Hold on a second, Alex,' said Brett as he put his hand on her arm.

'What's the matter?' Alex asked.

'See that black car over there,' said Brett, pointing down the street.

'Yeah.'

'It's been following us.'

'You what?' said Steph, suddenly coming to life as she leaned into the space between the two front seats.

'Don't panic. I think we're about to have our picture taken, that's all,' he said as if that sort of thing happened to him every day, which, of course, it probably did. 'Would you like to make any minor adjustments to make-up, clothing or hair before we get out?' he joked.

'Maybe this is an opportunity for us to really get some tongues wagging, Brett,' suggested Alex. 'What do you reckon? Fancy putting on a bit of a show?' Brett was a more than willing participant and eagerly agreed. 'You don't mind, do you, babe?' said Alex as she turned round to look at Steph. 'I'll make it up to you later, I promise.'

'Go for it. Anything to wind up that dreadful Quentin bloke. You two go into the restaurant − the table's booked in my name − and I'll follow you in in a couple of minutes. OK?'

Brett knew all the moves. He put his arm round Alex and started blowing in her ear to make her go all girlie and giggly. He was an expert in the art of pretending not to want to have his photograph taken and when the guy rolled down his window and started snapping, Brett pulled Alex closer into him and made sure he got some good shots before using the familiar 'hand in front of face' camera-parry.

Over dinner Alex and Steph regaled Brett with the whole background to Alex's relationship with Quentin and he was shocked.

'And I thought my manager was ruthless!' said Brett once they had finished.

'We were wondering whether you'd go along with our little plan to get our own back on him?' said Alex.

'Sure thing, babe. What did you have in mind?'

Alex explained to Brett that the best way to get Quentin really nervous was to carry on pretending that they were an item. Her plan was to attach more and more conditions to her contract and wait until the wrap party to let him know what she really thought of him.

'Excellent,' said Brett gleefully, rubbing his hands at the unlimited amount of Buck-a-roo this plan implied.

With 'business' out of the way, the conversation turned to lighter topics and by the time they left, it was little more than salacious gossip. Although Steph had really enjoyed her evening, she was beginning to feel a little left out with all their shop talk and jokes about people she'd never met so was quite pleased when Brett said he wouldn't be going on anywhere with them. It also meant that they could go somewhere a little more interesting than the obvious venues. A quick look out of the doorway was enough to confirm that the black car that had followed them to the restaurant had gone and Brett was safely bundled into a cab while the two women went on their way.

'Did you have a good time?' asked Alex as they strolled along the front.

'Yeah, it was great. I didn't realise that Brett was so witty,' said Steph who had been kept in stitches for most of the evening by his stories and observations.

'So where are we off to now?' asked Alex who was beginning to feel much more relaxed about life now that she had a plan of action for coping with Quentin.

'I hope you're in the mood for some serious dancing,' said Steph.

'I didn't really have dancing or anything serious in mind.'

'Well, from what I've heard there is a variety of entertainment on offer.'

'Lead the way then.'

Five's Company

Having made a couple of phone calls and made a few discreet enquiries, Steph had been given the name of a club that she thought sounded interesting. It wasn't too far away but her heart sank when they arrived at the address she'd been given. From the outside it looked far too salubrious to be much fun but it was getting late, too late to alter their plans, so they decided to go in for a drink anyway. They walked through the door and were shown down some stairs at the bottom of which was a heavy metal door. The contrast between the slightly genteel doorway they had initially walked through to the room they now arrived in was stark. The floor, walls and ceiling were covered in a reflective, chrome-like material embossed with shapes that caught the light and produced tiny holograms of colour when they picked up the flashing lights. The further they went into the space the more the light generated by the somewhat surreal surroundings was absorbed by the throng of sweaty, swaying bodies. They made their way through the crowded space and, bruiseless but breathless, they arrived at the bar and ordered two vodka Red Bulls.

Steph moved closer to Alex so that her mouth was over her ear. 'You OK with this?' she asked. Alex nodded and smiled as she moved to the music. The atmosphere was charged with chemical energy and they made their way into the mass of people and started to fall into their rhythm. Steph looked around for signs of the back room she had been told about, but couldn't even see any cruising going on let alone anything else, so she gave up looking and just started dancing and enjoying the feeling of various parts of various people's bodies brushing up against her from time to time. The fleeting contact with anonymous, naked flesh coupled with the 'I want you' look that Alex was giving her was really turning her on. Alex was kissing her hard when Steph felt a hand on her arse. Thinking at first it was Alex's, she enjoyed it but didn't think too much of it. When she felt both her lover's hands on her waist, however, she looked round and discovered that the actual owner was in fact a Chinese woman dancing next to her. She smiled at her and turned her attention back to Alex, but the woman didn't stop touching her up. The stranger started to move close in behind her so that Steph could feel her thighs on the back of her legs. She turned round to see the woman smile at her and back away in the direction of the bar. She beckoned at Steph and Alex to follow. Steph turned to Alex who had become aware of what was going on. Steph's expression asked 'what do you think' and Alex's implied 'why not'. They followed the woman past the bar and down a narrow corridor into a dark, cavernous, alcoved room. It was littered with women having sex together. Their guide ushered them into an unoccupied alcove and Steph and Alex lay back on the cushions wondering what was in store but the woman promptly disappeared.

'Maybe she didn't want to join in after all,' said Steph, as she started to undo the buttons on Alex's shirt.

'Shame,' said Alex, allowing herself to be undressed. It wasn't long, however, before the woman was back. She'd obviously been rounding up a couple of friends as it was three women who re-entered their space. They were all wearing large, black strap-ons and had clamps on their nipples that were poking out of their leather cupless bras. Alex and Steph exchanged glances. It was too late to back out now, even if they had wanted to, which they didn't. Gently the Chinese woman eased Steph away from Alex and started taking off Steph's clothes, leaving the other two to finish the job Steph had only just started. It was strangely titillating for both Alex and Steph not only to have someone else touch their bodies, but to be watching the other's reaction to it. Their admirer was stroking Steph's naked thighs, torso and arms with firm deliberate movements. Climbing in between Steph's open legs the woman started to bite on her nipples, gently at first and then hard enough to make Steph flinch.

'Just relax,' soothed the woman and once again Steph felt the stranger's mouth on her nipple, her hair on her chest and the weight of the dildo resting on her stomach. The sight of Alex's open cunt not more than a metre away simply added to Steph's desire. Her lover's labia were red and engorged and her clit was practically twitching with lust. She watched as one of the women parted Alex's legs even further and started to bite and lick her way up her inner thigh while her friend twisted Alex's nipples with her fingers. The woman's head was in the way, so Steph couldn't see it when she put her tongue in Alex's sex, but she could see what was going on by the look on Alex's face.

The stranger made her way down Steph's body, brushing it with her hair as she went, until she got to Steph's cunt. Steph could feel her hot breath on her fanny and opened her legs wider. The woman parted Steph's labia and dragged the very tip of her

174

tongue over her hole and up to her clit. Her touch was tantalising and just when Steph thought she couldn't stand any more, the woman rolled off her onto her back.

'Sit on my face,' came the order and Steph willingly complied. As Steph pumped her clit in and out of the woman's mouth she was staring at Alex. Both women were now between her legs.

The sensation of having two tongues working on her clit and cunt simultaneously was new and amazing for Alex. Her pleasure was so intense that she had to prop herself up on the cushions in order to breathe properly. She opened her eyes and saw Steph watching her. Steph eased her body away from the other woman's face so that she had to strain to reach her fanny with her tongue. The sight of the woman's tongue flicking Steph's large, hard clit had the desired effect on Alex as she felt her juices streaming out of her cunt. Alex saw Steph was about to come and released the orgasm she had been holding onto for what seemed like an eternity.

The women in between Alex's legs kissed each other voraciously while they slipped condoms onto their rubber cocks. They got up and one moved towards Alex, one towards Steph. Steph could feel the dildo pressing into her back as the women slipped into the space behind her. Without saying a word she got Steph to manoeuvre herself backwards onto her dick. Steph had seen how big the strap-on was but it was only when it was forcing its way into her cunt that its size really hit home. She felt the woman's cock stretching and stimulating the walls of her cunt as she slowly lowered herself onto it until it filled her completely. Half-kneeling over the woman's body, Steph felt her partner's dick moving slowly in and out of her. With each stroke she felt the tip connect with the place inside that was designed to make her come. The other woman was now crouching behind her and had reached round to stimulate Steph's clit while her friend continued to fuck her from below. Steph felt the woman's breasts brushing against her back and could feel another orgasm growing.

She looked across at Alex who was being fucked by the third woman on the cushions next to her.

'Harder!' was the only word Alex said to the woman she was

having sex with and her request was immediately complied with. Alex felt the woman's finger nudging her arsehole and groaned with pleasure. The woman reacted to Alex's feedback by gently probing a little deeper and Alex moaned again.

'Do you like that?' asked the woman. Alex nodded. Without missing a stroke the woman produced a butt-plug from nowhere. Steph's orgasmic cries made Alex look up just as the lubed, condom-coated toy penetrated her arse. The feeling was excruciatingly pleasurable and Alex came as noisily and violently as Steph.

FIFTEEN
Friendly Advice

The napkin bearing Brett's signature that Steph presented to Bev when she got home went down a storm. She bombarded Steph with a million questions but was stopped in her tracks when Steph uttered those immortal words, 'Brett touched my hand.' Steph thought it was all getting far too bizarre when Bev started going down the sexual 'six degrees of separation' route.

'So if Brett's snogged Alex and Alex has snogged you, then –' said an overexcited Bev.

'Don't you even think about it!' Steph laughed as she pushed her advancing friend away. Finally Bev calmed herself and they settled down for the night in they had planned. They swapped thoughts about the fast-approaching graduation show and shared just how nervous the whole thing made them.

'Do you realise that our show is a week today?' said Bev, just in case Steph wasn't scared enough.

'At least that means that this time next week, it'll all be over!' Steph replied, trying to look for the positives.

'Have you got anyone coming, Bev?'

'Yeah. A couple of agents have said they'll try to come and a casting director or two.' Her voice was flat with the horror of it all.

'Do you reckon Alex'll be able to come?'

'Hope so. It depends on her schedule though.'

'So how's it all going with her?' asked Bev as she topped up Steph's wine glass.

'It's fantastic, Bev. Really, I've never felt like this before about anyone.'

'Well, you certainly look better than you have for a long time. I was seriously worried about you for a while.' Bev's concern was genuine and she was pleased that Steph was getting her life back together so quickly. 'So much change in so little time,' mused Bev.

'I guess it has been a bit of a whirlwind, hasn't it?' agreed Steph.

'So what is Alex like, then? What do you two do together?' probed Bev, eager to find out what it was that had nearly sent her friend over the edge.

Steph thought about the question and wracked her brain for an example of something she'd done with Alex that hadn't been geared towards or involved having sex.

'Come on, Steph, out with it,' encouraged Bev.

'Well, we have sex quite a lot . . .' she confessed.

'Understandable. But what else? What films does she like? What's her background? Where have you been in town – galleries, walks? You know, normal stuff.'

Steph hung her head and bit her bottom lip as she struggled to provide Bev with answers to her questions. She suddenly felt very ashamed that she didn't even know if Alex had any brothers or sisters and they hadn't even talked about going to the movies together, let alone set foot in a gallery.

'You mean to say that after all the time you've spent with this woman, all you've done is fool around?' gasped Bev. Steph shook her head in disbelief. She had to laugh and admit that that would be about the bottom line.

'Maybe it's time to develop a different side of your relationship, hen.' Bev laughed.

'I know you're right, Bev. But what if we find out that we don't have anything in common? That would be awful.' Steph was panicking.

'Well, if you find you've got nothing to talk about, you could

always just go back to what you do best. You see, problem solved.'
Bev was finding Steph's predicament terribly amusing.

'I can recognise jealous laughter when I hear it!' teased Steph as
she chucked a cushion childishly at her friend.

'When are you seeing her next?' asked Bev.

'Tomorrow night,' replied Steph.

'Well, there's your opportunity, then. Present her with an
agenda for a day out and see what she says.' Steph thought about
what Bev was saying.

'Yeah. You're right. I'll pick up a *Time Out*, see what's on and
suggest something.'

'You're pretty serious about her, aren't you, Steph?'

'I am . . . I think I . . . you know, I really believe I'm . . .'
stammered Steph.

'Shite, babe, you're not going to say the "L" word, are you?'
Bev chortled.

'Oh, fuck off!' said Steph coyly.

Had It Been Nine and a Half Weeks?

The candles had burned down and fizzled out so the light coming
from the open fridge door was the only thing that lit up the room.
Steph could feel a pleasant breeze waft through the open window
of Alex's kitchen every so often but it was still a hot, sultry night.
The perspiration on Steph's body was making the tight, white vest
that Alex had lent her cling to her torso even more tightly. She
shifted slightly to make use of the cooler air that was coming from
the fridge and waited. Steph thought about how the soft piece of
fabric that Alex had used to blindfold her was pressing into her
temples and, surprisingly, making her feel very relaxed. Was it that
or the fact that they'd been smoking? One of the two. She leaned
back against the cupboard and planted her feet on the lino in front
of her to stop herself from sliding down. Thinking back over the
evening, she realised that she had never gone round to someone's
house before and eaten a meal they had prepared for her in her
pants and vest. It made her giggle. She heard Alex's footsteps on

the wooden floor in the hallway and then on the lino in the kitchen.

'Thought you'd abandoned me!' said Steph.

'Now why would I do that?' Alex sat down on the floor in front of Steph and reached into the fridge that she had stocked up specially for the occasion. She picked up a bright, ripe strawberry and dipped it in an open tub of crème fraiche. She put the cream-covered strawberry to Steph's lips and watched her lover slowly start to lick the fruit and bite into its flesh. Alex held the fruit in place and watched Steph's tongue wind round it, greedily and sensuously lapping up its flavour. Alex took what remained of the strawberry away from Steph and, putting it in her own mouth, leaned in to share it with her before kissing her lover's open, receptive mouth and licking the creamy substance from around her lips. Steph moaned with delight as their tongues touched. Steph pulled away.

'I have to take this vest off, Alex,' she said softly, not wanting to spoil the mood.

'It's OK; let me do it,' was her lover's reply.

Steph heard the sound of a drawer above her being opened and the metallic clashing of cutlery and utensils being moved around.

'What are you looking for?' asked Steph, who was feeling frustrated by her blindfold but didn't want to remove it.

'Don't worry, Steph, just lean back.' Steph did as she was told and felt Alex lift the bottom of the vest away from her body and then sensed something hard and cold on her skin. She recoiled in surprise.

'Jesus, what are you doing?' she gasped. Then she heard the sound of scissors cutting fabric and felt the garment she was wearing slowly peel away from her body. The pointed tips of the blades nudged her skin as Alex cut her way up the centre of the top with slow, steady movements. Steph held her breath as she felt the sharp, metal object slide in between her breasts. Alex put her hand under Steph's top and, lifting the ripped fabric, caressed her lover's breast as she carried on cutting the material. Steph's body was tense with anticipation but she tried hard to regulate her breathing so that she didn't make any sudden movements. She heard the snap of the final thread being cut and the parted fabric flying open and almost immediately the feeling of Alex's tongue on her nipple. She sighed with relief at having got through the procedure unscarred and slid down the cupboard she had been leaning against so that she lay, panting, on the floor.

Alex produced a bottle of chocolate sauce from the fridge and poured a trail of the goo over Steph's breasts and down towards her belly button. Sitting astride her lover, Alex proceeded to massage the sticky sauce into Steph's skin with her hands, while she sucked and licked at Steph's chocolate-coated breasts with her mouth. Alex felt her partner bend her knees and push her pelvis up into her crotch. Sitting up Alex pulled off her T-shirt and, filling Steph's hands with thick cream, guided them up to her own breasts. Steph's hands slid all over Alex's body as the cream ran down her torso in glutinous rivulets. She sat up and her mouth found one of Alex's nipples. She sucked it hard and flicked it with her tongue until she heard Alex sighing with pleasure. Steph felt Alex's body twist round to reach for something else from the fridge. She heard the sound of a carbonated drink being opened and shivered as a flow of ice-cold, fizzy water cascaded over her head and body. The tingle of the bubbles and water made her laugh and, drained of her strength, she fell back onto the floor. Alex brushed her soaking hair from her face and kissed her deeply and slowly before climbing off her prone body. Steph was disorientated for a moment as she lost contact with her lover until she felt Alex pulling at her knickers and slip the scissors either side of the fabric. She flattened her stomach and snapped her legs shut anxiously.

'Be careful, Alex!' urged Steph.

'Trust me,' responded Alex. It only took one snip for the crotch of Steph's knickers to come apart and roll up over her abdomen. Once more, Steph could breathe again.

Alex parted Steph's legs and put her wet, sticky fingers into Steph's wet, sticky sex. She felt the muscles of Steph's fanny contract around her fingers and slowly twisted them around inside her lover, a move which elicited more moans of pleasure.

'Don't stop, Alex,' protested Steph as she felt Alex move away once again. There were more sounds of containers being opened and, not wanting to have to wait to find out what was coming next, Steph lifted her hand to remove the blindfold. Alex gently caught her hand and put it back down by her side. Alex quickly opened the tub of ice-cream and the next thing Steph felt in her fanny was extreme cold. It took her breath away and sent shivers shooting up her spine. The warmth of Alex's tongue mixed with the slick coldness of the ice-cream was tortuous and Steph moved her hips in time with Alex who was using her tongue to swirl the grainy chunks in the ice-cream around Steph's pussy. She dug more ice-cream out of the tub with her fingers and spread it over Steph's clit before plunging her cold fingers into her lover's sex once more. Alex could feel the muscles in Steph's cunt drawing her fingers further inside. She thrust harder and deeper with her hand while she smeared the ice-cream around her clit with her tongue. The blend of textures and temperatures was unbearable and Steph abandoned herself to the feelings that were growing in her body and climaxed in an explosion of sensations that consumed her entire body. Steph ripped off her blindfold and stared into her lover's smiling face. Alex took Steph in her arms. 'I love you, Alex,' were the words that slipped quietly out of Steph's mouth. She cringed the moment she realised what she had said. Alex didn't say a word and Steph thought she'd got away with it.

As Steph lay next to Alex in bed later that night, she was thinking about her conversation with Bev. When she had turned up at Alex's for dinner, she hadn't planned for the evening to unfold quite as it had. Not that she was complaining at all, but she was determined that the next day they would go out and do things that other normal couples did. She had to find out whether there was anything more to their liaison than their frequent desire to rip each other's clothes off. Quite literally, in retrospect.

The Real World

'You know, Alex, I've been thinking . . .' said Steph the following morning as she blew on the steaming mug of Earl Grey Alex had passed her.

'Yes?' Alex got back into bed and started to flick through the paper.

'Does it ever bother you that we don't really do much together?' Steph's question was nearly swallowed up by her mug but Alex heard what she said.

'What do you mean?' she replied, turning on her side so she could see Steph better.

'Well, you know. Haven't you noticed that all we ever seem to do is make love, which is great,' Steph added hastily, 'but sometimes I just feel that I don't really know you very well.'

Alex tossed Steph's remarks around in her mind. 'Well, my favourite colour is purple; I was born in Cheltenham; I got BAGA awards 1–4 at school –'

'I don't mean you have to blurt your life history out in list form!'

'Yeah. I know. I suppose I can see what you're getting at. I'm sorry if I haven't treated you better but, you know, it's been a long time for me!' said Alex, laughing.

'I guess it has,' realised Steph. 'It's just that . . .'

'What is it, hon?' Alex squeezed Steph's arm, concerned by her sudden change in mood.

'Well. You're not only interested in me because of *that*, are you?' For someone who could be so forthright at times, Steph was feeling very awkward with the subject matter.

'You think I see you as my own personal sex slave, is that it?' Alex said through her laughter.

'Kind of. Not that that would be an altogether undesirable role, but I just want to know where I stand with you. You know, what your expectations are?'

'Oh blimey. "Expectations"!' said Alex, trying hard not to be amused by Steph's ultra-seriousness. 'I tell you what, why don't we spend some "quality time" together today? What do you fancy doing?'

'There are a few exhibitions on that look really interesting,' said Steph, pleased at the way Alex was taking on board what she'd said. 'Or we could go out to the East End, have lunch in Hoxton, a couple of beers, take in a film – whatever. The world's our lobster really!' Steph picked up the paper that was lying on the bed between them. 'Does it have listings in here?' she asked.

'TV and tits – that's about it,' said Alex. Steph opened the paper and her screech nearly gave Alex a heart attack.

'Look, Alex! Look, it's you and Brett!' screamed Steph. Alex grabbed the paper away from Steph and poured over the picture.

'Jesus! That is just too fucking weird!'

'What have they written?' said Steph, trying to pull the paper back. Alex skimmed what in some circles passed as an 'article'.

'It's exactly what we wanted. "Young lovers, Brett Torento and Alex Dechy, blah, blah, blah, enjoying a romantic dinner whilst on location shooting Torento's latest film . . . A close friend of the couple say they are very much in love . . . yardy, yardy, yah!" That's amazing!' Alex was totally thrown by the experience.

'Is it the Brighton photo?' asked Steph, managing to get the paper back.

'No. We went for a bit of a walkabout in town earlier this week. I didn't notice anyone around though,' pondered Alex. 'You know, that's a bit creepy. It's one thing when you know what's going on, but something else when you didn't even know there was anyone there.'

'Still want to go out today?'

'I'm not that spooked. They're not interested in me anyway: it's Brett who makes the story. Come on, honey, let's go and have a shower.' They made their way into the chocolate-stained, cream-covered bathroom.

In the end they decided to walk along the canal to Camden. The weather still hadn't broken and, walking along the tree-lined banks, they could have been way out in the countryside. Given that their brief was to 'get to know one another better' the atmosphere was slightly strained between them at first.

Alex was wracking her brain to think of something to say as they strolled past the zoo.

'Ever been in there?' she asked.

'Yeah. Would you believe our voice teacher sent us all down here once to do some research.' Steph's memory of the project was still vivid.

'Don't tell me, you had to do the "let's pretend we're animals" thing too!'

'I spent the next month being a giraffe in class.'

'But giraffes don't make any noise, do they?'

'Not really; but my giraffe-walk was a real talking point.'

'I can imagine.'

Steph quizzed Alex about her life before drama school. She found out that Alex had moved to London when she was 17 years old and spent a year working in bars, auditioning for drama schools and getting involved with what she loosely referred to as 'avant-garde' fringe theatre which conjured up images of lots of nudity and dancing with chiffon scarves in Steph's mind.

'So what about you? Have you always wanted to act?' asked Alex.

'Not really. Not in the way that people say they've had a burning ambition to tread the boards since they were two years old. It kind of crept up on me really. I did my A Levels – one of them was in drama. My teacher said I was good and encouraged me to apply for places. When I came to London to visit a friend at university, I knew I wanted to live here and so when I got the offer, it all just sort of fell into place,' she explained.

'What are your plans for after you graduate?' Alex guided Steph over to a bench and they sat down to soak up the sun.

'I haven't got a clue really. I've been a bit preoccupied with the show – and you – to think too deeply about that. Not that I needed much of an excuse to avoid the issue!' The thought of leaving college and walking out into a big hole of nothingness did give Steph the willies for sure. 'When do you go to the States?' asked Steph. That too was an issue that had been avoided.

'Soon after I finish shooting my scenes here, so about ten days' time.' It was a statement that hung heavily in the air.

'How long is it you're going for again?' ventured Steph.

'About three months in all.'

'Oh,' said Steph as she felt her heart sink to the bottom of the canal.

'Come on, there's lots of stuff to do before then!' Alex jumped off the bench and, taking Steph's hand, hauled her up too.

Laying Foundations

Quentin had popped into the office that weekend to pick up some papers he'd forgotten and couldn't resist having a quick flick through the newspapers that lay on the mat. He grinned smugly as he saw the latest picture of Alex and Brett in one of them. Although Alex hadn't quite come running to him for protection from the invasive press coverage her relationship with Brett was getting, Quentin was more than pleased by the amount of interest her high-profile was generating. He had taken the liberty of entering into negotiations with one company who wanted to use Alex in an advertising campaign to sell their cosmetics. From the approximate financial package he had got them to put forward, he knew he was sitting on a goldmine.

As he put the paper down on his desk, he saw the light on the answer machine blinking so pushed the play button to see who had called. The machine, which was as antiquated as the man, whirred and then clunked into action.

'Hello, Quentin, it's Alex here, Alex Dechy.' Quentin stopped what he was doing in surprise. He hadn't heard from Alex for a couple of days and had been getting a little anxious about the still unsigned contract. He licked his lips in anticipation. 'I was just calling to run a couple of amendments to the contract by you,' wafted Alex's voice out of the machine. 'It's just that I've been talking to a couple of people and have come to the conclusion that maybe your percentages aren't terribly competitive. Anyway, I won't go into details here, but maybe we could talk on Monday? Hope you're well. Speak to you soon. Bye.'

Not the response Quentin was hoping for. He played the message again. What did she mean when she said she'd been 'talking to a couple of people'? She didn't sound in the least bit intimidated by the exposure she was getting. He realised that the impressionable young woman he had signed up all those years ago had suddenly become more savvy. His old shock tactics weren't going to do the trick this time. He was reluctant to cave in to her demands, but if it meant that she stayed with him he would have to take it in the wallet. That said, he didn't have much more time to get her to sign on the dotted line and was going to have to speed up negotiations.

'Come on, let's do it again,' said Alex as she got up off the living-room floor.

'You want your pound of flesh, don't you!' sighed Steph in a heap at her feet.

'Wrong play, sweetheart!' replied Alex. 'Come on, we'll take it from Orlando's entrance . . .'

'But –'

'You were the one who wanted to come home and work, Steph. I was quite happy strolling around Camden, but, oh no, Little Miss I've-Got-A-Show-To-Put-On had to come home, didn't she?'

'Ms, please, Alex, Little Ms!' quipped Steph, weak from the effort of it all.

'I seem to remember last time we worked on *As You Like It*, you were rather keener to rehearse with me,' coaxed Alex as she dug Steph's limp body in the ribs with her toe.

'If my memory serves me correctly, I don't think we actually got round to working on the play . . .' Steph reached up for Alex's hand and drew her down onto the floor with her. '. . . Unless you count the wrestling scene.'

The kiss that Steph planted on Alex's lips tasted of beer and a day in the sun. 'You've changed my life completely, Alex.'

'Is that a good thing?'

'I've never felt so happy,' answered Steph.

'Me neither,' whispered Alex. Steph watched Alex peel off her top and undo her trousers.

'I thought we were going to try not to do this,' said Steph.

'I have tried.' Looking at her beautiful, naked lover, Steph couldn't believe there would ever be a time when she didn't want to make love to Alex. Steph followed Alex's lead and discarded her clothes. The feeling of Alex's naked body on top of her made her heart pound even harder. Slowly they explored each other's bodies with their hands and mouths. Having left no expanse of flesh uncaressed, Alex gently eased Steph's legs wider apart to expose her lover's fanny which was wet and aroused. She licked her finger and rubbed it over Steph's clit in slow, deliberate movements. It was erect and hard. Alex lowered herself onto Steph's open cunt so that their clits were rubbing together. Alex saw tears start to well up in Steph's eyes as she came.

'I love you too,' confided Alex softly.

'Maybe this no-sex thing isn't such a good idea after all,' Steph said when they were in bed later that evening. 'What am I going to do for three whole months when you're away?'

'You? What about me?'

'Do you know what I think?' Even in the moonlight Alex could see the familiar sparkle light up Steph's eyes as she said the words and knew exactly what she was thinking. 'I think it's my responsibility to give you one last goodbye challenge. Something that will make you remember me throughout all those lonely days and nights when you're holed up in your trailer with only Brett and Kerplunk for company.'

'Oh Jesus, what is going on in that depraved little mind of yours?' demanded Alex.

'And I think I know just the occasion.'

'No, Steph, please. Not the wrap party. Please say you're not going to do something at the party!'

'You always have the power to say no.'

'That's not fair. You know I can't resist you.'

'Well, by my reckoning you have about six days to learn how!'

SIXTEEN
The Graduate

Judgement Day had, at last, arrived but Steph wasn't handling the thought of being evaluated too well.

'I don't think I can go through with it, Alex,' said Steph as she stared into the bowl of cereal in front of her.

'Don't be ridiculous. Once you're out there, you'll just focus on what you're doing. You'll be so into it that you won't even be aware there's anyone watching you. You are going to be absolutely wonderful.'

'What time are you getting there?'

'I'll be on time, don't worry.'

'And you'll come and meet me at the stage door straight afterwards?'

'Of course.'

'Jeez,' said Steph as she put her hand on her heart. 'Feel that? You haven't got any Valium, have you?'

'Steph, stop being such a frigging drama queen and pull yourself together!' Alex was trying to lighten the situation. 'You know your stuff, you're good; and everything will be fine. Just hold those thoughts.'

'I'd better go if I'm going to meet Bev and the others,' croaked Steph. She got her stuff together and went to the door.

'Hold on a sec!' called out Alex from the other room. 'I wanted to give you this.' She put a small purple crystal in Steph's hand. 'It's meant to help calm you down, but it's kind of my good luck thing. I wanted you to have some too.'

'Alex, that's so lovely of you. Thanks.'

Alex kissed her on the lips and bundled her out of the door.

Alex had managed to avoid Quentin's calls and messages and was revelling in the fact that his voice was sounding ever so slightly more hysterical with every day that passed. Although nothing had ever been said, on set people were now treating her and Brett as if they were love's young dream and she thought what a callous bastard Quentin was. She wondered what they would think when they realised that the nearest they had come to a bona fide clinch was during their first game of Twister when they discovered it really needed to be played with more than two people to totally rule out the possibility of breaking limbs.

Rachel stepped into Quentin's office to announce that his cab had arrived just as the phone rang.

'Pick it up then, woman!' he barked at his assistant.

Rachel leaned over his desk. 'Good morning, Mr de Fleur's office. I'm afraid Mr de Fleur is just on his way out of the office at the moment, Ms Andretto . . . calling from? . . . cosmetics . . . Alexandra Dec–' The moment Quentin heard the word 'cosmetics' he realised who she was talking to. He flung himself across the room and wrenched the phone out of Rachel's hand.

'Antonia!' he bellowed. 'How ni– . . . Francesca, of course! How could I have forgotten?' He rolled his eyes and slapped his greasy forehead for having been so stupid as to have forgotten his meal-ticket's name.

'I know you're very anxious to meet her. She's looking forward very much to discussing the campaign with you too, but, you know, she is so terribly busy at the moment. You see, they're just putting the finishing touches to the scenes they're shooting in Britain, so the schedule is changing from moment to moment . . . To be honest we have been inundated with various offers such as your own, but I feel that a quality line like your own would be perfect for Alexandra . . . As I said, some offers have been higher but it's really up to Alexandra to decide . . . No, there's no problem at all! You will be able to meet with Alexandra within the next few days; you have my word on that, Francesca.' Quentin was practically puce by the time he came off the phone.

'Are you all right, Mr de Fleur?' asked a concerned Rachel. 'Can I get you a glass of water?'

'That bloody girl!'

'Who?'

'Alexandra!'

'But I thought what with this cosmetics campaign thing every-thing was looking really good for her.' Rachel was now slightly confused.

'Yes, but she hasn't signed her new contract with me yet, has she, you fool!' screamed Quentin. 'Without the contract I can't get her to sign the deal and if there's no deal there's NO BLOODY MONEY! Capiche?' Rachel certainly did and scurried out of the office as fast as she could.

Alex wished Quentin wasn't coming to Steph's graduation show because she didn't know if she would be able to stop herself telling him to shove his stupid contract up his arse there and then. She had gone through it with Brett and Steph, however, and they both agreed that Quentin would feel altogether more humiliated if she told him at the end of shoot party rather than in front of a bunch of desperate drama students. The prospect of finally being set free from the tyrannic hold she had allowed Quentin to have over her filled her with nervous anticipation and delight but it was the thought of the kind of plan Steph was concocting that really made her head spin. She couldn't deny that Steph really had her over a barrel. Their whole affair had been feeding a desire she had somehow managed to suppress for years. What Steph had put her through in the restaurant had been bad enough, or good enough, depending on which way you looked at it, but at the party? She told herself it would be an outrageous and absurd thing to do. The tingling in her crotch, however, told a different story.

★

Alex met Marsha on the steps of the theatre and she was pleased to see a friendly face in amongst the rather motley collection of people that these kind of events attracted.

'Alex, darling, you're looking well!' Marsha kissed Alex on both cheeks and held her at arm's length to inspect her in more detail. 'I'm glad to see my soon-to-be client so happy!'

'Things are good at the moment, Marsha. And I can't wait to get shot of Quentin, if you know what I mean?'

'Not long to go now, my dear.' They were handed a pro-gramme as they made their way to their seats in the stalls. 'How's Stephanie?'

'Nervous,' replied Alex. 'How was she doing in rehearsals?'

'I think you'll be suitably impressed.' They sat down and the lights dimmed. They were about halfway through the third scene when Alex became aware of some movement at the back of the auditorium. She turned round and saw a figure squinting into the darkness. She realised it was Quentin and sank down in her seat. It was too late, however; she'd been spotted and Quentin began to creep from seat to seat in her direction leaving a chorus of 'shhs' in his wake. When he eventually squeezed himself into the seat behind Alex, she felt the hackles rise on the back of her neck. She felt his hands grab hold of the back of her seat as he pulled himself forward to speak to her.

'Alex, so pleased I bumped into you,' he wheezed.

'Quentin, I'm here to watch the show, so just shut up and we'll talk afterwards, OK,' she hissed and turned her back to punctuate the end of her sentence. She felt him fidgeting behind her all the way through the performance.

The performance went off without too many glitches and, as Marsha has predicted, Alex had been impressed and proud of Steph. There was no way she was going to avoid having to speak to Quentin, so she decided to get it over with while Marsha went and lined them up a couple of drinks from the bar.

'I take it you want to talk to me about our contract, Quentin, don't you?' opened Alex.

'And to say hello. We haven't spoken in a while and I thought maybe I could take you out to dinner and we could discuss future plans . . .'

'Look, I'm really sorry, Quentin, but I've left the contract at home and I can't make dinner tonight.'

'You did get the amended contract through the post, though, didn't you? The one with the adjusted percentages and other provisos you mentioned?'

'Yes. I tell you what, why don't you come along to the party the production company are holding on Friday and I'll hand it over to you then?'

'So you're totally happy with it now?'

'As happy as I'll ever be.'

'So it'll be a sort of celebration, you mean?' Quentin wanted some sort of confirmation that the outcome would be positive for him.

'Celebration is exactly the word I'd use.'

'Fabulous!'

'I have friends to meet now, Quentin, so I'll see you on Friday, yes?'

'See you there.' Quentin did a funny little punching the air thing with his fist and Alex laughed politely before making her way backstage.

As she waited for the stage-door keeper to let her through, all Alex could hear were the sounds of excited voices and the popping of champagne corks. Steph had gone with Tina and the others to Bev's dressing room to celebrate.

'I can't believe that it's all over,' said Sarah, as she grabbed a bottle from a bucket of ice and peeled off the foil.

'Did you hear Jason forget his words in the *Chess* medley? I thought I was going to pee my pants!' Kylie laughed.

'Twist the bottle and hold the cork, Sarah,' instructed Bev as she lined up the plastic flutes on the side.

'Well, I was still on the loo when beginners was announced!' screeched Steph.

'To never having to wear black lycra tights ever again!' It was Bev who proposed the toast and they all clashed flutes. There was a knock on the door and Alex poked her head round. Steph saw her and went over.

'Thought I heard a familiar voice,' she said. The chat died down as everyone turned round to see who the interloper was.

'Everyone, this is my friend Alex.' The women all said hello and waited for Alex to say or do something.

'You were all fabulous!' she commented finally. 'Look, Steph, I won't spoil the party. I'll go and wait for you out front with Marsha, OK?'

'Hold on.' Steph slipped out of the room and shut the door behind them.

'How does she know her? From acting class?' Sarah was stunned by Alex's appearance in their dressing room.

'They're . . . you know . . .' Tina flapped her elbow around and did an exaggerated wink to illustrate her unfinished sentence. 'Didn't you know?'

'Know what?' Sarah could never bear to be left out of any gossip.

'She's her girlfriend, you flamin' galah!' chirped up Kylie, in her best 'Kylie' voice.

'Well, bugger me!' was all Sarah could find to say.

Steph took Alex's hand and led her through the corridor to the room she was sharing with Kylie. 'So what did you think?'

'You were totally fantastic!' said Alex.

'You really thought so?'

'Really.' Alex kissed Steph and put her arms around her. 'Look, you'd better get back to your friends. You don't want to miss out on all the fun, do you?'

'Just show me once more how good you thought I was . . .' said Steph as she pulled Alex back into an embrace.

SEVENTEEN
Old Faces

Marsha was standing underneath the 'no smoking' sign, puffing on a cheroot and surveying the scene front of house. There were lots of faces she knew and even some she deigned to wave at. One face that she knew but couldn't quite place was making straight for her, however. Mid thirties, blonde, nice tits, no bra . . . Marsha scoured her memory and finally came up with 'Rebecca', private singing lessons circa 1999, as the woman arrived in front of her.

'It is Marsha, isn't it?' enquired the blonde.

'It is indeed. And you are Rebecca, if I'm not mistaken?'

'Rachel, actually, but it's close enough!'

'I do apologise.'

'That's OK. Look, I'm sorry to butt in, Marsha, but you know Quentin de Fleur, don't you?'

'You could say that.'

'You haven't seen him, have you?'

'What on earth are you doing looking for him?'

'I'm working as his assistant these days.'

'Oh. The musical didn't work out then?'

''Fraid not, no. It was a big disappointment to everyone.'

'And you were so perfect for that role.'

Rachel's eyes were flicking around the room in search of her prey. 'Ummm. You should have seen him, Marsha; he left the office in such a foul mood that he forgot to take his tablets with him. He looked like he was going to have a seizure or something and I don't want him keeling over after all the pressure he's been under recently.'

'Pressure?'

'Yes. It's all happening at our office at the moment,' said Rachel, momentarily forgetting her potentially dying boss. 'He represents Alexandra Dechy – you know, the one who is going out with Brett Thingy?'

'I had heard something about that, yes.'

'Well, he's got some sort of mega deal lined up for her – to be the face of some cosmetics company or other – and it's likely to rake in a fortune, but Alexandra is dragging her feet over renewing her contract. He's absolutely paranoid that she's going to go and find someone else to look after her and came down here to get her to sign on the dotted line. It's driving him up the wall, Marsha, I swear!'

'I can imagine.'

'So have you seen him?'

'I caught a glimpse of him at the end of the performance. As far as I could make out he was still standing then, but I haven't seen him since.'

'Lordy! Maybe I'd better go and check the Gents. Nice seeing you again, Marsha.'

'You too, Rachel.'

Soon after Rachel's whirlwind visit, Marsha spied 'her girls', as she had grown to think of them, coming in the room. She went over to Bev, Tina, Sarah, Kylie and Steph and congratulated them heartily on their achievements.

'It looks like you've already been at the champagne, but maybe I could tempt you all with another glass of the devil's work?' she asked. Alex, who had slunk into the room a minute or two after the others, now moved up to the bar to join Marsha.

'Have I got some news for you, young lady,' said Marsha out of the corner of her mouth.

'Sounds fascinating,' said Alex, amused at her friend's attempts at being surreptitious.

'Oh, believe me it is.' Marsha turned to pass Alex the bottle the bartender had given her. 'By the way, darling, your chemise is on inside out.' It took Alex a couple of seconds to realise that Marsha was referring to her top, which was, indeed, on inside out. Alex left the room in the same manner she had arrived and headed for the loos.

When Alex rejoined the group, she tapped Marsha on the shoulder. 'Are you going to tell me what this amazing news is then?'

'Oh my dear, of course. Let's find somewhere quieter where we can talk. Follow me.'

Steph, who was standing in the group Marsha had been entertaining with her 'when I was an actress' stories, caught Alex's eye as she left the room with Marsha.

'What's up?' she mouthed at her. Alex shrugged and disappeared out of the door. Steph was lost in thought when she realised someone was calling her name.

'Steph, hi. Steph? It's me, Angie. How are you?'

'Angie! What are you doing here?'

'Maggie and I came along to see Bev . . . and you,' she said shyly.

'It's so nice to see you.' They stood there slightly awkwardly not really knowing what to say to each other. 'So, did you enjoy the show?' said Steph eventually.

'Yes. It was great.'

'Would you like a drink?'

'No, I've just got one in.'

'OK.' Another awkward pause.

'I heard from Bev that you finally got it together with that woman you were involved with.'

'Yes.' Steph felt the ice break and the tension go out of her shoulders.

'That's fantastic!'

'Yes. I'm really happy.'

'Is she here?'

'She's around somewhere. How about you? Anyone on the scene?'

'I have met someone but, hey, you know me. I like to keep my options open!'

'I seem to remember that, yes . . .'

Rachel's Big Mouth

Marsha had dragged Alex off to one of the boxes in the Upper Circle.

'What's with all the cloak and dagger stuff, Marsha?' said Alex as they finally sat down in the worn red velvet seats.

'I have just been talking to a young woman called Rachel,' said Marsha.

'Rachel . . .?' repeated Alex, trying to place the name.

'Rachel from Quentin's office.'

'Oh . . .' Once again Alex felt her blood run cold at the sound of that woman's name and wondered what on earth Marsha was going to come out with next.

'She has told me something very interesting. Very interesting indeed.' Alex was still slightly worried as to the nature of Marsha's new-found knowledge.

'Marsha, please, get to the point!'

Marsha duly repeated what Rachel had said to her about the deal with the cosmetics company Quentin was orchestrating. 'I take it you had no idea about this.'

'No. No! So let me get this straight,' said Alex who was a little bemused by the information she had been given. 'Quentin has as good as signed me up for some advertising campaign and is waiting until I renew my contract with him until he tells me about it?'

'I think that is an accurate appraisal of the situation,' confirmed Marsha. 'You hadn't said anything about it so I didn't think you knew.'

'Good God! I didn't think that man could get any lower!'

'So what are you going to do about it?'

'I don't know.' Alex thought for a moment or two. 'I really don't know. Is Rachel still around?'

'I haven't a clue.'

'Do you reckon you could find her and wheedle some more information out of her?'

'For you, my dear, I'll try my best.'

Alex was still feeling a little shell-shocked when she walked back into the bar with Marsha. She looked round for Steph when she bumped into a pie-eyed Bev weaving her way towards the loo.

'Have you seen Steph, Bev?' asked Alex.

'Yes. She's over there talking to you!' Bev blinked hard, laughed and staggered off.

An even more confused Alex looked in the direction Bev was pointing and peered at the woman Steph was talking to. The resemblance, from the back at least, was uncanny. She walked over and stood at Steph's side, surprised by the feelings of jealousy that she was experiencing. Her lover looked round, put her arm around her waist and drew her into the space next to her. 'Angie, I'd like you to meet Alex. The woman I was telling you about earlier.' Angie and Alex looked at each other quizzically.

'You're the woman from the paper, aren't you?' Angie declared after a moment's reflection. She looked from Steph to Alex and shook her head as the pennies started to drop like tokens from a pokie.

'And you are?' asked Alex.

'It's a long story,' said Steph.

There was one of two places that Rachel might be if she were still in the building, so Marsha headed for the Gents as her first port of call. It wasn't a place Marsha was used to frequenting but she adapted to the conditions admirably by using her velvet scarf to cover her mouth and nose to mask the smell of piss that wafted out with every swing of the door. Once she was happy that neither Quentin nor Rachel were holed up inside, she headed for the lounge bar where many of the 'guests' of the college were being entertained with a buffet and piped music. Marsha knew that Rachel wouldn't be able to resist doing a little schmoozing while she was out of the office and Quentin's sight and, sure enough, there she was wiping bits of vol-au-vent off the jacket of an up-and-coming musical theatre director.

'. . . and you would have been so perfect for that part,' said the man with his eyes firmly planted on Rachel's unfettered breasts.

'My dear, I need a word,' declared Marsha as she swooped into their conversation and scooped Rachel up.

'But I'm –' Rachel was powerless to resist.

'I have been so anxious about Quentin that I just had to make sure that the afternoon had passed by without calamity.'

'That's so sweet of you, Marsha,' said Rachel kindly. 'Actually, I found him soon after I spoke to you. Between you and me, he was a bit agitated but I think he's going to be all right. He made a few calls and has gone back to the office now. I'm so pleased! He looks so relieved.'

'So his client signed the papers then?'

'Well, no, not exactly but she invited him to a party at the end of the week. I think it's to celebrate the end of the shoot over here or something, and she's going to give him the contract then. Isn't that a nice idea?'

'Oh, yes. Very thoughtful.'

'It's like a celebration. Well, a double celebration really, because he's going to bring the people along from the cosmetics company as well so they can meet Alex and he can close two deals at the same time! You know, Marsha, I was really worried about my job for a while. Things have been a bit tight for Mr de Fleur and my job was going to be the first to go, so it was touch and go there for a while.'

Marsha's expression showed that she needed more explanation.

'If Alex had found someone else to look after her he was just going to say to the company that she wasn't interested and no one would have been any the wiser. So as far as I was concerned it was no deal, no job! But, don't worry, Marsha, we're going to be fine. Mr de Fleur's going to be fine.'

'Well, that is good news.'

'I'll tell him you were asking after him –'

'No. I wouldn't if I were you. I'm sure he wouldn't like to think that we'd been talking about him like this. Besides, I'm sure he wouldn't remember me anyway.'

'Oh yes. I see where you're coming from. "Mum's" the word,

then!' Rachel had half her attention on the young man she'd been talking to who was now being preyed upon by some other young musical theatre hopeful and started edging back towards him.

'Good luck then, Rachel. Don't forget to give me a ring if you'd like some more singing lessons.' Rachel blew a kiss in Marsha's direction and had expertly nudged her rival out of the frame by the time Marsha had left the room.

We Meet Again

The champagne had done a lot to loosen tongues and Alex soon found out that the long story Steph had advertised as describing her relationship with Angie wasn't such an epic after all. In fact she felt strangely touched that Steph had gone for someone who was so similar, physically, to herself.

'It was all Bev's fault really.' Steph laughed, once she had explained the fact that she had slept with Angie. 'If she hadn't persuaded me to go to that health club, then maybe nothing would have happened.'

'You met in a health club?' asked Alex.

'Yeah. I work in a club in the City,' explained Angie. It was then that Alex realised that she had been jealous of Angie once before.

'Oh,' was all Alex managed to say. She remembered the night vividly and was wondering what Steph would say if she knew that she had been there too.

'I'm sorry,' apologised Angie. 'I didn't mean to upset you.'

'No. You haven't,' answered Alex although the women found it hard to read the tone of her voice.

'It was just sex, Alex,' explained Steph anxiously.

'Yeah. Really, that's all it was . . .' Both Angie and Steph looked at each other, worried that they had taken their openness a little too far.

A waiter passed by and they all took another drink off her tray. Steph and Angie turned their attention to their drinks while they waited for Alex's mood to change. The last thing they expected her to do was laugh.

'What's up?' asked Steph.

'I don't know if I should tell you this or not . . .' Alex said, still not sure whether to bite the bullet and tell them how she'd happened to be there.

'What?' coaxed Steph.

Alex took a deep breath. 'I was there.'

'You were where?' asked Steph again.

'I was at the health club that night,' Alex blurted in a mouthful of drunken laughter.

'How? . . . When? . . . What do you mean?' asked Steph.

'I mean, I was in the steam room when you two were doing it!'

'No!' exclaimed Angie.

'Yes,' said Alex.

'You mean you were watching us?' cried Steph who was still trying to get her drink-addled mind round the conversation. 'How come? What were you doing there?'

'OK, OK. You two have been very honest with me so I suppose I have to do the same. Marsha told me that she overheard you talking with Bev about going to a women's night at a health club and I knew where it was so I thought I'd go along. I just wanted to see you, I suppose.'

Steph and Angie just stood there silently for a second, aghast.

'And I thought doing a mock audition to get your address was extreme!' Steph slipped her arm round Alex who didn't know whether to look ashamed or to join in the laughter.

'Well, I don't think we can deny that, can we?'

'And did you like what you saw?' asked Angie.

Alex didn't get the chance to answer the question, however, as at that moment Marsha arrived at her elbow.

'Alex, I have done some sleuthing –' announced Marsha, before turning her attention to Angie. 'Well, excuse me. I didn't realise you had company. I'm Marsha, and you are . . .?'

'This is our friend Angie,' said Alex, not really knowing which conversation she wanted to continue with.

'Pleasure to meet you.' Marsha took Angie's hand in a firm handshake.

EXPOSURE

Alex could see Steph's reflection in the mirrors on the toilet wall opposite them. The anticipation of being discovered and the reflection of Steph tonguing her in this public place were more erotic than any of her fantasies. It made her more turned on than ever. She wanted and needed to come. It needed to be quick so she put her hands behind Steph's head and guided her mouth gently towards her clit.

'It's locked,' came a posh, pissed voice from the other side of the door.

'Oh, for pity's sake, Flicky, it can't be locked; it's probably just stuck,' came another voice. 'Let me have a go.'

Alex was on the verge of coming. 'Don't stop,' she mouthed to Steph who was looking towards the door. Just as a broad, horsey shoulder heaved against the flimsy door, Alex grabbed Steph and hauled her into a cubicle, swinging the door shut just as the outer door crashed open.

Steph quickly took up where she had left off, massaging her hard clit with her left hand. Just as Alex was about to come, Steph covered her mouth with a juice-soaked hand.

Flicky and horsey friend were washing their hands when they heard Alex's stifled groan. Horsey leaned towards her companion and whispered, 'There are people having sex in there!'

EXPOSURE

JANE JAWORSKI

First published in 2001 by
Sapphire
Thames Wharf Studios
Rainville Road
London W6 9HA

ISBN 0 352 33592 0

Cover Photograph by Michele Serchuk

Typeset by SetSystems Ltd, Saffron Walden, Essex
Printed and bound in Great Britain by Mackays of Chatham PLC

CONTENTS

ONE

Come Here Often?

'For pity's sake, Stephanie, you're desperate for this woman. You want to spend the foreseeable future shagging her sense-less. Your one and only aim is to get into Alexandra's knickers right now; not after a period of prolonged courtship, but now. So what are you doing holding her hand?' asked Marsha incredulously.

'I didn't –' Steph tried to explain herself as she squirmed in embarrassment.

'Use your body, Stephanie. Get close to her, touch her, domi-nate her because at the moment she's dominating you.'

'Do you really think –?'

'Make her look you in the eye. Look at her. She's crying out to be fucked until she screams. She's not going to say no, but you've got to persuade her that what you've got between your legs is worth sticking around for,' Marsha continued, now on a roll.

'But it's really hard doing this in front of all these people,' Steph blurted out with enough force to stop Marsha as she started to move in on a nervous-looking Alex.

Stephanie was ruing the day she'd clapped eyes on the notice advertising this particular acting workshop on the notice board at drama college.

1

'But this is a sexuality and gender class, petal. So like it or not, you're going to explore sexuality and gender.'

Steph wanted to kill her mate Bev for encouraging her to get involved in this ridiculous scenario. She glared at her best friend who was among the fifteen other students sitting crossed-legged on the floor of the draughty drama studio watching her feeble attempts at portraying a predatory male. Bev was the one with her hand over her mouth snorting with laughter. 'Manly' wasn't the first word that would leap to mind when describing Steph. In her clingy jeans and spaghetti-strap top, she liked to think she looked a little like Davina McCall and, with a few minor adjustments, she wasn't far off. But, in spite of her voluptuous tits and curvaceous hips, a 'masculine' side had been known to rear its head on occasion.

Tuning back into her tutor's voice, Steph heard Marsha ask if she was uncomfortable playing the man. Not wanting to appear prudish or unable to push her acting ability to its limits, the fiercely competitive part of Steph made her protest that she was perfectly fine with the situation and that she would like to continue with the improvisation.

'That's the spirit, luvvy. It's all about understanding power dynamics,' encouraged Marsha. 'When I was in Rep back in the 70s, I had to go on as Macbeth for a couple of nights, would you believe! Yes, it's a long story, but the point is I would have given anything for a forum like this to help me understand just what it's like to have a bloody great donger hanging between your legs.' There was a slight titter at Marsha's sudden enthusiasm for bloody great dongers.

'That's enough of that,' she said sharply. 'There is nothing amusing about this whatsoever. After all, you boys will be up here in a minute.' As she concluded her lecture, she spun round in a flurry of chiffon and silk and said nonchalantly to her assistant, 'Remind me to bring the strap-ons in tomorrow, will you, Glenda, darling?'

Steph turned her attention to Alex who had been standing patiently in the centre of the room during this interlude. Alex was playing what Marsha called the 'gender anchor' in this exercise in order to keep some semblance of reality. They had only met about three hours previously and until that moment Steph had been too intimidated to look at her fellow performer properly. She knew from the introduction circle earlier that morning that Alex was a little older – 28 to be precise – and a far more experienced actress than herself. She'd got her Equity card and had done several tellies already, whereas Steph, a mere kid of 20, was still stuck at drama school working her way towards her graduation show, an event that could make or break her career.

Eventually Marsha stopped talking. Dramatically, she hunched over, backed off the stage and into the audience leaving the women to pick up the scene where they had left off. She pressed 'play' on the beaten-up portable CD player and the Isley Brothers' swirling guitar riffs filled the room. Marsha had obviously never left the 70s.

Steph took in the way Alex's black, curly hair licked round her neck. Then she stared at the face it framed and thought she looked like one of those gorgeous models you see splashed on the side of buses advertising clothing for Gap – all lips and eyes. One of the store's most recent advertising slogans, 'Everybody In Leather', flashed across her mind and an image of this sensuous woman clad only in tight black leather pants replaced the real image of cord bootlegs and tight T-shirt that stood before her. No stranger to Sapphic sexual fantasies, Steph tried to put the bright blue eyes, slender nose and full, parted lips into a sexual context she could recognise and was not surprised to find that flirting with this woman was incredibly easy.

The scenario Marsha had set for them was simple and left lots of scope. Steph's character had taken Alex's character to a bar with the express purpose of getting off with her.

'So . . . do you come here often?' Steph's opening gambit provoked unanimous groans from her audience.

'Why don't we go and sit down?' asked Alex, as she directed Steph to the shabby sofa that the class had set out to represent the interior of a bar.

'Control, Stephanie!' Marsha's voice wafted through the music. Twisting round to face Alex, Steph flung her arm loosely over

Alex's shoulders but although she had started talking she didn't have a clue what she was saying. Her mouth had gone into seduction autopilot because her attention was being diverted by the way her body was reacting to this situation. Far from taking control she was quickly losing it and getting more and more unwilling to rein herself in.

Alex's brief was to respond to Steph positively if she felt like it or not if she didn't. It was up to her to react to what she was offered. As Alex ran her hand up and down Steph's thigh, it was obvious that she wasn't going to 'block' the scene that Steph was now directing and the younger woman automatically flexed her muscles so that they strained against the faded demin of her jeans.

Steph had come up with a line about the music being loud so they were wedged together on the sofa with each woman's mouth hovering over the other's ear as they talked. Steph was aware that Alex's breath on her skin was really starting to turn her on and silently praised herself for being so into the role. She slipped her hand round Alex's neck to pull her in closer and daringly kissed the soft skin just below her ear.

Enjoying her fellow performer's audacity, Alex moved her hand further in between Steph's thighs that were spread wide apart. Steph remembered what Marsha had told the class about what it might feel like to have a cock instead of a clit. Judging by the throbbing in her fanny, hers would have just grown into a good seven inches. No, make that eight. Alex's hand nudged the fabric covering Steph's crotch, brushing against her cunt lips. It was a fleeting and almost imperceptible movement, but Steph had to stifle a moan. Nobody would have believed a reaction like that wasn't real.

The two women explored each other's bodies with their hands as they talked until Steph gently guided Alex's face up to her own. Not a very brutal or aggressive move, but it felt right and Steph wasn't really thinking about acting any more. For a brief second they looked at each other, wondering if they should go this far. Lust got the better of caution, however, and they kissed each other in short, tentative bursts. The attentive atmosphere in the room changed completely as the women felt fifteen pairs of eyes not just watching them but boring into them.

When they parted their lips and Alex thrust her tongue into her partner's mouth, Steph felt as if a fireball was surging through her veins. She was practised in the art of stage kissing and no one had ever stuck their tongue in before. All mouth, no tongue action; that was the unwritten rule but Steph wasn't complaining. All the right parts of her body were throbbing and wet, when the music faded and Marsha's hushed voice broke into the scene.

'Now, Mike, you're this man's girlfriend,' interjected Marsha in a semi-whisper to the class. 'Let's say your name is Kathy. You've arrived at the bar with some friends and have just seen your boyfriend locked in an embrace with this other woman. Go into the scene and let me see what you do. Now remember, you're a woman so be aware of how that might inform your whole physicality. OK. And, enter Kathy.'

Stupid bloody 'Kathy', thought Steph to herself as she felt Alex instinctively pull away from their embrace.

As You Like It

'You ever snogged a woman before, Steph?' asked Bev as they made their way up the metal stairs to the canteen for lunch.

'What kind of question's that?' Steph asked nervously, wondering whether it had been obvious to the whole group just how turned on she was.

'Looked pretty damn horny, that's all, hen,' joked Bev.

'Let me put it this way. Who would you rather snog? The gorgeous Alex or the less than gorgeous Mike Lomas?' replied Steph as she gave her friend a playful poke up the arse as they neared the top of the narrow stairs.

'Oh yeah. Point taken,' said Bev without needing time to weigh up the pros and cons.

'Get a move on then. At this rate all the strawberry Slimfasts'll be gone by the time we get there.' Steph had tried all the diets in all the books in all the world, but whether she was currently trying to lose weight or not, she did favour a Slimfast for lunch.

As they troughed down their food in a small, afterthought of a room that passed as the canteen, Steph scoured the room for Alex. She wanted to find out more about this alluring, somewhat enigmatic woman but Alex was nowhere to be seen. Steph was always open to having adventures, but she'd never before experienced anything like her adventure that morning and, after years of dreaming about doing it with a woman, was hoping she might be able to engineer an opportunity to do a bit more exploring.

A fart and a belch from Bev signalled that lunch was over and the two friends went down to look at the notice board to see what the afternoon held in store for them. Steph's moist crotch still reminded her of the morning's activities, and her heart beat faster as she ran her finger down the list hoping that she'd see her own name in a pair with Alex's. She searched for a way to hide her excitement at seeing she was going to be rehearsing a scene from *As You Like It* with Alex. All she could blurt out was: 'Oh no! Not frigging Shakespeare!'

'I'd take Shakespeare over Adrian Mole any day,' said Bev when she saw she'd been cast as the schoolboy secret diarist. Bev's words fell on deaf ears, as Steph was already on her way to the rehearsal studio.

Flinging the door open, Steph's eyes scanned the room hoping to find the newest object of her obsession. Alex was the only person in the room and Steph watched her as she lay on her back, knees bent, lost in a typical relaxation pose. She hadn't had a chance to speak to Alex about the improvisation they'd done earlier on, but she hoped her gut reaction that it had been a mutually agreeable experience was right. Bev came tumbling in the door behind Steph and broke into both women's dream worlds.

'Oh, hi, Steph, I didn't know you were there,' said Alex as she rolled over onto her stomach and looked up at the two women.

'Yeah, hi, Alex,' stammered Steph, a little ashamed at being identified as a voyeur. 'Have you met my mate Bev?'

'Pleased to meet you, Bev.' Alex got up off the floor and came over to shake hands. It struck Steph as being rather formal considering she and Alex hadn't so much as said 'g'day' before sticking their tongues down each other's throats. 'I gather we're going to be working on a bit of Shakespeare together this afternoon, Steph,' said Alex. Steph wondered whether it was her imagination or whether Alex's voice had been that deep and sexy earlier that morning.

'Yeah. Who do you want to be, Rosalind or Orlando?' joked Steph.

'Oh, I think it's my turn to be the man, don't you?' replied Alex. Steph was amazed that her clit started to throb at the mere thought of it. She wondered whether this woman was the one who would finally make her fantasy world redundant. The other students began to enter the room and Marsha took centre stage to address her class.

'Now, I know there's not a lot of space at the moment, so we're going to have to use the rehearsal rooms in shifts. It's up to you to work out who goes first, but don't forget that you've got to present these scenes in less than forty-eight hours, so going off to have a cigarette and a bit of a sunbathe in the garden isn't going to be a productive use of time,' barked the tutor. 'Now, I'm going to be roaming around the building all afternoon and will drop in on all of you at one stage or another to see if you need any help. So don't panic, you won't be on your own.'

Alex led Steph out into the garden for a fag, a coffee and a bit of a sunbathe while they waited for a room to become free. Steph suddenly felt a little nervous about being with this woman without any class or character to hide behind.

'What made you sign up for this class then, Alex?' asked Steph in her 'polite conversation' voice.

'Marsha.'

'You know each other?'

'You could say that. She used to teach me voice at drama school and often phones up when she's got these kind of things going on.'

'You've done this class before?'

'No. I have to say that this is one of her more interesting ventures.' Steph took the fag that was being passed to her and smiled at Alex as the smoke seeped from between her lips. Alex smiled back. From the way Alex was looking at her, Steph knew that nothing had to be said about the morning's performance. They sat in silence for a moment or two, enjoying the cigarette and the warmth of the spring day.

'Why don't I give you a neck rub while we're waiting?' Alex asked out of the blue.

'Sounds good,' replied Steph as she swivelled round so her legs were astride the back of her chair. With her head lolling forward Steph saw Alex's cigarette being tossed onto the grass and ground out by a pair of heavy leather boots.

'So where do you live, Alex?' Steph managed to squeeze the words out through her compressed windpipe, such was her enthusiasm to know more about this woman.

'Questions and neck rubs aren't really a good combination,' replied Alex, not wanting to give away a thing. 'Just relax into my hands.' Alex pushed her hand up through Steph's shoulder length brown hair and started kneading her scalp. She moved her body closer so that Steph could feel the warmth of her thighs pressing against her own. She was so aroused by this woman's touch that it was fast getting to the point where either a wank or a fuck would have to take place. Steph had had enough of being brought to the brink of orgasm by Alex and was eternally grateful when she recognised Bev's voice shouting out that there was a room free and that they should go up and grab it. Steph was not at all nervous or apprehensive as the two women made their way silently up the stairs and along the corridor to Studio B. She knew Alex wanted to shag her and as a total dyke virgin whose dreams were about to come true, Steph had never been so turned on in her life.

They walked into the room and Steph shut the door and pulled the roller blind down over the glass panel so nobody walking past would get a glimpse of what they both knew was about to happen. The door didn't lock, but neither Steph nor Alex were worrying about intruders. Dropping her bag onto the floor, Alex moved in on Steph and kissed her hard on the mouth. She pushed against her so forcefully that Steph started to stagger backwards. Sensing that she was going to break away from her, Alex grasped her around the waist and guided her over to the wall.

'You know, I haven't been able to stop thinking about fucking you since we kissed this morning,' gasped Alex as she leaned over her and reached down to run her hands over Steph's arse.

'Me too,' confessed Steph.

'Do you want me to show you exactly how turned on I am?' Alex said, toying with her eager partner.

'God, yes!' said Steph, wondering what she was going to do. Alex plunged her hand down into her own trousers, dipped her finger in her fanny and, with it soaked in her juices, used it to trace the moist outline of Steph's lips. Steph's tongue licked her lips, hungry for the taste of Alex's sex.

'I would say that is the taste of a pretty horny woman.' Steph's expectations about how the afternoon might pan out were being surpassed already.

Intoxicated by the strong smell of sex, Steph reached inside Alex's T-shirt and dragged the material up and over her breasts. She thanked her lucky stars that there was no bra to contend with and pulled away from Alex's demanding kiss to get a better look. Alex's tits were beautiful; round, firm and a perfect handful. Mesmerised by this stranger's body, she ran her fingers over the dark red nipples that were erect and aching to be licked. Alex let out a gasp of excitement as Steph bent her head and ran her tongue over her expectant flesh. Steph looked up to see Alex's blue eyes looking down at her, her kiss-smudged lips were slightly parted and her breath was coming in short, sharp gasps.

'Christ, that feels so good,' moaned Alex, 'but if you don't lick me pretty damn soon, honey, I'm going to explode.' With her mouth still exploring every inch of Alex's breasts, Steph reached down to Alex's crotch. She rubbed the seam that ran in between Alex's legs and heard her partner groan with pleasure.

'Easy! Someone might hear us,' said Steph. She turned round to look at the door for reassurance, suddenly scared by the thought of being so exposed.

'That's half the fun, don't you think?' Alex whispered huskily in Steph's ear as she reached down and cupped her new friend's crotch in her hand. Her mouth was so close to her ear that Steph could feel Alex's lips touching her skin as Alex reminded her about the job in hand. 'Now, what's more interesting: Marsha paying us a surprise visit or my cunt, which, I can assure you, is wetter than you could ever imagine and crying out for your mouth.' Alex reached for the waistband of Steph's jeans and flicked open the button. The only sound that filled the air was Steph's zip being pulled down, slowly but surely. Leaning against the wall and almost forehead to forehead, the two women stared into each other's eyes, mouths open, sweat glistening on their skin, anticipating what was to come. Never breaking eye contact, Steph reached down, slipped her hands inside Alex's trousers and watched the pupils of the woman opposite her dilate with desire.

'They're too tight,' declared Alex, 'undo them.' Steph found the button and released it from its hole just as Alex had just done to her. Steph pushed Alex's trousers over her hips and pulled at the elastic of the black cotton pants she found underneath. The feel of Alex's pubic hair was driving her crazy, but the clothes were still preventing her from reaching her fanny.

'Take your trousers off and open your legs,' Steph hissed. Alex wasn't about to argue and struggled to release one leg from her cords to allow Steph to get at her crotch. Pulling her pants to one side, Steph plunged her finger into Alex's sex. Using one hand to keep her underwear out of the way, Steph began to move her middle finger in and out of Alex's moist cunt.

'Jesus, that feels good,' said Steph. The smell of Alex's juices rose between them and Steph inhaled them readily.

'Eat me, Steph. I want to feel your tongue in my cunt,' Alex commanded. 'I can't wait any longer.'

Suddenly the sound of the bell that signified lesson changeover filled the room. With Steph's finger in Alex's cunt and Alex's hands massaging Steph's tits, the two women froze. The sound of feet could be heard tramping along the corridor and voices dissected some class that had just taken place.

'I want you to make me come, Steph,' whispered Alex as the noise got closer to their studio.

'But what if they're coming in here?' argued Steph who for once was being outdone in the risk-taking stakes.

'Then they'll get the thrill of their lives.' Alex smiled. Spurred on by Alex's bravado, Steph let herself be pulled away from her position against the wall and allowed her head to be guided down between Alex's legs. Using the wall for support, Alex tilted her pelvis forward and presented her aroused cunt to her lover. With the school alive with the noises of students on the move, Steph parted Alex's fanny lips to reveal her protruding clit. There was a bang as someone lurched against the door.

'What the fuck . . .?' asked Steph urgently pulling away.

'Steph! Do you wanna have sex with me or think about them?'

'Jesus, Alex, you're good!'

'Steph, please,' groaned Alex, seemingly oblivious to the potential intrusion. She placed her hands on the back of Steph's head and guided her into her crotch. Alex's knees buckled slightly with the intensity of her desire.

'Get on the floor,' ordered Steph. Alex did as she was told and let Steph spread her legs as wide as they would go. Steph marvelled at the beauty of the cunt that was being presented to her.

'So, you want me to lick you out, do you?'

Alex shut her eyes and nodded in reply. With that, Steph plunged her tongue into Alex's hole and tasted a woman's juices for the first time. She replaced her thrusting tongue with her thrusting finger and turned her attention to her partner's clitoris.

Next door, a rehearsal of *Whistle Down the Wind* had started up and singers of various standards were warming up. 'Oh, yes. That's beautiful. Oh, babe, right there,' said Alex, her voice rising with her impending orgasm.

'Shhh!' urged Steph. Protected by the building noise in the adjoining room, Steph abandoned the slow, tantalising route and started to tongue Alex's clit faster and faster as Alex's hips bucked up to meet her mouth. Totally intoxicated by Alex, Steph had ceased caring about intruders when she heard her gasping cries: 'I'm coming. I'm coming! Oh fuck, Steph, I'm coming!'

Steph hung on to Alex's waist and continued working on her clit until her hips stopped thrusting and her orgasm subsided. Sitting up, Alex took Steph's face in her hands and licked her own juices from her partner's face and mouth before quickly pulling her trousers back on.

11

'I never thought I'd say this, but thank fuck for *Whistle Down the Wind*!' Steph said, laughing, elated at the thought of having made Alex come so violently.

'What are you doing with these still on?' Alex teased as she fingered Steph's gaping trousers. 'Don't you fancy me?' Alex went to pull the offending trousers and knickers off, but Steph suddenly wanted to feel this sensuous woman on top of her. She opened her legs and let Alex's lithe body slip in between. Alex covered her face with soft kisses and began rubbing her pelvis up against Steph's fanny.

'You want to come like this?' she asked. Steph nodded. 'Will you be able to come like this?' she probed, concerned that Steph shouldn't miss out on the fun.

'What do you think?' replied Steph who grabbed Alex's arse urging her to thrust faster. 'Just being in the same room with you would be enough to make me . . . oh my God!' Clutching Alex's arse with her fingers and sinking her teeth into her shoulder, Steph's climax was intense. With Alex between her legs and a post-orgasm flush taking over her face and chest, Steph ran her fingers lightly over the smiling face that hovered above her.

The opening door sounded like a gunshot to the two women who were lost in each other's bodies and their own thoughts. Alex turned round quickly to see Marsha standing just inside the doorway looking slightly puzzled.

'We thought we'd work on the wrestling scene instead of going straight into the main text,' piped up Alex, thinking on her metaphorical feet. 'That's OK, isn't it, Marsha?'

'Oh, yes. Lovely. Perfect actually. Clever girls!' said Marsha who seemed to be satisfied with this explanation. 'Wonderful idea for finding a way into Orlando,' she continued. 'So which one of you is playing Orlando?'

'I am,' chorused the two women from the floor. Marsha raised an eyebrow and gave the women a knowing smirk. In their heart of hearts, Alex and Steph knew they'd been rumbled.

12

TWO

Falling Off the Wagon

That evening Steph was sitting in her north London flat wondering whether her afternoon of sex had been a figment of her imagination or not. Alex had left shortly after Marsha had walked in on their 'rehearsal' but there had been no reference to what had happened between them, no 'we must do it again sometime', no hint of how she felt. As a result, Steph was in the rather unusual position of feeling slightly used. Bev had called to ask if she wanted to go for a few jars down the pub, but she was too busy feeling incredibly turned on at having finally discovered the delights of lesbian sex and also a little put out that Alex hadn't been more . . . well, 'friendly' was the only word she could think of that fitted her expectation.

She cracked open a bottle of Australian chardonnay and poured herself a glass. Learning lines seemed more than a little dull in the circumstances so she flicked the TV on. Soaps turned into quiz shows which turned into the drone of a newsreader's voice which, mixed with the wine, succeeded in sending her to sleep. When the doorbell went at around 10.30 p.m., Steph thought it would be Bev, pissed and too lazy to get her keys out of her bag. Begrudgingly, she heaved herself out of her TV chair and went to answer the door. As soon as she saw Alex standing in front of her,

JANE JAWORSKI

she regretted the manky old track-pants she was wearing and the unattractive sneer on her face.

'Hello,' said Alex as if it were the most normal thing in the world for her to turn up unannounced at strange women's houses after the nine o'clock watershed.

'What are you doing here?' asked Steph in astonishment.

'I was in the area, so . . .'

'But you don't know my address!'

'I am quite friendly with the course tutor, you know.'

'Oh, yeah. Of course,' said Steph, feeling a bit silly.

'So, are you going to let me in?'

'Oh, yeah. Of course!' Steph moved aside and let Alex through.

'Are you OK?' Alex asked, noticing that Steph looked a bit flustered.

'I'm just a bit surprised that you're here, that's all.'

'Surprised? In case you'd forgotten, we've got a scene to put on and, as I recall, we didn't do an awful lot of rehearsing today.'

'But you practically ran out of the studio after Marsha burst in on us this afternoon. To be honest, I didn't think I'd be seeing you again.'

'I had an audition I had to be at, that's all. Sorry, hon,' soothed Alex as she reached out to run the back of her hand across Steph' cheek. 'But look, I'm here now, so why don't we get down to some work?'

'Fucking weirdo!' Steph said, trying to hide her delight, and showed her into the living room. Steph retrieved her abandoned book from the floor and the two women worked their way through the scene, talking about motivation, objectives and all the other wank that actors love to bang on about. Around 12.30 there was a phone call from a very drunk Bev. She wanted to let Steph know that she was going to stay over with Tina and that she shouldn't worry about her. She told Steph that she loved her very very much, that she was the best mate in the world and that she would see her tomorrow in class.

'So we've got the place to ourselves?' said Alex who had discarded her script and was stretched out on the TV chair tossing back the last of the wine.

14

'But it's gone midnight, Alex, and surely way past your bed-time,' taunted Steph.

'Come here and say that!'

Steph couldn't resist sinking to her knees in front of Alex to accept the long and luxuriant snog that was being offered. Alex automatically reached for Steph's tits but was pushed away.

'Not going all coy on me now, are you?' asked Alex in surprise.

'As much as I want to spend all night fucking your brains out, there are too many questions I need answers to,' declared Steph, amazed by her self-control.

'What do you mean?'

'Christ, Alex, we've groped each other in front of a class of students and had fantastic sex in one of the drama studios but I don't know anything about you!'

'And you want to?'

'Yes!'

'So what do you want to know?'

'Why you're being such hard work would be a good place to start.'

'Steph, do you really think I go round hitting on every cute woman I work with?'

Steph thought about this for a moment and then had to admit that she did. Alex burst out laughing at Steph's image of her.

'Well, I'm sorry to shatter your illusions, but I don't. Although after today, I am beginning to think that I should!'

'So, what then? You've got a boyfriend, is that it?'

'Good God, no!'

'So why are you being so goddamn secretive?'

'I want you to try and understand, Steph, that it's not because I don't like you. This is going to sound really odd, but I have an arrangement with my agent. Really I shouldn't be here at all.'

'What? Some sort of business deal?' Steph was fascinated and apprehensive about where this was leading.

Alex looked as if she was having a hard time deciding exactly what she was about to say but eventually came out with: 'I've kind of made a promise to my agent that I will remain celibate.'

Steph started to laugh and was pleased that Alex's imagination seemed to be as fertile as her own. 'It's no joke, Steph.' The seriousness of Alex's tone meant Steph knew immediately that this outlandish statement was not some sort of bizarre wind-up after all.

'Why on earth would you do that?' asked Steph, despite being a little wary of the answer.

'This is really hard to say without sounding totally hypocritical and arrogant, but I struck a deal with my agent when he took me on. He would only put me up for the high profile, starry stuff – you know, movies, big tellies, blah, blah – if I kept the dyke thing completely under wraps.'

'So you are gay?'

'As a goose, sweetheart!'

'Fucking hell,' exclaimed Steph.

'I know. It's shit. It is like selling your soul to the devil, but I've dreamed about being in the movies all my life and now I've got someone who's powerful enough and interested enough to help me make it happen. Believe me, Steph, when you're standing in front of someone who's offering you a screen test for "the next big movie", giving up sex doesn't sound like such a big deal.'

'You're not doing a very good job then, are you!' Steph laughed at Alex's serious tone. 'So where do I come in? Are you going to cut off my tongue and condemn me to a life of kiss-and-tell-silence?'

'You wouldn't be much good to me if I did that, would you?' Alex started to lighten up.

'So this is sort of finishing something that should never have started?'

Alex paused and silently nodded her head. 'I know I have no right to ask you, but will you keep quiet about what happened? Not a word?'

'Not even to Bev.'

'So why did you have sex with me in the studio, Alex? Anyone could have walked in and seen us. Why would you do that if you're so scared about people finding out you're a raving lesbo?' Steph was tired, disappointed and confused.

'I can't help what turns me on, can I?' Steph waited for her to

16

continue. 'I just find the idea of having sex in unusual places really horny, that's all. I know it's stupid, but that's how it is.'

Steph was beginning to wish she hadn't opened this conversation as she was approaching information overload.

'Trust me to land a freak like you on my first go.' Steph got up from her position at the foot of Alex's chair and produced a bottle of Grouse and a couple of glasses from the cabinet. Serious drinking seemed like the right thing to do at this stage.

'You are allowed to drink, aren't you?' remarked Steph sarcastically as she poured too much Scotch into the tumblers. 'No deals, pacts or restrictions on that one?' Alex dealt with the jibe by just ignoring it totally.

'Today was really your first time?' Alex's surprise seemed genuine. She took the drink that was passed to her, but held on to Steph's hand.

'Yeah,' Steph admitted shyly and looked up at Alex hoping she wasn't going to be made fun of.

'Well, you were wonderful.' Alex slid off the chair to join Steph sitting on the floor. She swung herself round so the two women were sitting face to face, their bent legs entwined. Alex took Steph's hand again. She guided Steph's hand up to her mouth and gently sucked on her fingertips and licked down the shaft of her fingers.

'This is the first time I've fallen off the wagon, you know.' She was trying to make her feel better.

'Am I meant to be flattered?' Steph was almost in a sulk.

'When you kissed my neck in class, I thought I was going to come on the spot.' Alex continued sucking and licking and caressing Steph's fingers.

'That's only because you haven't had sex for God knows how long. How long has it been?' Steph suspected Alex knew the precise answer to her question but instead Alex just shrugged her shoulders.

'What made you think you could trust me though?' The thought of Alex choosing her to have sex with did make Steph feel a bit special.

'I don't know. Instinct. Gut reaction. We clicked, didn't we?'

17

Flattered by her comments, Steph was still aware that her click had been bigger than Alex's. 'Steph, I'm trying to tell you how much I fancy you!' said Alex, apparently eager to get some sort of reaction from her.

'Yeah, well, I'm trying to tell you that I'm sick of fantasising about various unattainable women and this afternoon I really thought I'd finally found someone I might be able to start a real relationship with and now you turn out to be a complete fucking ambition-crazed wacko!'

They sat in silence both trying to digest what the other had said. Steph watched Alex as she glanced round the room taking in the *My Friends & Neighbours* poster on the brightly painted green walls, the books lined up on the shelves according to colour and the solitary customised Ikea cabinet in the corner.

'So which unattainable women have you been fantasising about?' She smiled at Steph, took her glass from her hand and put it on the carpet beside them.

'I'm allowed to have secrets too, you know,' Steph teased.

'Well, you're not going to be doing that tonight.'

'Really?' Steph was fascinated by the way she could say something like that and not sound arrogant.

'Why should you have to touch yourself when you've got me to do whatever you want?' Steph's heart raced. She knew it would be madness to have anything more to do with this woman, but some reactions can't be controlled by logic.

'Just for tonight?' asked Steph, hoping that she'd misunderstood the whole warped scenario.

'Just for tonight,' confirmed Alex. Steph put her hand on Alex's thigh. 'But not a word.' The touch of her bare leg made Steph tingle with desire. 'Promise?' Steph kissed Alex full on the lips in a move that sealed their pact.

She ran her hands through Alex's soft curls and pulled her tighter into her body as their tongues met. As she pulled away from the kiss a string of saliva joined their mouths for an instant and glistened in the light of the muted TV. Steph's hands were shaking as she reached for the buttons of Alex's shirt. Slowly she undid the first button to reveal her bra. She ran her hands over the

18

flimsy material that covered Alex's body, wanting to savour every moment of this affair. Motionless, Alex offered her body to Steph's exploring hands. Steph popped open the buttons one by one until she was able to push the garment off her lover's shoulders and onto the floor. Alex's tanned, semi-clothed body was more erotic than Steph could have dreamed. Reaching behind her, Alex undid her bra and let it fall to the floor before easing herself down onto the cushions behind her.

'I don't know if I can,' Steph whispered almost overcome by the sensations that were wracking her body.

'Give me your hand,' Alex murmured. Gently, Alex placed Steph's hand on her exposed breast. Steph felt the nipple harden underneath her palm and squeezed, enjoying the soft moan that escaped from Alex's lips. Sitting astride her hips, Steph bent over and dragged her tongue from the hollow of her neck round to her ear. Pinning her arms to the floor she breathed in this beautiful woman's scent and took her earlobe between her teeth, biting it just as she liked hers to be bitten. Steph could feel Alex's hips grinding against her. 'Not so fast. This is my night, remember,' she chastised Alex, pushing her pelvis into the cushions with her crotch. 'I'm going to get up now, but I don't want to see you with your hand in your crotch, OK?'

Alex nodded and seemed to be pleasantly surprised by the way Steph had decided to take control. Steph stood up with her legs either side of Alex's body and peeled off her T-shirt. She hooked her thumbs inside the waistband of her track-pants and pulled them down and off. Instead of the white, lacy knickers she'd had a glimpse of earlier that day, Alex found herself staring up at Steph's naked cunt instead. Unable to contain herself, she sat up, wanting desperately to plunge her tongue into Steph's sex. Steph tutted as she held Alex's head inches away from her fanny. 'I thought we were doing things my way . . .'

'But I just –'

'You can look, but don't touch. Not yet.' Steph was really getting into her role now. She could feel Alex's breath on her clit and although she yearned to have Alex touch her, she was enjoying the woman's desire too much. Steph ran a finger over the length

19

of her cunt so it was covered in her juices and put it in Alex's open mouth. 'Think of that as an appetiser,' she teased as Alex licked the offered finger noisily. Moving away from Alex's impatient tongue, Steph turned her attention to her partner's remaining clothes. Assessing the situation, she guessed that the cotton skirt wouldn't pose much of a problem and began to pull it down over Alex's legs. The prostrate woman lifted her hips obligingly. The wet crotch of her pants confirmed just how turned on Alex was. Steph couldn't resist taunting her even more and ran the finger that had just been in her own wet hole over the drenched material. Alex gasped and thrust her hips forward but, knowing that she had to let Steph orchestrate the scene, made no move to touch her.

Kneeling between her open legs, Steph lowered her head and brushed her lips across Alex's navel, pulling her pants down as she went so she could reach in and touch her pubic hair. She reached behind to the small of Alex's back and gripped onto the only item of clothing that was left and tugged the pants down over Alex's arse. Lifting her crotch, the offending article was eased away from her body.

'Sit on my face,' Alex hissed, impatient to get to the main course. Steph positioned herself so that she was kneeling astride Alex once again.

'Wait for it,' she whispered, lowering herself so that her fanny skimmed over Alex's stomach, smearing it with her wetness. 'Everything comes to those who wait.' Gradually she moved up Alex's expectant body and, running her hard clit over Alex's erect nipple, she shuddered with excitement. Not wanting Steph to come before she'd got a chance to taste the cunt she'd been deprived of earlier, Alex took this as her cue. She moved down between Steph's legs so that her lover's swollen red lips were inches over her face. Alex ran her fingers down either side of Steph's erect clit so it thrust out of her cunt even further. Flicking it with her tongue, Alex plunged her tongue into Steph's sex. Steph's groan of relief at finally giving in to Alex's tongue came from deep inside her and Alex could feel the thighs either side of her head trembling with lust. Steph's breath was coming in short, heavy bursts as she thrust her clit hard into the mouth below her. Taking her weight on her arms she started to slide her cunt over Alex's mouth so urgently that Alex didn't know whether she was tonguing her cunt or her clit. Her face covered in Steph's juices, Alex grabbed hold of her hips so she could force her tongue even further inside her hole. Steph's moans were turning into screams of delight and she pumped her taut, throbbing clitoris into Alex's mouth.

'Jesus, Alex, you're going to make me come!' She could feel her clit grinding against Alex's teeth. 'Jesus Christ!' she screamed as her orgasm built inside her. With one final thrust Steph let out an enormous groan as her climax thundered through her whole body and her come poured into Alex's hungry mouth.

Steph leaned down to lick her own come from Alex's face. Reaching behind her she ran her hand in between Alex's legs and felt the stickiness that had seeped out of her sex and onto her thighs.

'I want you to fuck me with your clit.' Alex's voice was husky and barely audible but straight to the point. Steph didn't need to be asked twice to try out her favourite sexual fantasy. Alex looked almost pained with anticipation as she lifted her right leg up to let Steph position her open cunt lips over her own. Between their scissored legs, Steph could see Alex's clitoris was engorged with lust. Alex put her hand in her cunt and parted her lips further to give Steph a better view of her sex.

'I want to feel you rubbing against me, babe,' Alex demanded. 'I want to feel you against me.' Steph was frozen with intense excitement. 'Fuck me, Steph.' The command was enough to stir Steph into action and she lowered herself onto Alex's clit. She heard the sound of their drenched fannies coming together and thought she'd died and gone to erotic heaven. Both women gasped loudly when they felt the pressure of the other's clitoris on their own.

'I never thought anyone could be so –'

'Oh yeah!' shouted Alex as her lover hit exactly the right spot. Steph was once again building towards a climax. Concentrating hard on giving Alex pleasure, she moved her hips in time with the thrusts coming from below. Steph saw Alex's face start to contort and knew from the way Alex was digging her fingers into her arse that she was about to come.

'Come with me, Steph. Come with me!' Alex screamed as her orgasm swept through her entire body. The noise, the sweat and the smell of two women coming together was intense.

As Steph sank into Alex's arms, there was a bang on the wall from jealous neighbours. The two women grinned at each other, proud that their performance had provoked such a reaction. Steph looked at the clock. The realisation that it was nearly four o'clock suddenly made her yawn. Alex twisted round to look at Steph who had curled herself around Alex's body. 'You're not going to sleep, are you?' she said, disappointed.

'I'm exhausted.'

'But we've only got a couple of hours left together – you can't go to sleep.'

'How about we just go to bed then?'

'OK.' Leaving the room strewn with their clothing and reeking of sex, Steph led Alex into her bedroom. Under the duvet Alex put her arm around Steph and pushed strands of sweaty hair away from her face. 'I can't get close enough to you,' said Steph who was already beginning to panic about Alex leaving and walking out of her life. Alex drew Steph in tighter and trapped her between her legs.

'Close enough?' she asked.

'Ummm, feels good.' Alex began to stroke Steph's back and arse and neither woman was surprised to feel their bodies start to respond. Pelvis to pelvis, their hips started to rock backwards and forwards and they started to make love all over again.

Stupid Mind Games

It was Alex's mobile phone that eventually woke the pair up. Alex leaned over the side of the bed and scrabbled around in her bag trying to locate the source of the intrusion. Tipping the bag upside down, the phone came tumbling out. Alex looked at the display and recognised Marsha's number.

'What does she want at this time in the morning?' groaned Alex as she let it click onto voice mail.

'Who?' croaked Steph who was even less awake than Alex.

'Marsha.' Alex turned and looked at the clock. 'Jesus Christ, it's 11.30!' she yelled and leaped out of bed. 'Come on, Steph, you're going to be late.' Steph gripped on tightly to the covers that Alex was trying to pull off her.

'I'm not going.'

'What do you mean, you're not going?' said Alex as she looked around the room for her clothes and then remembered why they weren't there.

'I can't go back there and work on a scene with you after all this!' Steph mumbled through the duvet. Alex sank down onto the bed.

'Look, you go and I'll phone Marsha and tell her that something's come up, OK?' enthused Alex.

'I'm not going, Alex, and that's final.'

'What are you going to do all day then?' Alex appeared reluctant to leave whilst Steph was looking so unstable. 'For Christ's sake, Steph, we hardly even know each other. We had a shag –'

'Or two.'

'Or two,' continued Alex. 'It was fun. It was good sex. But a couple of orgasms and a shared fag doesn't automatically make us lesbian-fucking-life-partners, you know!'

'Why are you talking like this, Alex? Stop it.' Steph was disappointed by the sudden change in Alex's attitude but knew exactly what she was trying to do. 'I'm not as naive as you think, you know,' she said sharply, too tired to play stupid mind games. 'I know you're panicking because you don't know any more if you can trust me, but that's just something you'll find out in time, won't you?'

'Steph, I thought we'd agreed . . .'

'Look, Alex, I really like you. Fuck knows why, because anyone who agrees to obliterate their private life for some tenuous promise of money and fame must be a total idiot, let alone a complete bastard for taking out their frustration on defenceless young women. But I do like you. You are the horniest, most gorgeous

23

woman I've ever clapped eyes on and I think that what you're doing is just such a fucking waste!' Steph was pleased that she'd said her piece and flopped back down on the bed, pulling the duvet back round her.

'I'm sorry if I've hurt you, Steph,' replied Alex. 'I never thought it would be like this. I fancied you in class but should never had let it all get out of control. I really am sorry.' There was no reaction from Steph and Alex looked a little frustrated that things hadn't turned out as neatly as she'd planned.

'I mean, how was I to know that I was your first?' Alex continued. 'It wasn't very fucking obvious in the studio yesterday!' There was a humpf from under the duvet. 'Well, it wasn't,' protested Alex.

'It shouldn't make any difference whether I've shagged one woman or a thousand. The fact is that you shouldn't go round giving people a bite of the cherry then whipping it away!'

'So you only want me for my body?' asked Alex. Another humpf from under the covers. 'Jesus, Steph, all you've got to do is put yourself around a bit in some of the bars in town and you could shag a different woman every night!'

'Well, I might just do that!'

'Good.' Alex's phone went again. This time she saw it was the number of her agent's office. What impeccable timing she thought to herself, smiling at the irony of the situation. She answered the phone and went over to the other side of the room to speak to the caller in hushed tones. Steph pulled the covers down slightly from over her face to try and hear what she was talking about. She only caught a couple of words but could tell it was an important call.

'Alex, it's Quentin.'

'Quentin, this isn't a good time.'

'I don't think there can be a bad time to tell you that you've been called back to read for the Brett Torento movie, is there?' came the voice of Alex's agent down the line.

'Seriously?'

'Couldn't be more serious. They want you to do a couple of scenes with Brett this time. It's a good sign, Alex. A very good sign.'

'That's fantastic, Quentin. Listen, I'll finish up here and call you when I get home. OK?'

'Speak to you later.'

Clicking the phone shut, Alex returned to sit on the bed. 'Look, honey, I'm really going to have to go now; there's somewhere I have to be.'

'OK,' said Steph calmly, rolling over to look at Alex.

'Mind if I take a quick shower before I go? I'll have all the dogs in the neighbourhood following me down the street if I don't!'

'Sure. Take some clean underwear too if you want.'

Alex went over to the drawer Steph was pointing at. 'Cheers.' Holding a pair of Steph's knickers in her hand, Alex walked slowly towards the door.

'I'll let you get some sleep then, yeah,' Alex whispered to the shape under the duvet.

'Whatever,' was the muffled reply. Alex gathered up her stuff, grabbed a towel off the back of a chair and made her way to the door.

'So you won't go saying anything –' Alex tried one last time to get some reassurance before she left.

'Oh, please!' said a frustrated Steph. Alex paused a moment.

'Don't forget to go and cruise around some of those bars I mentioned,' said Alex in lieu of a goodbye.

THREE

Cruising and Surfing

A slurping noise echoed round the sides of the glass as Steph sucked the last of her vodka Red Bull up through her straw. She looked intently at the mound of ice lurking in the bottom and knew, if she wanted to avoid making eye contact with anyone and have something to occupy her attention, she would have to go to the bar and order another one. Going out alone wasn't something that Steph usually did. Going out alone to a women-only bar was something she never did and now she was there felt so nervous that she'd made a big dent in the contents of her cigarette packet and downed three vodkas – she'd only been in the bar an hour. Even Bev would think that was quite impressive.

Steph smiled as she remembered the look on Bev's face when she told her she was gay. Her friend's Glaswegian accent had got broader and broader as she gasped and howled and finally squealed with delight. Bev had trotted out a couple of stories including one about an experience she'd had with some chalet maid on a field trip to Bognor and then suggested they go down to the pub to celebrate. They had had a good time in the pub and talked about all kinds of stuff that Steph couldn't now recall and was sure wasn't worth remembering anyway. She had alluded to her liaison with Alex but had stopped short of mentioning her by name. By the time Steph had got to the end of her confession, which had got